THE OPPOSITE OF FALLING

Jennie Rooney was born in Liverpool in 1980. She read History at the University of Cambridge and taught English in France before moving to London to work as a lawyer. Her first novel, *Inside The Whale*, was a Richard and Judy debut choice, Tesco Book Club selection and shortlisted for the Costa First Novel Award.

D0733822

ALSO BY JENNIE ROONEY

Inside the Whale

JENNIE ROONEY

The Opposite of Falling

VINTAGE BOOKS
London

Published by Vintage 2011

2 4 6 8 10 9 7 5 3 1

First published in Great Britain in 2010 by Chatto & Windus

Vintage
Random House, 20 Vauxhall Bridge Road,
London SW1V 2SA

www.vintage-books.co.uk

Addresses for companies within The Random House Group Limited
can be found at: www.randomhouse.co.uk/offices.htm

The Random House Group Limited Reg. No. 954009

A CIP catalogue record for this book
is available from the British Library

ISBN 9780099523475

The Random House Group Limited supports The Forest
Stewardship Council (FSC), the leading international forest
certification organisation. All our titles that are printed on
Greenpeace approved FSC certified paper carry the FSC logo.
Our paper procurement policy can be found at:
www.rbooks.co.uk/environment

Mixed Sources
Product group from well-managed
forests and other controlled sources
www.fsc.org   Cert no. TT-COC-2139
© 1996 Forest Stewardship Council

FSC

Printed and bound in Great Britain by
CPI Cox & Wyman, Reading, RG1 8EX

To Pluse and Mart

Part I
1862

One

The letters

All her life, Ursula Bridgewater had been building up to something. She felt it as a bubbling restlessness inside her, a straightness along her spine that occasionally came across as terseness, but which she did not really intend. She was of the opinion that one really ought to *do* something with one's life, especially if one had the necessary resources, but she had not yet fixed upon what this should be. Her brother called her a Presbyterian, but this was not the case. It was not religion; it was just restlessness.

She did all the normal things. She went for walks and to ladies' luncheons and did not raise a fuss at her exclusion from dinner parties where spinster ladies were not to be unleashed upon the men. She was immaculately well-behaved. She did not shout out any of the things which squeaked and fidgeted inside her. She did not clap her hand to her forehead at the banality of polite conversation – sofa cushions and drapes! – nor did she allow her tongue to sharpen for her own amusement as it did at home with her brother, George, who allowed it, encouraged it even, and she restrained her eyes from rolling helplessly in the manner which used to upset her mother so much. She did not drum her fingers on tabletops, nor did she tip back her head when she laughed so that the veins pulsed in her neck.

Oh no. She did not let on. She simply smiled and nodded, drinking tea and hmming at embroidery displays, and she continued to smile even as she fixed her hat and retrieved her umbrella and waved farewells from the window of her hansom, and only then could she relax, could she puff out her cheeks and blow out all those church-mouse sentiments which she kept scurried up inside herself. It was in these moments that Ursula Bridgewater supposed the problem was quite simple. She assumed she wanted a husband.

George also attributed his sister's restlessness to this absence in her life. Ursula was, on her twenty-fifth birthday, mostly untouched by man. She had once been engaged to Henry Springton, a young man who had proposed to her at a train station ('of all places,' she would add carelessly when recounting the incident from a distance, although at the time she had thought his spontaneity quite romantic), before boarding a train for London. He had asked for his release three years later, telling her that he had fallen in love with someone else, a widow called Imelda who was ten years older than him and had two children from her previous marriage.

They had agreed to remain friends, and Henry Springton had continued to write to Ursula as he had done during their engagement: long, careless letters in which he told her about trips to the opera with his new fiancée, theatrical evenings, hansom carriages decked out with cut flowers to surprise her. Ursula was not the sort of woman who would have wished for such extravagances, and she suffered from terrible hay fever in any case, but she found it an exquisite form of torment to read about them in his letters.

Ursula imagined Imelda to be one of those translucent, willowy women with an array of silk dresses and an earnest manner, adored by men and with whom Ursula could never really get comfortable. It was not that these women were ever unfriendly towards her – quite the opposite – but she just did not fit. She envied their charm, their sprinkled smiles and delicate wrists, their way of perching on chairs with knees pressed together, and Ursula found that she lacked the endurance to keep up. Their effusiveness left her numb and breathless.

'Ursula, dear, you *must* come up to the Lakes for the shoot this autumn.' Mrs Holboy invited her to the Lake District at the end of every summer, clutching at Ursula's arm as she did so. 'Perhaps you might bring your brother too. It is so much more comfortable to be an even number, don't you think?'

And Ursula would smile. She would feel the muscles in her cheeks doing as they were bid. 'But of course it is!' she would chime. 'How delightful!'

Of all the social virtues, Ursula did not see why charm should be the one which caused her such jarring difficulty. On occasion, she attributed it to the fact that she had not been allowed to go to school like her brother, and had been flung unprepared and unfinished into society. Her mother had given her lessons in the library, of course, but these had always seemed tame and insufficient in comparison with the adventures George recounted from his days at school. There were no ink pellets on her collar, no balanced water buckets or cricket bats or Classics masters to contend with, and Ursula was of the opinion that her French was bound to suffer as a result.

She had tried to educate herself. When they were children, Ursula had insisted upon a nightly recital of everything her brother had learnt that day, even if she did not understand it. She would make George stand at the blackboard in the nursery and write sums for her to do on her slate. George's multiplications were long and convoluted and he made them up on the spot, so he could never tell if the answers Ursula produced were correct or not. He instructed her in the passive voice, in which people did not *speak* but *were heard*, which seemed to Ursula an unnecessary complication, and he inscribed long lists of Latin derivatives on the blackboard which Ursula would copy into her notebook and recite to George's chess pieces when he had gone to school. He told her that her name meant 'little bear' in Latin which delighted her, and from that day onwards he never called her anything else.

But, in Ursula's opinion, it had not been enough to compensate. She knew that she was still viewed by some of her circle as a little *arriviste*. Her wealth was steam-powered and fired by the great furnaces which churned through the night in the tea factory inherited by her brother from their uncle. Her dresses were heavy and unfashionable, dark crinolines which she now saw were too fussy, too buttoned-up. Imelda Springton would not wear such garments, Ursula thought with a sigh, and who could blame her? They were certainly not charming. So perhaps it was all for the best anyway, if charm was what Henry Springton wanted in a wife.

'We were more friends than lovers anyway, weren't we, dearest Bear?' he wrote ruminatively in one of his letters, two years after his marriage to Imelda and not long after his first child was born.

No, she thought, we were not. And if we were, perhaps you might have told me. She signed her next letter 'Ursula' rather than keeping up the affectionate 'Bear' which he had so readily adopted when trying to woo her, but Henry Springton was not the sort of man to notice such subtleties. She left longer and longer intervals before replying to his letters, so that these missives gradually faded into quarterly updates of his continuing happiness.

Her own letters were jovial and brief, filled with dashes and exclamation marks, portraying a jaunty, exaggerated version of her activities and appointments, whilst also dropping hints of flirtations. 'My great friend, C—,' she wrote, 'finds me ever so hard to pin down!'

She had not seen Henry Springton again after releasing him from the engagement. She was not the sort of woman to hold a man to his promise once he had confessed his love for somebody else, but the thought did occasionally strike her that she could have tried a little harder. She could have threatened him with a breach of promise action, as a few people had suggested to her at the time. But then she would have denied him all the happiness he was so willing to document in his letters, and she would not have wanted to carry that responsibility on her narrow, upright shoulders.

Ursula sometimes wondered if she would even recognise him if she were to see him now. He had been, at the time of the proposal, a young man with chestnut hair and dark eyes. Autumnal features, Ursula would think later when she knew him to be an ending rather than a beginning.

In her brother's opinion, it was this experience that had left Ursula with inclinations which, left unfulfilled, had transmogrified into restlessness. George observed how she subscribed to geographical journals and read Royal Society reports, how she studied geological formations and attended lectures of the Liverpool Literary and Philosophical Society, and he imagined that it was all part of the same urge. He saw how his sister's days were kept busy with rational endeavour and good works. In the winter she knitted scarves for orphans at the Holy Innocents' Orphanage in South Liverpool and donated a box of apples to them every October, collected from the orchard at the bottom of her brother's garden. She entered into correspondence with the secretary of the Royal Geographical Society in London on the subject of the proposed colour-coding of atlases, and she took out a subscription to Mr Thomas Cook's monthly magazine, *The Excursionist*.

Of course, Ursula did these things because she enjoyed them, but at the same time she also knew they were not enough. Her life did not seem to be progressing in the manner she had expected. Yes, she had anticipated a certain loneliness after the abrupt conclusion of her engagement, but she had thought it would have a sharp, new-pin quality to it. She found that, in reality, loneliness was not much more than a muffling of the senses. It had nothing of the new pin about it. It did not sparkle or break the skin. It was just a grey, mouth-dry silence, and it bored her.

She knew she must *do* something, only she did not know what. She did know, however, that she was unlikely to find it whilst sitting here in the drawing room of her brother's house, mooning on the chaise longue like the Lady of Shalott. She also knew that she would not find it on a shoot in the Lake District, or over luncheon, or in the offices of her brother's factory. She needed to go further than the Forest of Bowland. She needed an adventure.

It was this conviction that prompted Ursula's maiden voyage with the Thomas Cook company in the early summer of 1862. George came to see her off at Lime Street Station. There were pipers on the platform dressed in breeches and velvet waistcoats, and women whose parasols fluttered under the arched glass roof. Ursula's compartment was already nearly full. She nodded at the two other women passengers, both dressed as if they were going to a carnival with puffed sleeves of bright crimson and layers of petticoats, and whose three children were lined up next to them on the benches.

George opened the carriage door and supported Ursula's arm as she stepped up. She knew he only meant to be helpful but it unbalanced her. She did not need doors to be opened for her. How did he think she got from room to room when he was not there?

George peered forwards. He saw playing cards, red and black and shiny, spread out upon the seat where his sister would be sitting. The colours of the devil, George thought, even though he did not really believe in such things. He saw the cards gathered up a little too expertly, and he leant forwards into the compartment, suspecting gambling. He did not see any money – not even matchsticks – but all the same he pulled at his sister's elbow.

'I shall come too,' he whispered suddenly. 'You shouldn't be going on your own.'

She sighed. 'Really, George,' she hissed. 'I'm only going to Wales.'

She stepped into the compartment and closed the door. The window was pushed down and her brother looked in from the platform. Ursula sat down and arranged her skirts. It struck her that she had never really been anywhere in all her twenty-five years; or at least, nowhere important.

As well as not being allowed to go to school, Ursula had also been the youngest child in her family and, like so many youngest children, had grown up with the sense of having missed out on something, some youthful, unreclaimed happiness to which George occasionally alluded when he spoke of the years before she was born. There had been another brother and a sister between them, both lost to tuberculosis within the space of one cold year, whom George had known and Ursula had not, and Ursula attributed a certain amount of her current restlessness to this unspoken difference between them.

She was also the only girl in a family of male cousins. This was, in Ursula's opinion, the main problem, as it meant that she was the one most likely to be prohibited from doing things. In their games in the nursery, she had not even been allowed to ride the packing-cases which they used as horses, except occasionally when she was being captured by George and rescued by Jacob, the middle cousin, and even then she was merely flung from one packing case to the other, and on neither packing case was she allowed to hold the reins.

'You can't hold the reins if I'm supposed to be rescuing you,' Jacob had whispered crossly to her on one particularly fraught occasion. 'You're supposed to be swooning.'

'I'm bored of swooning,' she had retorted, and then had sat on the back of Jacob's horse with her arms folded, refusing to cooperate with her rescue.

'I want to be a soldier in the next game,' she announced. 'Or the jester.'

'You can't,' George had told her, patting her head in a manner that only infuriated his little sister further. 'You're just a girl.'

It was this comment, Ursula later supposed, which had tipped her over the edge. She remembered the navy-and-white sailor dress she had been wearing that day, her mousey-brown hair falling in unregimented spirals from her crimson ribbons. She had adjusted her neckerchief and narrowed her eyes at her brother, and then she had lifted her chin and straightened her back.

It was a tiny change, barely noticeable, and indeed George had not noticed it at the time. When she was older, he would call it terseness, this uplift along her spine, but at the point of its origin, unversed as he was in the subtleties of female body language, he mistook it for a yawn.

But now Ursula leaned her shoulders out of the window to wave to her brother as the train pulled out of the station. Her skin goose-pimpled in the early morning air. She had not felt like this since childhood, or perhaps since the proposal, and maybe not even then because there were other things to think about with that. Marriage had a solemn edge to it. There were no solemn edges now. The day was bright and sunny, salty and fresh where the wind blew in from the Mersey. The station echoed with seagulls, perched on the iron rafters above the platform. It felt like a dream.

It was here that Henry Springton had asked her to marry him, under an arched roof hot with steam and farewells. He had pressed her hand when she accepted, but she had not kissed him. She had turned her head decorously, thinking it better to wait. Such restraint! And for what?

She shook her head, trying to dislodge the image of Henry Springton. Flecks of soot landed on her face and her collar, and she drew back into the carriage as the train lurched out of the station.

Her companions in the compartment were chatty and excitable. They told her about other trips they had taken, to the great house at Chatsworth, with Joseph Paxton's famous glass conservatory in which there were water-lilies so large and rubbery that the children had sat on them like frogs; to Brunel's steamship with the iron hull that had lost its bearings and run aground at Dundrum Bay in Ireland; to Belvoir House where the Duke of Rutland himself had delivered the tour.

They offered her a boiled egg. She accepted it out of politeness, but also out of curiosity, as she had never eaten an egg with her fingers before. She peeled it carefully as she saw the children doing. The shell fell away easily, revealing the smooth and delightful whiteness, and she felt the soft weight of it in her hand. She took out some slices of roast beef which she had intended to save for lunch and offered them around.

How George would hate this! Ursula thought gleefully, amused by the prospect of her dear brother's horror at so many fingers picking at his food.

After they had eaten, Ursula sat back and clasped her Tourist Handbook to her chest. She had already folded down the corners of the pages she needed to have handy – Welsh phrases and route markers for the proposed ascent of Mount Snowdon. Her mind was full of lakes and mountains, of never-ending train journeys and water-lilies. Her fellow travellers told her about a tour to Paris to see Napoleon III's Universal Exhibition on the Champs Elysées. She heard of steamboats on the Rhine, of Cologne, Mayence, Mannheim, Frankfurt and Heidelberg. They showed her their sketches of Strasbourg, of Dijon and Rheims: terrible drawings, but onto which she could implant her own images of low, timbered houses, grand cathedrals and rivers. She heard about the difficulties of changing money, of francs and centimes, of groschen and pfennigs and kreutzers, of boats from Newhaven to Antwerp, of trains to Brussels, to Aix-la-Chapelle.

Ursula smiled. She was only going to Wales. She still could not really claim to be *doing* anything with her life, but the excursion had the flavour of a trial run, an experiment. It was, she thought, a build-up to something else. She leant her head against the back of the seat and closed her eyes. She felt the sun on her face as it streamed into the carriage, warming her skin and imprinting darts of silver and blue behind her eyelids; a bright nothingness which filled her head like a laugh. She wanted to hold onto this delightful feeling, capture it, rest it in her palm like a seashell; a small, pretty thing washed up by a great, wide sea.

Two

A soft, white arm

Sally Walker had not been to this part of Liverpool before. On the occasions when she had been allowed to accompany her mother into town, she saw only the bustling centre, the tall ships in the docks and the belching factories and warehouses which towered over the water's edge. Then, there had been errands to run, orders to collect. She had clung to her mother's hand as they hurried along the rutted, cobbled street and she had not let go.

Sally sat now in the carriage with a parcel of clothes on her knees, her short legs swinging where her feet did not reach the floor, and she did not recognise a single building. She was homesick for the sea at New Brighton, for the sound of the waves and the rub of salt in the air, for the people who came in and out of the tea shop on the Parade where her mother had worked, and the smell of ham and eggs. Where New Brighton was curved and expansive, Liverpool was sharp and tightly-packed. The narrow roads ran up from the docks, channelling the wind to make Sally's eyes water, her skin crack.

The Orphanage of Holy Innocents stood to the south of the city, backing into fields which stretched out to Speke and then on to Manchester. It was large and gloomy with a pinched chapel at its centre, and low, symmetrical buildings attached to each side. The dining hall and schoolrooms were built from the same stone as St George's Hall in the city centre – grey, the colour of damp clouds – but the orphanage did not catch the sun like that grand music hall, did not gleam almost white in the bright winter mornings.

Inside, its windows were high and grimy, with blue curtains that matched exactly the robes of the Virgin Mary's statue in the chapel. There was a laundry room with vats of caustic soda and a sewing room with wooden stools arranged neatly around the long tables. There were no mirrors on any of the walls as there had been in the tea shop, no paintings of women in white dresses like those at which Sally's mother had once gazed so dreamily. There was nothing light, nothing pretty. The only decorations were gilt-framed oil paintings displaying the Passion of Christ and the Martyrdom of the Saints, oases of devotion amidst the grey.

Sally did not like these pictures. She did not trust Jesus's fingers, the way he pulled at his own flesh to display his Bleeding Heart. She could not bear the pleading eyes of the saints as they bore their agonies in this dark-brushed, papery silence. At night, she imagined them calling to her for help, and she had to cover her head with her blanket, because how could she have helped them if she could not even help her own mother?

On the day following her admittance, Sally was taken to the mortuary in town by Sister Thomas of the Holy Ghost. Sister Thomas of the Holy Ghost was a tall woman with a long stride and an iron core. Sally found her impossible to navigate. Every word, every arc of the hand, displayed a propensity for dominance, a sort of natural aggression, which Sally found unsettling.

'Before we go in to see The Body, you must shut your

eyes and imagine your mother's immortal soul,' Sister Thomas of the Holy Ghost had hissed in her ear as they stood together outside the door of the mortuary. Sally felt a small spray of spittle land on her skin. She pictured the soft whiteness of her mother's stomach.

'Well? Can you see it?'

'No,' Sally whispered, her eyes fixed on the taut boot-laces of Sister Thomas of the Holy Ghost.

The nun sighed.

Sally Walker screwed up her eyes and tried to imagine her mother's immortal soul. The image Sally had of her mother at this time, so soon after her death, was pearly white and entirely unembroidered. She held a perfect likeness of Elizabeth Walker in her mind. She could shut her eyes and picture her mother's thin toes, the second one longer than the first, and remember the exact sound and pitch of her voice in the mornings. She could recall the firmness of her mother's arms, the narrowness of her waist, the way she wrapped her beautiful blonde hair up in a towel after washing it like the Indian women on the packets of tea that lined the walls of the tea shop where she had worked.

Her mother's immortal soul, however, was another matter altogether. Sally did not know where to begin. She looked up at Sister Thomas and her eyes grew cloudy with tears. She shook her head again.

'The immortal soul should look like a dove,' Sister Thomas said, her voice betraying a slight impatience. 'Oh, that I had wings like a dove,' she intoned crossly, 'then would I . . .' She stopped and looked at Sally. 'What then would I do, girl?'

Sally looked at her in alarm. She was not yet acquainted with the religious habit of breaking into verse, and she found herself uncertain whether or not she had heard properly. 'Would you fly, ma'am?' she asked tentatively.

'I would fly away and be at rest,' Sister Thomas announced. 'Such is the mystery of the immortal soul when breathed upon by the Holy Spirit.' There was a slight pause during which Sister Thomas fixed Sally with a disapproving eye. 'You have to concentrate if you are going to see it.'

Sally nodded and closed her eyes. She screwed up her face and tried to concentrate.

'Well?' asked Sister Thomas, a certain sharpness creeping into her voice.

Sally hesitated. No, she had not seen it, and yet she sensed that there would be no progress until she was able to picture her mother's soul in the prescribed form, so she held her breath and then smiled quite suddenly. 'Yes,' she said simply, opening her eyes. 'Yes. There it is.'

The nun seemed satisfied with this answer. She took Sally's hand to pull her forwards. A door opened and shut behind them. Sally shuffled her feet, short legs in grey stockings, until Sister Thomas came to an abrupt halt, causing Sally to walk into her thigh and catch the back of the nun's shoe with her foot. There was a general fussing, a straightening out of leather and wool, before Sister Thomas of the Holy Ghost placed her hands under Sally's armpits and lifted her up.

'Here,' she said, lifting Sally into the air and bumping the girl's knees on the shelf upon which the body lay. 'This is only the shell of your mother. It is just a body, and you must say goodbye to it, but it is not important. It is just dust. It is not the immortal soul.'

Sally was not listening. The room was dark, and the laid-out bodies were set like stones in the candlelight, four of them that she could see, colourless and smooth with carved faces. She held out her hands in front of her, trying to feel through the shadows while Sister Thomas's bony fingers wound around her body, compressing her lungs and bruising her back. She felt herself being tilted forwards.

There was a pause, a gap of perhaps a second as her eyes adjusted to the flickering gloom, before Sally began to scream. She did not pause for breath. She screwed up her fists and felt her lungs swelling as the noise reverberated against her throat. Sister Thomas clapped a hand over Sally's mouth, muffling the sound as it came out so that Sally gagged and struggled.

It is possible that, had Sister Thomas not been so insistent on Sally picturing her mother's immortal soul, the image of Elizabeth Walker would not have been quite so clear when Sally opened her eyes again, and perhaps she would not have reacted so strongly or screamed so loudly when she did. But there it was. The woman she was being lifted over in the mortuary had dirty hair and a grey neck. She was wearing a flannel tunic and heavy boots on her feet. This woman was not Sally's mother.

Sister Thomas of the Holy Ghost, however, remained under the impression that she was. Sally felt the hands around her ribcage tightening, lifting her higher, and then her face was touching the dead woman's face, and Sally felt the chill of the woman's skin against her compressed lips.

Sally could not turn away. She kicked her legs backwards. She did not mean to cause any harm. It was simply a reflex, an involuntary contraction of muscle. The first time she missed, and her legs swung ineffectually against the cloth of Sister Thomas's habit. The second time, she bent her legs and her right boot landed in the soft part of Sister Thomas of the Holy Ghost's midriff.

It surprised her, how easily the flesh gave under her.

And, at the same time, it did not really surprise her. Not any more.

When she later reported the incident to the Mother

Superior, Sister Thomas of the Holy Ghost delicately scattered the first seeds of Sally Walker's downfall with a knowing calm, hinting in a vague and indirect manner that this was more the sort of thing one might expect from a late medieval dissenter than from a parish orphan. She did not mention how she had dropped Sally to the floor, grabbing her by the arm and bruising the child's pale skin as she hurried her outside. Nor did she mention how Sally had cried out as they left the room, because she had seen something Sister Thomas had not: a soft, white arm protruding from a lumpy sheet on the other side of the room, its lovely fingers reaching for her.

Three

The Letter-Writer

Later that year, Ursula Bridgewater climbed Ben Nevis on a two-week tour of Scotland, conducted by Mr Thomas Cook himself. *'One hundred miles of sailing, railing and walking,'* as the brochure put it, *'all for four shillings.'* For the climb, Ursula wore soft leather boots and a crinoline dress which she had pinned up so that it did not snag. Her arms tingled in the cold mist and her breath parted in a white cloud around her.

After Ben Nevis, the tour group took a steamer down the Clyde to Glasgow, and from there boarded a train to Edinburgh, visiting Holyrood and the Castle. They passed near Balmoral in the hope of a royal sighting, but Queen Victoria did not emerge as she had once done to wave to the tour, remaining hidden behind the heavy stone walls. They went to the Firth of Forth and Arthur's Seat, to Bowling, Balloch and Loch Lomond. They visited Iona and witnessed the fleet of fishing boats donated by previous Cook tourists. After a bracing walk among the bright yellow gorse of Iona, Mr Thomas Cook mounted a large monumental stone and made a short speech about the joys of the island, about its lack of alehouses and the reality of history bursting through the ages into this forgotten place. He cast his arm towards the harbour and asked of his tourists: 'May we not claim for our labours the character of a mission?'

Such direction, Ursula thought admiringly. And from nowhere at all. Well, from Leicestershire if one was going to be precise, but from nowhere special.

It was on this trip that Ursula met Miss Joy and Miss Emma Clanthey. They were cousins, they informed her, and liked to plan an annual excursion to coincide with St Swithin's Day. They spoke of their travelling companions on the tour in a distant, amused manner which Ursula found at first exclusive, and then riveting. Each fellow passenger had a title by which they were known: there was Colonel Rhodes, red-cheeked and tweedy, who was dubbed the Artilleryman; Miss Davison became the Poet Laureate, an earnest lady who sighed breathlessly on the uphill scrambles and moved her lips when reading her leather-bound edition of Elizabeth Barrett Browning; Monsieur Bourdon, sharp-chinned and dapper, was the Silver Fox; Mrs Dilkes, a sad, drooping willow of a woman, the Solitary Chaperone. There were others to whom Ursula had not paid much attention previously but who now became characters of interest: the Continental Traveller, the Physician, the Fearful Bore, Mr Pieter the Great Dane, the Scottish Interpreter; a full cast list filled out with hotel-keepers and ticket inspectors and policemen.

And then Ursula discovered her own title: the Official Letter-Writer. The cousins had smiled when they said it, thinking it a compliment, and Ursula had smiled back, performing expertly. It shocked her, that this should be the thing for which she was known. She had not realised how much time she spent scrawling at the writing desks of the hotels. She had written to George of course, sending him amusing tales of the other travellers and sites of historical interest which they had visited, and she supposed that this letter was quite lengthy, although it had not taken long to write. She had also written to a few of her other friends from whose drawing rooms she had escaped with such aplomb, but these were, on the whole, short, unremarkable letters.

Mostly, she supposed, she had written to Henry Springton. Drafts of letters, written and rewritten until she despaired of her own voice. Yes, she had loved Ben Nevis, but it seemed facile to say so, and whereas to George she could use all the superlatives she wished, to Henry Springton she became reserved and cynical, trying to convey both delight and humour, whilst retaining a hint of self-mockery. It was not a task she enjoyed, and yet she forced herself to endure it because she could not bear to lose this connection with her past, and it was less of a burden to write to him from these excursions than from the drawing-room at home.

Miss Emma and Miss Joy, however, had not guessed at this. Ursula supposed they had befriended her because they imagined her to be a shrewd observational wit with a host of friends with whom she wished to communicate in neatly folded missives.

'Oh no,' Ursula demurred, 'not a *host*, as such,' but she did not protest any further.

Coming to Scotland had been Miss Emma (the Philosopher)'s idea, whereas Miss Joy (the Artist) would have preferred the Alps. She liked Scotland, being drawn to the facial expressions and sudden laughter of its inhabitants, but she compared it incessantly to Switzerland. She had once been to Switzerland when she was a child, and she remembered the crisp blueness of the sky, the lilacs and yellows of the flowers in the meadows. According to Miss Joy, there were no midges in Switzerland, no thistles or nettles. The hills were grander, their peaks more jagged and romantic, the heather more colourful.

Six months after she returned from Scotland, Ursula received a letter from the cousins which constituted a formal invitation to join the dramatis personae of a Swiss tour the following year. They told her she could resume her role as Official Letter-Writer if she so wished, but this time it would be in an honorary capacity, such as they held themselves. They had been considering Norway and the fjords, but had since read that it was as like Scotland in natural beauty as anywhere could wish to be, and this had put Miss Joy off. Happily, however, Mr Cook had intervened in the ensuing stand-off by announcing his intention to arrange a tour to Switzerland, and the matter was thus settled, and would be all the more settled if Ursula cared to join them. It was, they told her, to be their last, since both of them were to be married the following autumn and they feared their husbands were not Continental Travellers.

Ursula sighed at this last sentence – it would have been too much to expect this to continue – but she cleared this thought from her mind and issued an enthusiastic acceptance by return of post. She had been thinking of Scarborough for her next trip, perhaps with George if he could have been persuaded, although she knew he would have been churlish ('It is for children and invalids,' he had muttered when she made the suggestion), but Britain was starting to bore her. Switzerland, however, was intriguing: the land of Calvin and Lake Geneva, chocolate and cheese and ornate clocks, and the prospect of going with her two new friends was delightful.

They departed at the beginning of July and travelled first to Paris, and then on to Geneva. The Poet Laureate was on the trip too, which caused some hilarity at Newhaven, and there was an incident with a cut finger which induced Miss Joy to be appointed Honorary Physician as well as Artist, much to her pretended dismay.

'It is so unromantic to be deemed scientific,' she complained.

Dieppe was white-washed and religious, a carved crucifix marking the entrance to the harbour; Rouen, slate grey and twilit; Paris, cold and wet. Ursula was unable to form any real impression of the city, arriving some time after midnight and departing from the Paris and Lyons railway station located near the site of the stormed Bastille at five o'clock the following morning. They passed through Sens and Mâcon, endless fields edged with poplars and acacia, and thence to Ambérieu and on into Switzerland, where the women wore caps instead of bonnets. The fields rose up into those jagged mountains of Miss Joy's memory, and the moon shimmered in the dark, icy lakes which, as the train chugged sleepily on to Geneva, reminded Ursula of the shadows of the ships in the Liverpool docks at dusk.

From Geneva, they proceeded back towards the French border near Chamonix, and then up into the mountains, led by the Mountain Goat, a brown-hatted man with long legs and a bright smile, and for whom Miss Emma developed a small passion. They did not climb to the summit but walked up to the glacier above Chamonix, and crossed it using a series of iron ladders. There were nineteen in the party, with seven mules between them, and they walked in twos and threes, stopping occasionally for refreshments at small wooden chalets, where red-cheeked women would offer goat's cheese and freshly-baked bread from their dark, wild-flowered kitchens.

They walked for another five days to Courmayeur in Italy, following a path around Mont Blanc into its wide, green valleys and over narrow, daisy-strewn passes which climbed up through drifts of cloud. Ursula walked in an oilskin riding shirt and a light woollen dress she had designed herself, having threaded a cord into the hem so that it could be gathered up on the more difficult mountain paths. Her boots were hobnailed and heavy, and she wore woollen stockings to her knees. On her head she wore a wide-brimmed straw hat with a small velvet veil to protect her neck from the sun, and she sported a pair of green glasses.

George would have proclaimed the whole outfit scandalous. Ursula did not see the scandal. She never did. It was simply to overcome the perplexing trappings, as Mr Cook called them in his tourist guide, of the prevailing feminine fashions. Ursula felt that she was at last doing something with her life, seeing something, although she still retained the sense that all of it was part of a build-up to something else, some higher purpose which remained elusive.

She wrote to George, telling him how the Reverend Harper-Jones (the Redeemer) had leapt up ahead of the party on their way across the Col de Bovine and scooped a marmot into his arms, and it was the softest, oddest creature she had ever seen. She knew he would not like this – her brother had never taken to animals – but she could not believe that he would not have warmed to it if he could have only seen its small paws burrowing away at the dandelions and forget-me-nots in the cold, bright, slanting meadows.

And eventually, almost reluctantly, she wrote to Henry Springton from the hotel at Courmayeur – a shorter, more precise letter than her previous attempts but still witty, still cynical. Her new friends hustled and interrupted her while she wrote, curious for details of this previously unmentioned recipient whose letter caused Ursula Bridgewater to chew at her pen in such a manner.

'He's just an old friend,' she told them abruptly, her cheeks hot at their questions.

She sighed and sealed the letter, and slipped it into her bag. Her body felt suddenly heavy, and for a moment she thought of returning home, of the docks and warehouses of Liverpool, the low sky in winter; more appropriate to her mood somehow than all these wondrous mountains.

Oh Henry Springton, she thought, you will never know the bite you took out of me.

Three months later, back at her brother's house in Aigburth, a package arrived from Chamonix. Ursula unwrapped it slowly, and held it up to the light. It was a portrait of herself and Miss Emma and Miss Joy, both now married and lost to her, but for which the three friends had sat in Chamonix before their ascent of the glacier. She smiled and hung it on the wall of her dressing room. It would occasionally catch her eye during those dull, corseted mornings back in England, and then she would laugh a little, because, dressed in all that mountaineering attire, she thought she looked a little like a Red Indian.

Four

Charles Blondin and the lion

Sally Walker was not an hysterical child. She did not excite easily. When her mother died not long after Sally's seventh birthday, she had borne the pain of this crisis alone. She had not cried as the other girls in the orphanage did, had not bitten her nails or kicked the bedstead with her toes or screamed in the night. She had prayed instead to a God in whom she did not really believe to look after a mother she could not really remember, and she had not been hysterical about it.

She might have talked to Mr Fisher, the owner of the tea shop on New Brighton Parade where her mother had worked. Elizabeth Walker died on the London Road whilst collecting an order for Mr Fisher from Liverpool. When word got to him, Mr Fisher had rushed to the Royal Infirmary and held Sally in his arms, and he thought he would probably have wept if Sally had been older and able to absorb his grief along with her own. But she had wriggled free from his heavy, fusty arms and his tannic smell. There were no tears. She had held back from him, her face uncrumpled and smooth, and nothing betrayed the ache she felt in her stomach, or the heavy, waxy lump in her throat when she tried to eat.

Mr Fisher came to visit her at the orphanage once a week,

bringing small treats, tennis balls and ribbons for her hair, which were immediately confiscated by Sister Thomas of the Holy Ghost. He took her to the Punch and Judy stand in St George's Square and to the seaside. He would have done more but he did not know what to offer. On these small trips he tried to talk to her about her mother, but Sally merely nodded and would not speak about it. She remained polite and formal, sidestepping any mention. Mr Fisher did not understand. He could not tell if the child simply did not feel anything, or whether she felt too much.

But Sally understood. She knew that Mr Fisher could mention her mother so casually because he had not seen the accident, could not imagine it. He did not know, as Sally did, how the omnibus had veered towards them, how Elizabeth Walker had reached down and picked Sally up, her hands gripping her waist. He did not know how she had bent her knees and launched Sally onto the pavement, forced backwards as she did so by Newton's Third Law of Motion, into the path of the oncoming horses.

Sally had landed hands first, grazing her palms and mottling her knees, her breath caught in her throat, and she had thought – oh, how foolish she had been back then, how careless! – that she might be flying. She had lifted her eyes, turning to her mother to shout, 'Look at me! I just flew!' – and it was only then that she had seen the horses, their heads tilted at an awkward angle and their hooves stamping as the driver pulled the reins tight. And below the horses, on the cobbles, she saw her mother's arms stretched above her head, her legs twisted beneath her in a subdued S, a single spot of blood just above her mouth, unnaturally bright. Unlike Sally, Mr Fisher did not have to block out the sound of Elizabeth Walker's head against the cobbles, or the lingering scent of rosewater drifting up from her wrists.

So it was not that Sally did not feel anything. It was just that she knew, when she was far too young to know such a thing, that she was all alone in the world, and it was for this reason that she had chosen to deal with her loss, and by extension her loneliness, by herself.

She could not express this knowledge, and in any case she did not want to. But she understood why it was that Mr Fisher could come to the orphanage and talk about her mother in that way of his, playful and sentimental. She knew why he patted her head with his hand and bought sugared mice for her at the Punch and Judy show which she could not eat. She knew he was trying to be kind but she also knew she could not respond in the way he would have liked. And the reason was quite simple. It was because, when it actually happened, when Elizabeth Walker fell, he was not there.

But Sally was.

*

For a while, when she was very small and her mother was still alive, Sally had thought Mr Fisher might be her father. Or, more precisely, she had hoped he was. He was bright and jolly, with warm hands and thick white hair, and sometimes, when all the customers had left and Sally was polishing cake forks while her mother swept the floor, Mr Fisher would wink at her and then remove his patent leather shoes and his dusty brown socks, and he would waddle up and down the middle of the shop like a duck.

When Sally had asked her mother about this theory of her paternity, her mother had snorted almost crossly. Her mother had a habit of snorting at things she did not want to talk about. It was the one noise she made that Sally had never been able to interpret. Elizabeth Walker had a thin, delicate nose with light freckles on the very top of it, but when she snorted it wrinkled upwards and Sally did not like to look at it, scrunched up like that. She snorted about the cost of coal, at the bunion on her left foot, at the patches of eczema on her neck, and at any mention of Sally's father.

The only solid piece of information Sally had regarding her father's whereabouts was that he had sailed to Australia before she was born, and was probably (and here her mother would snort in that way of hers) lost at sea. Elizabeth would not offer any further details, except on one occasion when Sally had been biting her nails and her mother slapped her hand from her mouth, adding that she was just like her father. Her tone of voice made it clear to Sally that such a resemblance was not to be encouraged. But this was all Sally knew of him. There were no letters, no pictures, just a large, nail-bitten space where he had once been.

When she was a child, Sally's father lived in this gap. She worried away at his sharp-edged absence, unable to let it go. Every story she heard became, for Sally, a story about her father. He was a prince, a pirate, an explorer. He lived in a castle and ate stewed apple for breakfast. He was a hare *and* a tortoise. He was a seahorse, a starfish. He sang to her from rocks.

Before the accident, she would send messages to him in eggshells from the beach at New Brighton: a moth's wing and a sugar lump. Once she sent him a boiled egg yolk, perfectly round and slightly dusty, because she thought it might grow into a chicken. She wrote notes on small scraps of paper, asking him if he could breathe underwater and whether she could borrow his parrot.

Elizabeth Walker had not guessed the extent of her daughter's fascination with the subject of her father, being all too well-acquainted with the reality of the man's mortal flesh. When she thought of her husband, she thought first of his teeth, mildewy and soft, and his fingernails bitten down to the quick. He leaked occasionally into her thoughts, staining them with that rust-coloured dirt she remembered so well from his collars and cuffs and she would shudder at the very thought. She did not consider the possibility of her husband becoming a romantic figure for anybody. She did not think for a moment that when her daughter collected the eggshells from the table after tea, slotting them into each other and smuggling them up to her bedroom, that it bore any connection to her lost husband.

She did not know how Sally's father had become confused in the girl's mind with the stories Elizabeth told her at night, sitting on her bed while Sally tried to sleep. There were children locked up in ovens, wolves in night-gowns. She used to begin, *Once upon a time . . .* but this had unnerved Sally.

'Which time?' she would ask. 'Why *upon*?'

So Elizabeth Walker had stopped using this beginning and instead began each story in the way her grandfather had started all of the stories he had told her when she was a child: 'There was a time and there was no time.' Or some-times: 'There was, and there was not, a little girl . . .'

Elizabeth Walker thought this was less specific. She did not realise that it gave greater fluidity to the stories, so that every man in every story would seamlessly become part of Sally's made-up memory of her father. He was sealed in the glass bottle of her imagination, intricately crafted and immaculate, this man who had gone away to sea and would never be heard from again.

*

When Sally had been at the orphanage for six months, Mr Fisher sought permission to take her out to see Charles

Blondin walking the high wire in the Liverpool Zoological Gardens. He thought it would be a treat. He remembered how Sally's mother had loved to read about Blondin's crossings of the Niagara Falls in the *Liverpool Daily Post*, how she had marvelled at the descriptions of the three-inch hemp cord strung out over that great gush of water, huge and white beneath him. After her death, the reports had continued to arrive on the steamers from New York, accompanied by grainy photographic images. Mr Fisher cut these out to send to Sally, to show her he had not forgotten.

There were pictures of Blondin in grey-and-white striped trousers, balancing a chair on the high wire and waving to the crowd from his perch. There were pictures of him cooking an omelette on a small stove in the middle of the rope, and then lowering it to the passengers on the *Maid of the Mist* paddle steamer below. He crossed the Falls blindfolded and in a sack, and offered to carry the Prince of Wales across on his shoulders.

Mr Fisher sent all of these to Sally, folded lovingly, because he did not know how else to express that emotion to this silent child. He did not realise, of course, that Sally would be unable to look at these pictures. He could not imagine how they would terrify her, and how the image of the tumbling water would keep her awake at night, her eyes wide and dry.

But the newspaper clippings were not the only reason that Sally was unable to sleep. When she first arrived at the orphanage, Sister Thomas of the Holy Ghost had told Sally that she must always sleep with her hands folded over her chest, palms downwards, so that if she died in the night she would not scratch the coffin. Any scratches, Sister Thomas informed her, would indicate despair at the point of death, and there was no worse sin than despair.

So when Sally Walker lay in her bed at night with her

hands crossed over her chest, she was not just afraid of dying. She was afraid she might despair. And she was afraid of other things too. She was afraid of the dark, of Sister Thomas, of woodlice, of the Bleeding Heart and the Passion, of frogs and snakes and spiders, of King Herod. But most of all, more than anything else, she was afraid of falling like her mother, and when she looked at the newspaper cuttings of Charles Blondin on that high wire above the Niagara Falls, she felt it in her stomach, that same whooshing, giddying sensation she had felt on the London Road that day, and it jolted her awake every night.

When Charles Blondin came to the Liverpool Zoological Gardens in the summer of 1862 and wheeled a lion across the high wire in a wheelbarrow, Sally had just turned eight and was dressed in her best dress, grey wool with a blue sash. There were crowds of children betting with marbles and women with soft, blonde hair just like her mother's, the sight of whom made Sally stumble, her legs suddenly weak. Mr Fisher found a place where they could see, away from the main push of people, and he sat down next to her on the grass. The rope was strung from the top of an oak tree to the roof of the elephant house. It shivered in the breeze.

Sally could not look. She thought: Dear God, lift mine eyes.

Mr Fisher lit a cheroot and blew smoke rings in the cold air, nudging Sally gently with his elbow as they shimmered upwards and broke apart. He offered her a boiled sweet. He tugged a piece of grass to make into a whistle. He told her stories about the tea shop and described the new sign he had ordered from Manchester to go above the awnings. She could not listen. Every word, every gesture reminded her of that earlier, happier life she had known. There were birds perched on the tight rope. Sally smiled at Mr Fisher until her cheeks ached. She knew herself to be afraid and yet she also knew that she must do what was expected of her. She must gape and gasp and clap, and show Mr Fisher how grateful she was. She made these resolutions to herself. There was applause and general hilarity. The boiled sweet stuck to her teeth. She plucked at it with her tongue.

But I am not brave enough, she thought. And it was true, for when the moment came for Charles Blondin to step out onto the wire, Sally Walker felt an ache in her chest such as she imagined St Stephen must have felt when the stones hit his skin in the oil painting above the dormitory door, and she pressed her hands over her eyes.

'Ho!' Mr Fisher exclaimed as a guy rope seemed to get twisted in Blondin's feet, and he stood first on one leg and then on the other to shake it free. Mr Fisher nudged Sally. 'Are you watching, Sal?'

Sally hesitated, and then slowly parted her fingers. She peeped out. She saw a blur of sky, of red, heart-shaped leaves. She thought of the Bleeding Heart and shuddered. She looked up further, up and up, until she could see Charles Blondin dressed in white stockings and red-and-white striped plus-fours, hopping on the wire to untangle the guy rope from beneath him. She thought of horses, of their stamping feet, and then of her mother's hands around her waist as she launched her; a faint whiff of rosewater. She bit at the inside of her cheek as Blondin executed a final triumphant kick so that the tangled guy rope fell at last from the high wire, turning dizzily in the air before landing on the ground with a soft slap. Sally clapped her hands to her mouth. It was nauseating. It surged in her, a great wave of giddiness rising like a huge sob. She could have walked three steps forward and picked up the rope and it would have been the same as it had always been – after all, it was only a rope – but there was something broken about the way it landed, a subdued S-shape, which Sally had seen somewhere before, and which she could not, however hard she tried, erase from her mind.

Five

The bat

The bat arrived from England in a cardboard box. It had been dispatched from the office of the Royal Society of Taxidermists in Bloomsbury, London, by Miss Hammond, a Baptist lady of forty, pale-haired and marble-skinned, who did not like the practice of stuffing dead animals with rags and cotton and hanging them on walls. She had, however, remained in her secretarial position at the Royal Society because the President had received a mention in a footnote to the eighth edition of the *Encyclopaedia Britannica*, and she had never before met anybody who had appeared in an encyclopaedia, or indeed in any form of reference literature. It was for this reason that she had not yet felt bold enough to hand in the letter of resignation which had lain sealed in the drawer of her desk for the past three years.

The only concession she could make to her dislike of stuffing animals was that, when she packaged them up to send to various members of the Society in the outposts of the Empire, she would shroud them in white tissue paper as a mark of respect. She would then entomb them in a cardboard box before sending them off on packet steamers from Wapping.

This particular bat was sent in response to an order mailed from America several months previously, requesting a fruit bat with spread wings (this last part was underlined three times). There would be bats in America, of course – Miss Hammond had learnt this from the Society's treasured copy of the *Encyclopaedia Britannica* which, even after much thumbing-through, still fell open at a certain page – but they were not affiliated to the Royal Society. She felt that it was quite understandable, therefore, that the man placing the order, a Mr Edmund O'Hara, should want his bat to be properly affiliated.

Miss Hammond folded the tissue paper carefully and tucked it around the bat's wings. She wrote an address label and, more out of habit than because she expected to find anything in particular, ran a cursory finger down the index of the *Encyclopaedia Britannica* in search of an Edmund O'Hara. She just wanted to be sure, to check she was not missing anyone important. There were no entries.

'Oh well,' she thought to herself. 'I am expecting too much, now that I have my connections.'

She propped the cardboard box under her arm to take to the post office and, striding down the steps and into the white spring light of the London morning, she resolved to wait another month before handing in her letter of resignation.

The bat arrived in New England in June 1862, just as Miss Hammond was postponing her resignation for yet another month, and it caused the sort of commotion that Miss Hammond would have made herself, had such a thing arrived at her own doorstep.

The commotion sprang from the fact that Edmund O'Hara had not yet found a way of mentioning the imminent arrival to his wife. This was not a deliberate omission. It was just that there had never really been an opportunity and he lacked the courage to create one, knowing that the arrival of a fruit bat with spread wings was likely to induce a certain prickliness in her.

When Mary O'Hara sat on the wooden steps of the post office to open the parcel and was greeted with decorative folds of white tissue paper, she was not expecting a bat. She imagined the package to contain something pleasurable and delicate, perhaps a belated wedding gift from her husband's relatives in Ireland. White linen from Belfast, she thought, or lace from Limerick.

She knew this was unlikely. There had been no more than a single letter from her husband's family since the birth of her son, Toby, ten years previously, and it had done nothing more than list the childhood ailments of her husband and his brothers. Mary O'Hara considered that this might have been unsettling if she were the sort of woman who was easily startled, but this was not the case. Or at least, not really. There was only one thing which niggled at her, tugging at her consciousness while she tried to sleep. She could not describe it without considering herself irrational. Her husband called them dreams – oh, how she wished they were! – but she knew they were not. They were premonitions.

Mary O'Hara received her first premonition when she was seventeen years old and newly-married. She did not know what it was. She did not recognise the place or any of the people. It was only later when she read about the Cape Ann earthquake in the *Boston Daily Herald* that she realised she had known it would happen approximately seven weeks before it actually occurred. The sheriff of Cape Ann was a Mr Johnson and he was thirty-nine years old on the day of the earthquake. Five people and three dogs perished. Mary O'Hara knew they would. It was exactly as she had dreamed it.

Over the next twelve months she witnessed a tornado in

Gloucester and a tremor in Newport several weeks before each of them occurred, and it was after the second of these that she began to make notes of her premonitions in a small leather-bound journal which she would later mark with a small tick and the date on which the events actually took place.

She did not tell many people about this journal. She kept her dreams to herself and, at times, wondered if perhaps she was fitting the disasters to the dreams, as she could not always place her visions geographically until she read about them in the newspapers. This struck her as a rather self-aggrandising thing to be doing and she resolved to stop writing them down. She did this for a while, but it was no use. The premonitions stayed with her, being played back over and over again until she had recorded them properly and only then would she be free of them. Months later she would read about these things happening in places she had been unable to identify, and she would shake her head and wonder.

This did not happen every night. There were occasions when she could go for weeks at a time without any premonitions, entertaining instead perfectly normal dreams of cream cakes and perfectly knotted loaves of bread. These were the sorts of things Mary O'Hara considered proper for a woman like herself to be dreaming about; women with rational, New World educations such as her own would, all over America, be dreaming of bread, she was certain of it. They would not be foretelling disasters through dreams, and in the daylight, Mary O'Hara did not really believe that she could either.

However, this was not on her mind as she sat on the steps of the post office in Holloway Creek, New England, in 1862, untucking the white tissue paper from the cardboard box. She was thinking of curtains and bonnets. She felt the heat of the sun through the cotton of her dress as she picked at the parcel's sealing wax with her delicate, piano-player's fingers. She opened it carefully, not wanting the imagined swathes of silk to fall onto the dusty street.

When she saw that what she held was not linen at all, but a monster with pointed ears and glassy eyes and a translucent web of membrane strung between its outstretched cartilage, Mary O'Hara was startled. And she was not just startled. She was overcome. She did not think about what she was doing. Her rational education deserted her. What she felt was involuntary, a self-protective reflex she did not know she possessed. She threw the parcel from her knee so that its contents spilled onto the road and only then did she allow herself to scream, because she thought she had seen the devil himself.

Buster

Mary O'Hara was jealous of that bat.

Mary was a small, pretty woman with brown eyes and dimples in her cheeks when she smiled. Her husband, Edmund, was the opposite: tall and blue-eyed with hair the colour of maple-syrup. He was a toymaker, with huge hands and paint under his fingernails. To see him at work he was so messy, so fevered, that Mary O'Hara could hardly believe those tiny, intricate things were produced by those same hands. He made alligator masks and spinning tops, and he carved tiny dolls' houses from walnut shells. There were puppets who sat drowsily on a high shelf, until Edmund took them down and tugged at their strings to make them come alive under the web of his fingers.

Edmund had endless stories from his childhood, unlike

Mary who only had three. He would tell these stories again and again; his life in Ulster before emigrating, pitchforks and cabbage patches, sloops and cutters and muskets and landlords, ear infections and potatoes. Mary listened dutifully to her husband's stories even though she knew the endings already. His tales were like chapters from a favourite book, read and reread. Sometimes he would bend down when he spoke to Mary, resting his hands on his knees. Mary considered this slightly unnecessary – she was not *that* small – but there was something gentle about the way he did it which she grew to like.

She smiled when he told their son the story of the time they met: him, with wings strapped to his arms and legs, being hoisted onto the roof of the general store; and her, just a girl. A pepperpot, he had called her, and that was how she thought of herself when he spoke of that time. A pepperpot in a blue dress, with her dark brown hair twisted up into a tight chignon.

Edmund O'Hara emigrated from Ireland to America at the age of twenty. His family had not been poor, having seven acres of farmland in the countryside near Belfast. But – and his pop used the same words every time he told Toby the story of his escape – to the stomach of a hungry man, seven acres of rotten potatoes were materially no better than half an acre, and so he left anyway.

He arrived at South Street Seaport, New York, in the November of 1848. The harbour was a floating mass of filthy straw, of barrels and rags, of old clothes thrown from the sides of the immigrant ships. It was not what he had pictured when he left the lichen-covered stone of his homeland. The streets of New York were congested with pigs and dogs and rubbish. It was busier and bigger and dirtier than Edmund had imagined.

He pushed through the crowds with his bag strapped to his back, clutching a saucepan. It was raining, and there was such a jostle of people that he did not see the leaflet being pressed into his hand. He did not want it. He was about to drop it to the ground when he noticed the strange picture on the front. It was an advertisement for a demonstration taking place at the Tabernacle Church that very afternoon, a presentation of Mr Rufus Porter's Aerial Locomotive which would, one day soon, fly to the goldfields of California. Edmund looked at the drawing of a long basket attached to a hydrogen-filled gas spindle, with flags on the masts at both ends and a small puff of smoke coming from the rear. He squinted at it. He wondered how something so light and magical could rise out of all this muck.

Edmund O'Hara went to the demonstration out of curiosity, because he had nowhere else to go and because it was raining. He watched the cigar-sized model of Mr Porter's flying machine as it was released from the high pulpit. It hovered above Mr Porter's head, whirring and spluttering, and then quite suddenly it rose upwards and flew across the domed room to the opposite pulpit, where it was caught by a man in a top hat. It seemed like a small, clockwork bird, floating above the crowd, and Edmund felt a fluttering in his ribcage to see it: small, beating wings against his heart.

After the demonstration, Mr Rufus Porter explained the reasoning behind the rotating spindle, his estimates of buoyant lift and the speed of revolutions required of the steam-powered propellers to keep the locomotive airborne. The spindle of the real machine would be covered in cloth and coated in India rubber. There would be a hundred passengers, and a hundred parachutes. They would travel along the railroad in the sky and disembark three days later in Sacramento on a portable elevator. It would be a pivotal moment in the onward march of humanity: a four-month journey reduced to seventy-two hours.

At this, there was a loud cheer, a casting-up of hats (including that of Edmund O'Hara), a stamping of feet on the wooden floor of the church, and a ripple of confusion as the hats succumbed to the pull of gravity. Edmund bought a $50 subscription that very afternoon for a passage to Sacramento in Mr Porter's Aerial Locomotive. He queued in the rain to pay upfront and, after this outlay, had approximately $48 remaining to his name.

While he waited for the Aerial Locomotive to be completed, he found employment as a carriage driver for Mr Markham Reeve in Washington Square. During this time, he received regular updates from Mr Porter on the progress of the Aerial Locomotive: small booklets detailing progress and theoretical developments in flight. There was another presentation to demonstrate the work-in-progress, and Edmund was alarmed to discover how far behind schedule the engineers had fallen. Half the basket had been constructed but the materials for the spindle were not yet delivered, and would not be until final payment had been received from Mr Porter. There were requests for increased contributions included in each of the booklets.

This was not a good sign. Edmund inspected the plans for the design and read the calculations. He did this carefully, his brow furrowed while he chewed at his pen. It should work, he thought. It is quite straightforward, mechanically.

But at the same time he wondered why, if it were so straightforward, had it not been done before?

He began to design a wooden boat with a propeller attached to its stern. He did this absent-mindedly at first, more out of curiosity than design. He made paper birds which he threw from the top of his carriage while he waited for Mr Markham Reeve to summon him for an outing. His designs became more and more complex, weightier in terms of both materials and science. He began to sell his flying boats to toyshops. They asked for other things too, puppets and masks. He kept his tools in the carriage and worked on them during the long hours spent waiting outside his employer's club. For each flying boat, he earned twenty-five cents; for each mask, ten cents. He calculated it would take him approximately two years to earn back the money he had put into the Aerial Locomotive. He did not allow this to distress him too much. He would earn it back quickly enough in California, once he got there.

But then, on the back of one of Mr Porter's informative booklets, he noticed a small box of print at the bottom of the page. It was an advertisement for a flying competition to be held in a settlement in New England, 200 miles north of New York, near Boston. The first prize was $50. He found that his thoughts no longer drifted to the goldfields, but lingered instead on flight. He imagined the shape of the earth from the air. There would be coastlines, rivers, mountain ranges. He pictured farmhouses, barns, women with their faces turned to the sky. Pink cheeks and parted lips. His horse and carriage rattled over the cobbles of Washington Square and Edmund did not feel the jolts.

He thought: Well, there can be no harm in trying.

The first swoop of Edmund O'Hara

Edmund O'Hara's first life-sized attempts, if not exactly made up of feathers and wax, were primitive, flapping designs. Initially, Edmund had assumed that the downbeat of a bird's wing would produce a reacting air pressure equal to the bird's weight and that it was this which enabled birds to fly. He thought that, using this principle, he could propel himself upwards simply by beating his arms. He would later find that this was a common misconception among those inventors who had grown up in the vicinity of sparrows. You would not find such a thing being attempted in the southern hemisphere. The sparrow, Edmund O'Hara was to discover at great cost to his left leg, was a poor prototype for the emulation of orthogonal flight. It was an anomaly. Quite simply, it would not work.

Not that Edmund O'Hara attempted anything as ambitious as a simple vertical rise. He had read a paper published by the Royal Society in which there was a description of the effects of air resistance in its various forms. There was hull resistance to be accounted for, along with such things as drift, slip, skin friction. He read that, for large birds (a category which he supposed might include him), flight was often initiated by the act of dropping from an elevated perch in order to gain enough velocity to swoop upwards without the exertion of flapping.

Edmund made four wooden frames, each strung with wire netting. He nailed thin pieces of oiled silk to the sides of the wood, leaving them loose so that they billowed when he wafted them. He strapped them to his legs and arms with metal buckles, and then he lay on the floor with his chin resting on the cold matting to practise moving all four limbs at once. He jumped from a chair, and then from a table. He spread his arms and leant forwards, but did not even attain a full stretch before he hit the ground.

The next day, suitably harnessed, he leapt from the windowsill of the ground-floor room where he slept, and this time he managed to straighten his legs and execute three kicks. He felt the first gusts of flight against his stomach. He landed twenty yards from the window. There were tufts of grass in his hair, but there had been a brief moment of uplift, of elation beneath his silken wings, which remained with him.

I just need a higher perch, he thought.

And that was when he decided how he would win the competition. It was quite simple. He would fall from the roof of a house. In fact, he would not just fall. He would dive. And then he would swoop.

He arrived in Holloway Creek at the beginning of May, when the snow was beginning to melt in huge great clumps. He took a room at the boarding house, still dressed in his Washington Square livery, gold braid around his cuffs and a gold button pinned to the pocket of his shirt. He met Mary later that day on the steps of the general store, dazzling her with his gold braid and blue eyes.

'Are you here for the competition?' she asked, her dark hair falling around her face as she shielded her eyes from the brightness of the sun.

He nodded.

'Well, good luck then,' she said. 'I'll come and holler for you.' And then she walked on, whistling 'Loch Lomond' under her breath.

She saw him the next day, being hauled onto the roof of a house by a rope and pulley system. He was an oddly-shaped silhouette with the wings already attached to his legs and arms, a platypus rising up the drainpipe. There was a line of men holding the rope at the other end, Mr Mayhew and Mr James and Mr Hughes from the liquor store, leaning backwards into each other, hoisting him up.

Edmund O'Hara steadied himself against the weather vane. There was quite a crowd. He could see Mary's hat, dried flowers sprouting from the yellow ribbon she had tied around it. His clothes were tight against his skin. He stood with his arms outstretched and his eyes shut. He had to synchronise his arms with his legs, so that he moved his left arm with his right leg, like a horse. It was all a question of equilibrium. He opened his eyes and saw the chickens chasing each other in the yard. He saw their wings shuddering as they ran, their feet not leaving the ground.

Oh God, he thought.

The church clock struck noon. On the first stroke, Edmund O'Hara raised his arms. On the third stroke he took a deep breath and closed his eyes. On the sixth stroke he felt suddenly very light-headed. On the eighth stroke, he felt his knees buckle beneath him and he had to cling to the weathervane to stop himself from falling. And on the eleventh stroke, Edmund O'Hara dived from the roof of the house, head first, towards the river.

He was still in the air after the echoes of the twelfth stroke had died away. This, in itself, was something. He did not, however, swoop in quite the way he had imagined. He had drawn it on a graph, the proposed trajectory of flight, basing his calculations on Newton's equation for calculating air pressure as against the incline of a plane. He managed to sail over the roof of the barn, his legs and arms flapping wildly, and for a moment, just before he faltered and began to descend toward the river below him, it looked as though Edmund O'Hara was flying. There was a rush of wings flapping, of ducks taking flight.

Mr James was the first to let go of the rope and was already wading into the water when Edmund lifted his head out of the river, his snapped wings dragging at him. The men carried him to the riverbank, holding their hands over a cut in his leg.

Mary ran to the edge of the river and pressed her shawl onto the wound.

'Keep still,' she instructed, and it confused him. He thought he was keeping still. He did not think the movement was coming from him. He imagined it was external, and that his body was only responding to the spinning, rocking sensation of the earth beneath him.

'Does it hurt so much?' she asked next, her voice soft and apologetic, and he replied: 'Does what hurt?'

Mary thought his answer brave. She did not realise that, in fact, it was the opposite of brave, to be unable to feel anything. To be immune.

Edmund stayed in Holloway Creek for a fortnight while his wound healed under its careful dressing of muslin bandages. The skin grew back slowly, delicately; hairless and pale and slightly raised. By the time Edmund was ready to return to New York he had told Mary that he loved her. He sat on the floor at her feet with his legs stretched out in front of him – he would have knelt, but it strained the stitching in his leg when he tried; he felt it with his thumbnail, the drag of catgut through his skin, the redness beneath the white, and he did not want the embarrassment of his wound bursting, of the sympathy that would ensue – and he asked her to marry him from the rug, his large hand reaching up to hers.

Mary refused him. She was only sixteen, and she did not want to go to California on Rufus Porter's Aerial Locomotive. She said no, but she cried when she said it because he was so tall, so handsome with his blue eyes and gold braid. He accepted her refusal with such grace that if he had asked her again, right there on the floor, she might have changed her mind, but he did not and so she pretended to be quite decided on the matter.

Edmund O'Hara returned to New York and resumed his carriage-driving for Mr Markham Reeve, waiting for the day he would fly to Sacramento in a railroad in the sky. He had not won the competition exactly – the prize money being the object of some dispute as it was claimed that none of the contestants had actually flown – but Edmund remembered that moment of elation during the twelfth stroke, and he associated it in his mind with the softness of Mary O'Hara's voice. He wrote to her occasionally, and sent her a small wooden Noah's Ark filled with brightly-coloured birds which made Mary weep when she opened it, because she took it to be a tender symbol of ill-fated love.

Mary, at sixteen, was at a particularly romantic juncture of her life. Since Edmund O'Hara had left, torn from her (as she saw it) by cruel ambition, she had grown to love him from afar. She loved him at the back of her head, while she continued to embroider her trousseau and make scones for the church committee at her mother's request, and she told herself dramatically that she would continue to love him until the day she died.

This may have remained the case had the Aerial Locomotive not become bankrupt before it was even completed. The money had all been spent on the construction of the basket in which the passengers were to be transported. Edmund O'Hara, when telling this part of the story to his son, shrugged it off as if it were a great joke. He did not mention that, although it was not quite all his eggs that he had entrusted to the project of constructing the world's largest Aerial Locomotive basket, it was a sizeable enough proportion of eggs to ensure that he would not be going to the goldfields of California until he had, as it were, hatched a new plan.

And so he returned to Holloway Creek, having sold a large batch of toys to a store in Boston and with an order to deliver the same amount again in a month's time, and he asked Mary once more if she would marry him, on his knee this time. He did not know about her heightened romantic state and so was slightly startled when she flung herself into his arms and said, 'Oh Edmund, I will!'

She had hardly expected it herself. She knew that her acceptance had very little to do with the reality of him, and that her decision was based largely on the heroic qualities he had already demonstrated in her daydreams since his first departure. They were married three weeks on and, in doing so, she lost him. Or more precisely, she gained him – and lost something else.

So although this appeared to be a story about his pop, even when he was ten years old Toby knew that it was really a story about his mother. It was his pop who told it, a version of it – it was in his pop's nature to expand on things, to create histories around them – but Toby would watch his mother as his pop spoke, and he could see in her eyes that there was more to this tale than just the words.

Buster (reprise)

The bat was placed now on the mantelpiece in the drawing room. The room was full of over-large furniture: semi-circular armchairs of cracked-hide leather, tall dining chairs upholstered in green velvet set against the walls, patterned Alaskan rugs overlapping on the stone floor. Edmund had wanted to sell this furniture when they married, fifteen years ago now, but Mary had refused. She had grown up surrounded by it, and she liked the feeling of being entrenched in the house of her birth, not just by the stateliness of the furniture, but by the very practicalities of its weight.

A mirror with heavy bevelled edges hung above the fireplace, so that the bat seemed to float in a square of purplish light in the centre of the off-white room. 'Get away from me, you horrid thing,' Mary would whisper when she found herself alone in the room with the bat. She poked it with a feather duster, turning it so that it faced sideways, away from both the room and the mirror, but still she found it following her with its devilish eyes. 'I know your game,' she told it, her shoulders rounded and her chin held up, prodding it with the duster. 'Oh-ho, don't think I don't.' She called it names, Buster and Me Laddo, to make herself sound more confident. Her heart raced. She felt it inside her chest. Oh, how she hated that bat! She banished it from the house, insisting that Edmund take it to his workshop as she did not want it near her son, but still it repulsed her with its nonchalant expression, its horrid translucent skin.

It hovered above Edmund's workbench, hanging from a wire attached to a small hook in the shed's ceiling, and it swung as she opened the door. It was such a scratty thing, with its mangy stomach and one wing now stripped carefully away so that only the unadorned cartilage remained. She felt, as she always did when in the presence of the bat, an excess of emotion. She thought that perhaps it was fear, but in truth she knew she was not afraid; she did not mind touching it, spinning it with her finger so that it faced away from her. She would not have minded picking it up and removing its other wing altogether, and then perhaps burying it in the garden just as normal people might do with a dead animal.

Because this was part of the problem. Normal people, in Mary O'Hara's opinion, did not hang dead bats from ceilings and measure their proportions with pieces of string. But it was not only this that troubled Mary O'Hara. She fretted about the bat. It haunted her. It made her jealous, although jealous is perhaps the wrong word. It made her possessive, protective. She tried to write about it in her journal – she would not call it a presentiment exactly, as it

50

was vague and indistinct in comparison with her other, earlier dreams – but she found that the words she wrote were inadequate. Really, it was nothing specific; just a fuzzy, formless hint of disaster.

Mary was not used to disasters. She had been born in Holloway Creek on the New England coast just north of Boston, and had lived all her life in the same house which looked out over the river at the back, and across to the general store at the front. The house had a wooden porch and a white clapboard frontage, and huge sash windows. When she married, her husband moved in with her and her parents, and they had all lived together for a short while, until her parents died and it was just the two of them. It was quite simple.

Yet she did not aspire to simplicity. She had planned to have six children, three boys and three girls. Her sons would go out fishing in spring and her daughters would read novels to each other on rugs in front of the fire. They would sing songs around the piano in the evenings. It would be loud and untidy. But it had not happened like that. She had waited and waited, arranging things neatly, giving everything its place in readiness for the onslaught of disorder she had so wished for, but it had never come.

But then there had been Toby, a beautiful, delicate swelling of possibility. She had spent that summer baking sponge cakes, smothered with jam, for Edmund to eat, but mostly eating them by herself before her husband came in for dinner. Her stomach became round and stately, protruding from her white cotton dresses with such conviction that Mary O'Hara began to confuse this extension of her body with an extension of her own life. She thought she was being born again.

When the time came, she gathered up the force of each

contraction and held it inside her so that, when finally she pushed, it was with such force that Toby O'Hara came tumbling out onto the rose-patterned towel laid across the marital bed-linen before his mother was quite ready for the sudden emptiness inside her. He landed on the towel, the size of a quart pot, wind-blown and squashed from his precipitous descent, and romantically tinged with the cumulative possibilities of all six of her imagined children.

Whereas in the rest of her life, Mary was cautious and tidy, when she first held Toby in her arms, she lost all sense of control. She became profligate, reckless. She sensed there would be no other children and she no longer minded. She showered Toby with her love, every hoarded-up piece of it, every knitted stitch of it, every mast on every toy boat of it. It flooded her, leaving her exuberant and breathless, and she had to hold herself back so as not to alarm him. It was a whole lifetime's worth of love, blankets and sheets and sails of it, deposited at last in the galley-hold of her son's ribcage.

She stood in the doorway of the shed and prodded the bat with a stick. 'I'm watching you, Buster,' she whispered threateningly, but really, although she did not like to admit such a thing, she said it more to herself than to the bat.

Six

With Mr Thomas Cook and his representatives, Ursula Bridgewater toured Italy, Spain, Greece, Belgium, Bavaria. She visited the battlefields of Waterloo and the high-walled towns of the Netherlands. She was happiest when she was abroad, happy in a way she was not when she was at home, and yet this feeling was impermanent. It was a period of quarantine, a restorative, but it was not a cure. Yes, she had seen things, had felt the exhilarating effects of Alpine air, had spoken French in mountain-top crèmeries, but she still had not really *done* anything with her life. Upon her return from these excursions, she felt, as always, restless and impatient. Questing, she called it, although the object of her quest remained elusive.

As it happened, Mr Thomas Cook was also building up to something. It was the dream of all his life to lead a tour to the Eastern Lands of the Bible. He wanted to visit Bethlehem, Solomon's Pools, Mar Saba, the Dead Sea. He wanted to stand on the Mount of Olives, in the place where Jesus was last seen in his earthly form, and look down over the domes and towers of Jerusalem. He wanted to walk to where Jesus fell, where He was insulted, where Solomon dwelt and where Abraham spake. He wanted to see the burning bush at St Catherine's and climb Mount Sinai at dawn.

This was not a secret ambition. It was simply an extension of the first excursion he had ever organised while still an itinerant preacher in the Midlands. On that occasion, he had cobbled together a return tour from Leicester to a temperance meeting in a field in Loughborough. It lacked the exoticism of the Holy Land, but it was still part of the same project: bringing God to the masses. Although in Palestine, he supposed, there would be no cricket played on the lawn, no ham sandwiches. It would be too hot, too holy. It would be the grand triumph of his life.

Egypt also appealed to Ursula, but for different reasons. She knew of it from the Bible as a land of spectacular incident: Moses' call to the Pharaoh – Let my people go! – and the parting of the Red Sea; Joseph's betrayal by his brothers over a many-coloured coat; and the Nile, that majestic river, running with blood and cursed by frogs upon which the infant Moses had drifted in a basket of rushes. The tour itinerary read like a list of cities from a fairy tale, dusty and white with gleaming domes and spires.

And there was something else which attracted her. Mr Cook's ambition contained, she felt, something of the direction she wished for in her own life, and it was for this as much as for the destination that Ursula wrote to Mr Thomas Cook's offices in London that very afternoon and booked a Lady's ticket for travel in a first-class cabin.

When she announced her plans to George the following evening over dinner, he told her it was quite out of the question. There were bandits in Jerusalem and snakes in the Sinai Desert. Had she not read the Book of Exodus?

He stood up and poured brandy into a crystal glass. He swirled it in his hand. He did not understand his sister. When they were children, he had given her piggy-back rides around the drawing room and let her smuggle half-eaten Brussels sprouts onto his plate. He had shown her his special technique for climbing the walls of the corridor outside the nursery, clamped between the two walls, feet poking outwards and elbows upwards, like a crab. He was eight years old when she was born, and he often told her how he had picked her up and laid her out flat along the inside of his lower forearm and she had fitted exactly, her head in his palm and her feet against his elbow.

'Did I really fit, Georgie?' she would still ask him occasionally, when they found themselves sitting together in the drawing room and smoking cigars after dining out, both reluctant to go to sleep. 'Did I fit exactly?'

But in spite of their closeness, he still did not understand her insistence on excursioning. There were times when he wondered if Ursula was right when she claimed it was because she had not been allowed to go to school, as he had. He remembered how she had insisted on after-school lessons every day, but geography had never really come into it, as far as he recalled. There was only one particularly fraught occasion which niggled at him, when Ursula was six or thereabouts, and he had happened to mention that the earth was round, like an apple. Ursula had stamped her foot at him and stormed out of the nursery, telling him she would never believe anything he said ever again. He remembered that she had been utterly inconsolable, weeping into her blanket because she thought he was lying to her. George had resorted to scouring the books in their father's library, eventually finding one which separately described both the earth and an apple as an 'oblate spheroid'.

'So it is like an apple,' she had sniffed.

He had nodded, and had produced an apple from his pocket, biting into it twice – one bite above the other – tearing a strip between the two for Panama. 'This is America,' he had told her, 'North and South. And this is Africa, and this is the Holy Land, and this is India, and this is the Arctic and Greenland and this' – he picked at the skin of the apple with his nail, a tiny dent, not even as big as a tooth mark – 'is England.'

George sighed. Was it his fault? he wondered. Could all this gallivanting be dated back to that infernal apple? No, he decided. His sister was simply unusual. And she had been disappointed. She was not like the other women he knew, those he occasionally thought of marrying, but never asked, and of whom Ursula tended to disapprove. He might perhaps, one day, but he still considered himself too young for marriage. There was no time for such things in everyday life. When he went out for lunch, as he often did, he liked to be in the company of men with whom he could discuss practical matters: warehouses, transport, labour efficiency. Yes, he could also discuss these things with Ursula and she was a woman, but he knew that even Ursula did not always have the patience to cope with his liking for detail. She had no staying power. She would not stick. His sister had never stuck. She confused him with her schemes, her way of wanting one thing more than anything in the world and then quite suddenly another, as if she had no memory of the first. He supposed this had been the same with his mother, although he did not really remember. They had the same grey eyes, his mother and his sister, the same wide smile.

He drank the brandy in a single gulp.

Ursula put her foot down. She would go. She would go alone, as she had always done.

George poured another brandy. He held it up to the candle so that the light refracted through the glass, unfocused and sugary. He felt upset. His voice shuddered when he spoke. 'What is wrong with staying still for a while? Why must you always be off, gadding about the planet, like some . . .' He paused, not wishing to go too far.

'Red Indian?' Ursula offered.

'Exactly!' he bellowed, hardly noticing the delight with which Ursula was twirling her fork over her plate.

*

In the port at Alexandria, Ursula Bridgewater was rowed ashore by bronzed men, with lean, muscular backs. She saw her luggage being fought over by two of the men on the deck of the Mediterranean steamer, and being very nearly dropped into the sea. She would not have minded her dresses so much – they would dry out soon enough in this ridiculous heat – but she worried for her supplies. She had, on the recommendation of *Murray's Guidebook to Modern Egypt and Thebes*, brought insect powder and castor oil, laudanum and bandages and iodine, and also a small amount of opium which she had been informed was efficacious in calming disturbances of the bowel. She had magnesium wire to set alight when viewing the tombs (far better, she had heard, than an oil-burning torch) and she had purchased an Inodorous Sanitary Pail disguised as a bonnet box from Fyfe's Repository of Scientific Inventions for Sanitary Purposes, which she hoped would make it ashore. She sat in the small rowing boat and clutched her cabin bag to her chest.

Alexandria was a disappointment. It was not so very different from France, in Ursula's opinion, although perhaps a little dustier, and there were too many Englishmen in palm-leaf hats and long white socks. She found it too clean and ordered; where she had been expecting noise and muddle, she found only bureaucracy and afternoon tea. Cairo was more exciting with its exotic, rug-draped bazaars and gleaming turquoise domes. The streets were noisy with camels and flocks of goats being driven about by boys in red fezzes, and people were gathered around stalls of sugar-cane and bright red spices. And it was gloriously dirty; there were muddy stones and open drains across which she had to jump to keep her feet dry. She liked the exoticism of it, the hot breath of the sun at midday, the smells and the dazzling brightness.

From Cairo, Thomas Cook hired two steamers to take his party down the Nile. Later, it was reported in *The Times* that they were 'running in full cry up the river after the Prince and Princess of Wales', but this was only partly true. Mostly, they remained some way behind the six blue-and-gold steamers of the royal party in which, the report continued, were stacked 3,000 bottles of champagne and 4,000 bottles of claret, along with hunting guns and a profes-sional taxidermist.

It added a frisson, certainly, to know that the royal party were at Luxor only a few hours before they arrived, and that the old temple ruins at Karnak had been illuminated for the benefit of the Prince and Princess the night before Cook's steamers passed, but it was no more than that. Mr Cook reported these close encounters to the *Leicester Journal* with much glee, but Ursula knew perfectly well that this was merely an expression of his commercial persona. She knew it because she sensed in him that same bubbling of unfulfilled purpose which tingled along her own spine. There was a missionary gleam in the way he spoke of the 'wondrous, sacred Nile' and of the 'glorious desolation of the land.'

'Can you hear it?' he asked one evening, as the water lapped against the side of the boat and the sky glittered with stars.

'Hear what?' she asked.

'That whisper,' he replied softly, his hand pressed against his heart. 'The whisper of the Divine Word.'

No, she thought. I do not hear it. But I see it in you and I admit that it seems quite wonderful.

On some mornings, naked monks swam out to the boats to ask for baksheesh, and Ursula saw their shining backs from where she sat on the deck, dressed in full skirts under a netted veil. She saw snake charmers and conjurors on the banks of the river, jewellery-sellers and donkey boys. There were hippopotamuses with snub noses and horses' neighs, and craggy-looking crocodiles.

Ursula found the party a little wearisome after a while, and she tried naming the other tourists as she and the cousins had done in Scotland and Switzerland, but it was not so much fun without Miss Emma and Miss Joy. She wrote to the cousins instead – a joint letter – telling them that she was fulfilling her capacity as self-appointed Official Letter-Writer of the tour. She told them how her fellow excursionists dressed for lunch in colourful headdresses, purchased in the bazaars of Cairo, and afterwards jumped fully-clothed into the Nile to swim. Ursula did not join them, but during those long hot afternoons, she sat in her steamer chair with the Old Testament on her knee, watching the endless fields of wheat and the fat black cattle grazing on the shore, and the kingfishers darting in and out of the water amidst the weeds, and she felt perfectly content.

On the final day of the cruise, she wrote to Henry Springton. She told him how Mr Cook had attempted to bathe in the river's shallows, but had been swept away by an undercurrent and was obliged to be rescued by the boatman who cried out to Allah as he pulled Mr Cook to safety. She described the boats and the mosquitoes, the wine and the temples. When she had finished, she read the letter over. It had, she thought, a different tone from some of her earlier letters. It was still lengthy and amusing, but it was perhaps less cynical, and it had been easier to write. Whereas once she might have discarded this missive as a draft and started again, this time she did not. She folded the letter thoughtfully and slipped it into the Old Testament, to be posted later from Cairo, and then she sank back into her chair and closed her eyes.

When they returned to Cairo, the tour party travelled by donkey to the ancient pyramids at Giza. Ursula's donkey bore a golden brocade saddle and had a white and silver necklace. She had read about the pyramids in Herodotus, but when she saw them, she thought first of sand. They rose from the stony desert like great, triangular dunes, shimmering in the heat, their edges soft and melting. How Miss Emma and Miss Joy would have loved this, she thought.

She could see people on the pyramid, far away and small, their arms waving like the legs of spiders. Ursula accepted the help of three Syrian interpreters in braided jackets to help her climb, one taking each arm, and another to push from behind. The steps were higher than window ledges, and Ursula's skirts dragged and tore on the stones. The men went quickly, springing backwards up the steps, snatching at her arms and dragging her with them. She felt their hands on her wrists, their palms against her buttocks. She could hardly breathe. She felt her shoulder click as she was heaved up another step. She felt like a plough in a field, a towed cart.

At the top of the pyramid, the men whispered to her for baksheesh and, because she was so tired and the joints in her arms were aching from all that wrenching, and also because it was so very steep a drop (and she had been told that one never knew with Arabs), she emptied all the money she had from the cloth purse that hung on a string around her neck into the hands of one of the interpreters.

'Isn't it marvellous?' she heard an English voice ask of nobody in particular. She recognised the voice. It was a

Mrs Tattlesworth, also of Mr Cook's party, a sphinx-faced woman who had announced even before the ship had left the dock that she was blessed with the remarkable habit of always being able to hit the nail on the head. Ursula had mentioned this in her letter to Miss Emma and Miss Joy, and she smiled to imagine their delight at such a detail. Most of Mrs Tattlesworth's conversation was accompanied by a miming motion of a hammer being brought down onto the head of a nail, and she was doing this very thing right now, standing on the top of the pyramid.

'Marvellous,' she repeated.

'Yes,' Ursula agreed, but as she did, she looked out across the vast ocean of sand, the plain of unrelenting yellow beneath her, and she thought it was the loneliest landscape she had ever known.

It was a smaller party who travelled then from Alexandria by sea to Beirut, to begin the arduous journey overland to Jerusalem. They travelled in a huge cloud of horses, pack mules, tents, beds and kitchen equipment. There were iron bedsteads and white sheets and carpets and canvas basins laid out in the tents; tin baths and mosquito nets and woollen mattresses. The party consisted of eight women and sixteen men, travelling thirty miles a day on horseback. The saddle left Ursula's legs stiff and immovable – she did not know how Queen Victoria put up with it – and she wore a scarf of white cambric under her straw hat, with the material wrapped around her face and neck in the Turkish style.

Ursula had never stayed in a tent before, and she described to Miss Emma and Miss Joy the difficulties of avoiding the guy ropes at night, and the great rush in the mornings to get out of the tents before they were collapsed onto half-dressed tourists. The food was more plentiful than Ursula had expected. There was soup and wild boar for dinner, and boiled eggs for breakfast. At midday, lavish picnics were laid out under the trees for lunch – sardines in brine and cold mutton and bread. One of the guides, Ahmed, asked her if it was just like England.

'Almost,' Ursula replied, supposing that it was more English than Egyptian in any case.

When they arrived in Jerusalem, after the small excitement of a nocturnal robbery the night before, Ursula wrote in a letter to George that the whole city smelt of rosemary. The streets were cobbled and gleaming and busy with camels. On the first morning, they ascended the Mount of Olives and looked down across the city. It was surrounded by rock-strewn valleys and fields of high green grass. There were wild flowers, poppies and bluebells. A clergyman in the party took out his bagpipes and played the Highland Fling. They went to the River Jordan and bathed in its muddy waters, and Ursula noticed Mr Cook wading downstream to the bend in the river so that he was a little apart from the rest of the group. He was dressed all in white and Ursula watched as he lifted his face to the sky, and then submerged himself completely in the water. Some of the other tourists filled glass bottles with river water to take home and Ursula thought of doing this too until she saw how Mr Cook disapproved.

'Popish,' he called it.

For it was true that while Mr Thomas Cook had a reverence for the dust of the Holy Land, he also had a horror of icons, of candles and reliquaries, and he did not believe in visiting holy places for the purposes of prostration. On their second day in Jerusalem, he led his tour group along Jesus's path to the hill at Golgotha where He was crucified. Mr Cook walked this path with his eyes closed and his hands pressed together. He did this, and yet he also refused to kneel at the Church of the Holy Sepulchre with its gaudy side chapels and false claim to being the site of Jesus's burial. He would not queue with the rest of his party to see the Fragments of the True Cross and the Garden of Gethsemane, now an Italianate garden of marigolds and privet hedges maintained by prim monks. He would not accompany the party to see the grave of Adam and the centre of the earth. He shook his head at the pillar which claimed to be the *very pillar* where the cock crew and at the *actual* cradle of the Baby Jesus.

'It is all utterly ridiculous,' Ursula said to Mr Cook on the third day as they walked up the hill to the tomb where the angel had rolled away the stone and proclaimed: *He is not here!*

'Yes,' he agreed. 'What benefit can there possibly be in visiting Jesus's tomb when He has already arisen?'

This was not quite what Ursula had meant. She was speaking of one thing when she spoke of it being ridiculous, and he was speaking of another, but she remembered his face when he bathed in the River Jordan, dressed all in white, and she realised that she had underestimated the strength of what he called 'his faith'.

What a wonderful thing that must be, she thought wistfully.

Seven

Not the last straw

Sally Walker did not seem to take to religion. She slurred the words of her prayers so that they ran into each other, suggesting recitation rather than entreaty. Even her Ave Marias seemed to be lacking in – what was it? – passion, sincerity, and it was this to which Sister Thomas of the Holy Ghost took particular exception.

Sister Thomas of the Holy Ghost had a very practical relationship with the Virgin Mary. It was on the Virgin Mary's advice, as imparted through Sister Thomas, that the orphans were prohibited from eating apples whole. Each autumn, the girls would receive donations of them from local benefactors, left at the kitchen door in wooden boxes, and these would be distributed at dinner times. Sally remembered how she had eaten them in her earlier, happier childhood by the sea at New Brighton; that wonderful sweetness of apple flesh on her tongue, the tug on her teeth as she ripped it apart. At the orphanage, the girls were obliged instead to sit quietly at the dining table and cut their apples into small pieces, and then eat them with spoons.

Sister Jude would snort at this, and had even been heard to say that it was simply because Sister Thomas was getting a bit long in the tooth. Sister Thomas, however, maintained that you wouldn't catch the Virgin Mary biting into an apple, so you wouldn't catch her doing it either. She had a habit of dragging the religious into the temporal like that, but in such a matter-of-fact way that it was sometimes hard to distinguish between scriptural truths and snippets taken from home health manuals. It remained a source of concern to Sally that her doings were continually appraised by such a shadowy yet particular authority.

The reason behind this, however, was that Sister Thomas had a passion. It gleamed in her like rubbed brass. It was not a thing she liked to advertise. She feared it might be misunderstood, mocked, wrenched from her in the telling. As a child, Sister Thomas had confided in her elder sister, and even now she remembered her sister's laugh, surprised and sarcastic. But Sister Thomas of the Holy Ghost was now fifty-three years old and no longer paid much attention to her family's opinion. There was no question of it. Her sister had been wrong.

What Sister Thomas believed was this: she was going to receive a Vision. She knew exactly how it would happen. The Virgin Mary would appear, standing in front of her, palms outstretched, head tilted, eyes cast down. A blue dress and a bright light and, if she was feeling elaborate, a soft glow landing beatifically on her arms. Sister Thomas had pictured it so many times that she began to wonder if her ability to conjure up the Mother of God with such ease was, in itself, a Vision, and therefore worth reporting to someone more official than Father David. Someone who might realise the importance of what she was saying, like the Archdeacon, or even the Cardinal.

But, on balance, she had decided to wait until the Vision had been properly received and then she would report it through the official channels. That was the correct way of doing things. Until then, Sister Thomas was resigned to tolerating her current position as the senior nun for child welfare. She was, to this end, engaged in a constant battle with the education executive of the orphanage which presented itself in the form of Sister Jude.

Sally liked Sister Jude. She was a mild, gentle woman with something consoling about her, a hint of laughter about her mouth which surprised Sally when she saw it, because she had forgotten how it looked to see such jollity, such brightness. Sister Jude was an organiser, a reformer. She had been religious once, but she no longer cared for it. Her duty now was to her girls, not to a man nailed to a cross at whose body she had once gazed so longingly on her knees. When she was younger, she had wanted to run her fingers across his chest, feel the bumps of his ribs and muscles. Oh, she could hardly bear to think of it now! She had mistaken such sentiments for piety, but now she recognised them for what they were. Foolishness. Youth. Odd, misplaced desire.

Although, when she looked at it objectively, her decision to become a nun had not been entirely foolish. It had perhaps been an escape from the sort of questionable young men her sisters had married and to whom she would inevitably have succumbed had she remained in the secular world; men who were no longer young but old, who worked at the docks and came home with a reek of ale on their lips, and who had never held the tragic attraction for her which Jesus had inspired in his brass, classical form. She did not regret the life she had chosen, and felt no compulsion to confess this slow death of religion to anyone in the convent. She had always been comfortable, never lonely, and her youthful silliness did not distress her.

Sister Thomas disapproved of Sister Jude. She had also heard that same rumour about Sister Jude considering her a little long in the tooth. It was not true, after all. Her gums were perfectly fine. She had most of her teeth intact, which was more than could be said for some people she knew. She sat now in Sister Jude's office and ran her finger over her upper row of teeth.

'Yes, Sister?'

'It's about this teaching of mathematics,' Sister Thomas began, leaning forward on her chair and spreading her hands across the desk in front of her. 'I have read that it has been scientifically proven that excessive studying will render our girls barren. I have it on the highest authority.'

'Oh, is it in the Bible?' Sister Jude asked.

Sister Thomas ignored the interruption. 'It is in all the medical journals,' she said.

Sister Jude hesitated and coughed. She looked out of the window and nodded.

Deviating, Sister Thomas thought. 'Are you listening to me, Sister Jude?' she asked.

Sister Jude sighed. She had heard all of this before. She had, over the years, been obliged to deal with endless complaints from Sister Thomas that certain girls were developing over-emotional tendencies, or were sleeping with their arms askew instead of crossed over their chests, and that this was caused by too much study and not enough religion. 'Sister Thomas,' she began, 'the education of these girls is my responsibility and I must prepare them for a world which has no place for them. And as such, I wish for them to study mathematics.'

This was exactly the sort of response Sister Thomas had anticipated from Sister Jude, with her modern outlook and sharp chin. She sighed and shook her head, reflecting that it was the way of such things, that where there is talk of shining a light, there needs must be a shadow. In truth, Sister Thomas did not much mind about the prospective fertility of the orphans. Her main concern was that the study of mathematics was not only useless but also detrimental to the amount of time spent on sewing and polishing, which would, in Sister Thomas's opinion, be much handier in the girls' future lives, since most of them were destined for service. Some, of course, would stay on at the orphanage to teach, but these were the minority. These were the ones who had people to offer donations on their behalf, and there were not so very many.

The nuns had, in fact, received a donation that very morning. It had not come to them directly, but through Father Peter of St Helens, whom Sister Jude often pronounced to be wiser than the Bishop, but whom Sister Thomas of the Holy Ghost had taken against for his manner of seeming to take amusement from things she said which were not supposed to be funny. Smirking, she called it.

Father Peter was a friend of Mr Fisher, and Mr Fisher had confided in him that he was worried about Sally, but felt powerless to do anything. 'She will not talk to me,' he told the priest. 'The girl is too polite. Everything pleases her and yet she will not smile. I want to *help* her but I don't know how.'

It was in the spirit of *helping* the child that Father Peter had suggested a donation, along with a request that special care be given to the child's education. Mr Fisher did so, and included the request as a condition of the donation. A further sum was to be held in trust until Sally Walker attained the age of twelve, and Mr Fisher stipulated that this could be given over to the Order if Miss Walker chose to stay on at the orphanage as a teacher. If she chose to leave, however, then the money was to be Sally's own, to do as she pleased.

'Her own?' Sister Thomas exclaimed. 'What does a girl like Sally need with that amount of money? It will be better for her to be gainfully employed in teaching the unfortunates.'

Sister Jude pursed her lips. 'She can decide for herself when she is old enough.'

Sister Thomas pushed her chair away from the desk and stood up. She felt irritated by the donation's conditions, coming on top of Sister Jude's insistence on mathematics. A small fly buzzed against the glass of the window behind her. Sister Thomas swiped at it. She found her mind wandering back to its usual preoccupation of Visions and Archdeacons and, really, although she would not have admitted it to Sister Jude, it was this which made her upper lip so very thin and straight, her shoulders so square.

She was still smouldering about the Vision at Lourdes, and it was this which had made Sister Thomas more argumentative than usual. She had endured the Miraculous Medal of Sister Catherine Labouré, conceding that she had not actually been alive at the time of the sightings in 1831, so there were no real grounds for comparison. But all this talk of the holy spring at Lourdes had undone her. The girl, Bernadette, was clearly a lunatic. A golden cloud, indeed. And throwing in the Immaculate Conception. It really was very artfully done.

There was a rustling of papers behind Sister Thomas, and she heard the door of the study open and shut behind her. Brisk footsteps receded along the corridor.

Sister Thomas did not move. She stood at the window and thought once more how unfair it all was. She did not understand why the Virgin, if she were going to appear to anyone – at this, she nodded derisively, not wanting to trip herself up by such theorising – but *if* she were *really* going to appear to anyone, why not to Sister Thomas of the Holy Ghost? She felt somehow wronged by this French girl, this Bernadette, who had stripped her of her rightful place in the Catholic canon, relegated to a mere onlooker along with the likes of Sally Walker and her donation. It was, Sister Thomas thought, the last straw.

It was only later, when another straw presented itself, that it became apparent this was not the last one.

Eight

Audacity

The bat was a prototype.

Toby O'Hara did not know what the word meant but he knew that it was so. He did not question it. He also knew that the bat represented a sublime piece of audacity. Had anyone questioned him on this, he would simply have shrugged. It did not matter. These were the things his pop told him, so this was what he believed.

The bat hung in the shed above Edmund O'Hara's workbench. In the mornings, Toby would tiptoe down to the shed, wet-footed in the dew-bright grass, and he would touch the bat with his finger so that its shadow swooped across the earthen floor. He sat in the workshop during the long summer evenings while his pop worked on the machine, and he watched the shadow of the bat as it lengthened on the opposite wall.

His pop drew the bat from ten different angles. He filled sheets and sheets of paper with his designs, and then crumpled them into tiny pellets and flung them into the corner of the shed. He held a teacup in his left hand and a pencil in his right. There were pieces of wood lined up on the floor which he slotted around each other like an elaborate jigsaw skeleton.

'Utterly sublime,' he told Toby.

Mary O'Hara would come to collect them in for dinner, and when they heard her footsteps on the gravel outside the shed, there would be a hint of panic between them, the enticing sensation of a shared secret. Toby did not know why it was a secret, but he saw how his pop slipped the designs into a drawer and pulled out the toy house he kept half-finished under his desk. Edmund would clamp its walls between his hands as if he had just glued them together, leaving it out on the desk for the night and winking at Toby as they shut the shed door behind them, and then they would walk up the garden together, through the drifts of milkwood seeds and the dust of summer, and there would be a smell of fried onions coming from the open kitchen window.

It was in these moments that Toby came to fix upon the idea that the machine was a gift for his mother, an elaborate gesture of love, and that was why his pop was keeping it a secret.

These are the things Edmund O'Hara did not build in that hot summer of 1862:

He did not build a flapping wing machine. He had tried this and it had not worked, and so he had concluded that there was more to the internal science of birds than he had initially thought.

He did not build an aerial screw. He considered this for a time, after his early success as a toy-maker with the boats with two propellers (twisting in opposite directions) and the winding mechanism which, when activated, allowed the boat to achieve flight by boring through the air. He experimented with a mouse as a passenger, and the boat still flew, and for this reason, he concluded that it was all a question of scale. If a small one could carry a mouse, then surely a larger one could carry a man. But there remained the question of landing. Having no self-sustaining power of its own, it was likely to land harder when it came down. In spite of his optimistic assessment of achieving lift, Edmund O'Hara feared the bump.

He did not build a glider from which he could dangle, and whose wings he could extend and stretch according to requirements. This, he felt, required too much strength across the chest to compensate for the flexibility of the wings.

Instead he built a fixed plane machine. He took an inclined wooden surface which did not rotate or flap, and attached to this a small boat on wheels in which the pilot would sit. This was not an obvious design, and a certain amount of ingenuity was required to calculate that the sustaining power offered by a flat plane could actually be greater than that generated by a flapping wing. The crucial point – and this was Edmund O'Hara's main innovation – was that it would have to fly into the teeth of the wind.

This design was based on the observation of gulls. Edmund had watched how they could spring from the top of a cliff and float up into the air without flapping, simply by facing the wind and stretching their wings rigidly outwards. And there had been other precedents. Oliver of Malmesbury, an English Benedictine monk from the eleventh century, was reported to have fastened wings to his hands based on Ovid's description of those of Daedalus, and jumped from the top of a tower, also against the wind. He was reported to have sailed a distance of 125 paces before whirling to earth and breaking both his legs. The monk later attributed this misfortune to the lack of a tail attached to his feet, and it was on the strength of this that Edmund O'Hara included a tail in his design.

What Edmund O'Hara actually built that summer was a huge bamboo boat with two fixed wings, the frame of which mimicked exactly the bone structure of the bat. He built a box-tail and added a propeller to the nose. He strapped a chair onto the boat section for the pilot and then removed it again, deciding that it would be safer for the pilot to crouch on his front. He tacked oiled silk into the centre of each wing, waxy and heavy in his fingers as he threaded it through the wooden loops, but when he pulled it taut over the frame, he found that it became suddenly light and transparent. It sparkled and trembled before him.

During that warm bat-filled summer of his tenth year, while his pop huffed and puffed over his scribbled designs, Toby O'Hara sat on a small stool and worked on his own project.

At first, Edmund O'Hara did not pay it too much attention. He saw a mess of wood and paste, and his son's small head bent over his work. Toby informed him that he was also building flight. At this, Edmund had ruffled his hair but had let it go, the idea that flight was something which could be built. He did not know that Toby was, in a sense, right to label his project thus. He did not, at first, recognise the fields behind the house, the railroad station and the church. He did not see his son's project for what it was, a prototype of a different sort of flight.

Toby made his landscape on a piece of wood salvaged from his father's workshop. He tore strips of newspaper which he then dipped into a bowl of flour and water, and laid them messily across the board of wood, sometimes heaping them up and sometimes smoothing them flat with a fish slice. He made hills and plains and painted them green. He hollowed waves into a stretch of coastline and coloured them blue with tips of white. He made miniature buildings from cardboard with peppercorns for door-knockers and he pressed wet spinach around the edges of the fields which dried into crisp clumps of hedgerow.

When it was finished, he presented it to his pop. For such vision Edmund O'Hara would have given everything and anything. He looked at his son's model with that same moist-eyed look he usually reserved for the bat. Such perspective, he thought, and still so young!

It was from this moment that Edmund O'Hara stopped building the flying machine for himself, and started building it for his son.

Jam and pickles

Mary O'Hara learned of this in a dream.

She was already suspicious. There had been no new toys for Boston for two months, and yet there was always such a clattering in the workshop that Mary had, at times, been forced to stand outside and hammer on the door with a wooden spoon to get her husband to come in for his dinner. She would not look at his machine, even when he eventually invited her to see it, to inspect the ingenuity of it, to feel the lightness of the wings. She saw how her husband's eyes shone when he spoke of it and she thought him ridiculous.

But the thing itself was worse than ridiculous. It was terrible. To Mary O'Hara, it was an earthquake, a tornado. It hung in her nocturnal mind like a huge shadow, one wing outstretched and the other crumpled and spiky, and a small scarf trailing from the back of it. She lay in bed at night and clenched her eyes so tightly shut that they filled with luminous swirls of light. Her breath came in small, tight gasps. She could imagine it exactly, how it would end.

She confronted her husband about it in the kitchen one evening and, to her surprise, he admitted it. Not just admitted it but nodded delightedly and shushed her with his finger. 'Don't you see?' he had asked. 'It'll be such a wonderful surprise for him. He'll be famous.'

'Edmund, you must not.'

He smiled and patted her arm. 'It is perfectly safe.'

'If it is so safe,' she said slowly, 'then you fly it.'

'Oh no,' he said, stretching up from the table and slipping a piece of bread into his pocket. 'It is a gift. And besides, Toby is just the right height. The right weight. I'm too heavy.'

Left alone, Mary clattered around the kitchen and stabbed at the fire. It caught and spluttered. 'No, no, no, no, no,' she muttered deliriously to herself, her head shaking and her lips cracked. There was a square of moonlight on the kitchen floor. She moved an armchair into the silvery light and sat with her feet dangling in front of the fire. The effect was soothing and, for a moment, she allowed her eyelids to fall, remembering another, earlier summer, when she had dressed all in white and rested her arms upon her swollen stomach.

It was here, sitting in a square of moonlight beside her sewing drawer, that Mary O'Hara made her decision. She sighed and nodded, but it was not reluctance that prompted the sigh. It was relief. It surprised her that she had not thought of it sooner. The solution was obvious. She would fly the machine herself. It could not be so very difficult. Edmund would not allow it, of course. He would tell her again that he had built it for Toby. He was too stubborn to be dissuaded, but this in itself was not an obstacle. If necessary, she would simply get into the machine and refuse to get out.

So this is it, she thought. I thought I would have longer than this.

She did not want to fly. It was not her ambition. It did not occur to her that she might, in saving her son from her

76

husband's invention, pilot one of the first ever flights of a heavier-than-air flying machine, and have a stone slab engraved in her honour to commemorate the occasion. This sort of thing did not matter to Mary. She had no desire to feature on any more stone slabs than she needed to.

Mary O'Hara had never read Darwin. She believed in the Creation of the Earth in six days and six nights. She believed that there were birds for the sky and creatures for the earth and fish for the sea. She looked to the forgiveness of sins and the Life Everlasting. That was the main point, as far as she could see. She had no desire to imitate the birds as well. It did not really strike her as blasphemous as it might have struck others with a more literal interest in such matters, but, if asked, she would have declared the desire by humans to fly to be quite unnecessary, and she might have brought God into it if pressed. Just to back her up.

Her decision left her feeling edgy, not only because of this but also because she had seen Edmund O'Hara's first attempt at flight and it had not been a success. It scared her to think of it, and yet she must. It was the only thing she could do. She was quite determined that if somebody was going to be put into that machine and launched into the air, it would not be Toby. Oh no. She would not allow it. She would be a cage for him, a cocoon.

Because that is how it is. There is no proportion in love, no limit to such extravagance. In making this decision, Mary O'Hara gave no thought to the physicality of her own body. She ignored the pull of her arms and legs, the weight of her head on her shoulders. If she were called upon to fly, then fly she would.

'Are you coming to bed, Mary?' Her husband was standing in the doorway, his head bent forward to avoid the scratch of the door frame. He rubbed his eyes.

Mary O'Hara sighed. She looked at him and nodded again and then followed her husband up the stairs.

'Edmund,' she whispered as she got into bed, 'I want to fly that machine of yours instead.'

He laughed, thinking she was joking, but Mary O'Hara raised her small hand in the darkness and did not smile. *Look here, Buster,* she thought, not for the first time, although she did not say it out loud.

'But Mary,' he began sleepily, reaching for her small body under the covers, 'I've done all the calculations. The wings won't hold you.' He pulled her towards him, feeling the soft curve of her stomach under his fingers, smoother than the smoothest wood.

'If they'll hold Toby, they'll hold me,' she whispered and, although this was not mathematically true, it was near enough, for between mother and son it was only a case of a few inches.

Edmund laughed. 'Perhaps they would,' he said, 'but it is for Toby.'

He heard Mary's annoyance, her breaths too shallow for sleep, but there was such a lightness in his soul, such an excitement that he had nearly finished and that he would be giving such a wonderful thing to his son, that he was not really worried. He assumed his wife did not mean what she said. He lay on his side and moved his hand over her hair. So soft, he thought as he drifted into sleep. So delicate.

Mary O'Hara maintained her resolve all that night, crumpled in the bedclothes and surrounded by shadows, and went about her business the next day with the renewed fervour of a woman about to fly away into space and never be heard from again. She took down all the curtains in the house and stuffed them into the copper even though it was not a wash-day and she had steamed them only three weeks previously. She washed sheets and singlets and endless billowing shirts, puffing up in clouds of white. Her cheeks turned red with the effort of shoving the laundry stick into the treacly water, stirring it until it turned grey, and the sheets came out, heavy and dripping and pummelled white. She hung the rugs from the downstairs rooms over the branches of the tree in the garden and beat them with a stick.

Her arms ached. She took out her collection of jars. She soaked onions in vinegar and boiled apples into chutneys. She made jams and compotes. There is so much to do, she thought.

Edmund O'Hara watched his wife pickling vegetables and sugaring fruits, and he mistook this burst of activity for evidence that she had forgotten her plan to fly the machine. He was reassured by her new vigour about the house, not realising that his wife's sudden activity had nothing to do with jam, or pickle, or missing buttons. He did not know that what he was watching was channelled emotion. He watched her writing labels on the jam, her writing slow and loopy with slanting stems, and he saw the stack of jars growing higher in the cupboard, and he did not guess.

He smiled as he watched her, but when occasionally she stopped, put her hands on her hips and arched her chest backwards to stretch out her shoulders, he saw something in her eye that he had not seen before, a distracted, faraway look. He tried to work out where he had seen that look before – not realising that the look was once his own – and he did not think to connect it with the view from the kitchen window, the sun streaming through the clouds onto the hill to the east of Holloway Creek where he had laid the wooden launching track over the grass.

For the rest of his life, he would remember that look.

Part II
1872

One

When Sister Thomas of the Holy Ghost saw the window she stamped her foot like a horse. She imagined herself alone, unwatched. Sally Walker had been taken to the Mother Superior's office, and Sister Jude was mustering the girls from the doorway, gesturing with her modern hands that all the girls must congregate inside. Nobody was allowed to linger in the courtyard while the window remained as it was. A message had already been dispatched to the Bishop. There was talk of an archbishop, a cardinal even. Of course, there would have to be a thorough inspection before any declarations could be made. There was a process to be followed, a scientific procedure to attend to, in evidencing the presence of the miraculous.

The image in the dining room window was just as the girls had described. Head tilted, hooded robe falling in modest folds, arms outstretched, palms upwards. It was just like all the paintings. Sister Thomas crossed the courtyard, her heels clipping loudly in the silence, and the silhouette blurred from green to blue to red as she came nearer. She put her hand against the glass, her fingertips resting lightly against the outline of the Virgin Mary's hand. She pushed harder. She let her sleeve fall over her hand so that it hid the movement of her fingers. She wiped the edges of the

Vision, rubbing at it with her thumb, flattening her palm over the lower part of the glass and trying to make it smudge. It made no difference. The Vision remained as it was, shimmering and glowing in the morning sun.

Sister Thomas's face tightened. She brushed down her sleeves and realigned her collar, and then she stamped her foot once more. She felt an ache in her back. She bent over and twisted her arm around her waist and rubbed at the dull pain with her hand. She thought: how can this have happened *here* and happened not to *me*?

She remembered when Sally Walker had first arrived at the orphanage ten years previously, how she had kicked out in the mortuary and screamed, but how she had not cried at her mother's funeral. Quite unnatural, Sister Thomas had thought at the time, and she thought it again now. The girl has no inclination for the religious. She professes admiration for Darwin in her lessons, Sister Thomas mused, for fossils and dinosaurs, and she does not hear the clippety-clop of the devil's hooves following her up the corridor. And then that this, *this*, should be attributed to her!

Sister Thomas of the Holy Ghost stood perfectly still for a long while, staring at the window. She reached up quite suddenly and tapped it with her fingernail. The sound was firm and shallow. She put her ear next to the glass and listened. She tapped again, louder this time, pecking at the window, her head almost touching the glass. There was something affecting its sonority. Something internal. She was certain of it and yet, being unacquainted with the composite elements of glass, she had no way of proving it. It was nothing more than a hunch, but it was this sound, the clip of it, which convinced her of the absence of the miraculous.

It was while Sister Thomas was thus engaged that she

noticed a shadow moving in the recess at the side of the courtyard. She saw a grey stocking and a black smock. Not a child, but not a nun. Her hand stopped in mid-tap and she straightened her back. She coughed sternly.

The shadow moved into the sunlight and lifted its chin.

'Sally Walker!' Sister Thomas exclaimed. She spoke loudly, hoping to draw Sister Jude's attention from the schoolroom. 'I might have known it would be you. First this,' she gestured wildly towards the window behind her with its vision of the Virgin Mary, 'and now skulking in the courtyard. Malingering when you should be teaching lessons!' Her voice was becoming shrill and she could feel the blood pounding in her neck.

Sally took a step towards her. 'Sister Jude sent me out here to bring in the water bucket I was using when it happened. She says that the Bishop will want to see it as evidence.'

Sister Thomas paused and gave Sally a look as if to say – as she had said quite firmly on the day, many years before, when Sally had kicked her in the stomach – that no good would ever come of Sally Walker. She marched over to Sally and took her arm. She did not intend physical harm but her fingers were tightened by suspicion. She could not loosen her grip.

'Tell me,' she whispered. 'How did you do this?'

Sally shook her head. 'I didn't *do* anything.' She sounded almost impatient and Sister Thomas of the Holy Ghost took this as insolence. 'I was just washing the window and then Sister Bridget noticed it. I didn't even know it was there.'

'The Virgin Mary does not appear to girls like you,' Sister Thomas hissed, with the slight tremor of the dispossessed now evident in her voice. 'The Bishop will come and he will expose you as a fraud. He will be able to see what trick you have played on the window to make it glow like this and, when he does, do *not* think for a *minute*,' she breathed in dramatically through her nose, 'that I will stand up for you. I cannot vouch for this sort of behaviour. It does no good for the Order to have its beneficiaries, its teachers, playing along like this.'

Sally sighed. Her fingers were cold and numb. She did not believe it was a Vision any more than Sister Thomas did, although her reasons were quite different. She sensed the giddiness in Sister Thomas's voice, that same floundering sensation she felt in her dreams at night. She did not understand its cause but she knew its effects. 'I know,' she said, hoping to placate Sister Thomas by agreeing with her. 'I told them it must be the soap. It smudges. You need to rub it with newspaper.'

Sister Thomas opened her mouth and closed it again. 'I do not need to do any such thing. Besides, it is not the soap, my girl. That Vision will not rub off. It is not the right sort.'

Even as she spoke, Sister Thomas felt oddly hesitant, wondering if perhaps she should order Sally to fetch some newspaper before the Bishop arrived, but there was no time because Sister Jude appeared in the doorway and called to Sally to hurry inside with the bucket because it might start raining any second and then the evidence would be lost. Sally took a step away from Sister Thomas, glancing at the window as she picked up the bucket, then she ran back to the schoolroom.

The Bishop arrived in an emotional state, a plump, white-haired man who had forgotten his hat in his excitement and was still apologising for this omission as he ran a ringed finger over the glass. He ran it back again. He pressed harder and pushed downwards. He stopped talking and held his breath.

'By golly,' he said quietly, and his voice cracked slightly as he spoke. 'By golly indeed.'

Sister Thomas frowned as the Bishop continued to trace the outline of the Virgin Mary with his finger. She bent down and picked up a small pebble which she offered to him.

'Tap it, Father,' she said impatiently, gesturing towards the glass.

'Tap it?'

Sister Thomas sighed. She considered the man a simpleton. 'Tap it against the window.'

'Oh. Right.' The Bishop nodded and tapped the glass tentatively with the pebble, first on the Vision and then on the glass. He raised his eyebrows at Sister Thomas.

'The sound is different, is it not, Bishop?'

The Bishop inclined his head and tapped again, a little more forcefully this time.

'It all sounds true to me, Sister,' the Bishop said, placing the pebble in a small puddle of soapy water still present on the windowsill and pressing his palms together. 'As clear as the bells of heaven,' he added, slightly unnecessarily, in Sister Thomas's opinion.

Sister Thomas could not help but feel irritated. It was widely known that the Bishop was tone deaf. This affliction was, unfortunately, so severe that even the Bishop himself could not hear quite how far out of tune he was during the chants at Mass. He would, if pressed, have conceded that he was not good with the higher registers, but this was only because he considered himself a natural baritone. Of course he could not hear the difference.

What Sister Thomas sensed and the Bishop did not, was that the problem was internal rather than external. The windows of the orphanage were not weathering well. The pane in question was a fine example of cylinder sheet glass, constructed following the German method of swinging a cylinder in a trench to form a rounded piece of glass, and then cutting, reheating and flattening the glass to form a sheet. This method produced glass with no curve but with a gently distorting effect, caused by small imperfections in the glass which, as with most things, worsened over time. Now, in 1872, the imperfections had become such that, when Sally Walker took her sponge to the window in order to wipe the glass, the warmth of the sponge and the weakness of the seal holding the moisture out, had caused condensation to arise inside the glass itself. From a purely molecular point of view, this was what had caused the Virgin Mary to appear in the window of the dining hall on a cold Tuesday in January.

Of course, there was also another explanation entirely. It was the non-molecular version on which the Bishop pronounced and passed up to the Archbishop. There were visits to the school, daily showings of the glass between breakfast and lunch, and newspaper reports mentioning Sally Walker by name which were cut out and put aside to be framed.

At first, nobody noticed that the Vision in the window was starting to slip. Its chin sagged and its eyes drooped at the corners. Its hands were wrinkled and veiny and there were sinews protruding from its neck. It was Sister Thomas who was the first to notice this extraordinary rate of ageing. It was more obvious when considered from inside the dining hall, as the external side of the window had become so filthy from fingerprints and the hot breath of believers that it could hardly be called transparent. Indeed, Sister Thomas felt that, had you not been looking for her, you may not even have guessed that this silhouette was the Virgin Mother herself. She thought: Ah-ha.

At table that night, she swirled the water in her glass and said, 'But of course, we will only know it is a true

Vision if it remains so,' and then she paused so that others could make the observation themselves. But they did not. They simply nodded their agreement and continued to dip bread into their soup.

It was Sally who noticed it next. She was looking at the window across the courtyard when she saw that the Vision had slipped into a grotesque smudge. She was teaching letters to the younger girls, and her chalk stopped short on the blackboard. She smiled. She had grown tired of the fuss, tired of the whispering among the younger girls, and the stilted deference of the nuns. There was silence in the classroom, and all eyes turned to follow Miss Walker's gaze. One of the girls let out a small gasp and precipitated such a commotion along the row of pupils next to the window that Sister Jude was obliged to burst into the classroom to enquire as to the cause of such disruption.

'The Vision, Sister Jude. It's almost gone!'

Sister Jude tilted her head to the side and considered the window, and then rushed into the chapel to raise the alarm.

Later that day, Sister Thomas of the Holy Ghost swept silently into the chapel and removed the photograph of Sally Walker from the feet of the Virgin Mary's statue. She could hardly stop herself from smiling. Grinning, even.

She did not hear Sally Walker come in behind her. She turned around and saw the young woman watching her with those bright blue unblinking eyes of hers which had not shed a single tear at the funeral of her own mother – quite unnatural – and she forced her mouth to level out. She calmed her tongue and hid her teeth. She folded the photograph into a hymnbook and nodded at Sally. Sally looked down at the hymnbook and then up at Sister Thomas.

She is accusing me! Sister Thomas thought. But of what? Nothing. I have done nothing. I am not the one who has fooled everyone with a Vision in a window. I have no reason to feel guilty.

And yet she did, because within that unblinking eye she saw something that she did not want to see. She saw an 'Ah-ha' being cast back at her, and she did not like to think of herself as quite so transparent.

Two

Railroads

Ursula Bridgewater slit the envelope open and held the letter out in front of her.

'*Dearest Bear,*' she read.

She felt a pang of rejection and put the letter down. It is my own silliness that lies at the bottom of all this, she reflected. I should never have allowed him to call me that in the first place. It is George's name for me, not his, and he has stolen it from George. He has stolen it from me.

She drew a deep breath and took the letter up again.

He hoped she was well.

Of course I am, she thought. My health has never been an issue.

She returned to the letter, to learn that Imelda had contracted influenza over Christmas, and Ursula imagined the willowy body of her replacement reclining on a chaise longue with a flannel draped across her brow and Henry Springton's hand clasped in her own.

'*Mark and Leonard are both very well. Leonard loves his horse.*'

He is five years old and he has his own horse!

Ursula did concede that she was not underprivileged herself. She had grown up with prettily embroidered dresses and housemaids to boil the water for her bath, and she appreciated this. She took food in wooden boxes to the slums of

91

Birkenhead and the local parish orphanage, and distributed heavy, woollen scarves. She did this even in summer, as scarves were the only item of clothing she could knit although, she had to admit, they were not up to much. She suspected that her scarves did not always remain in their original form. She had seen other things being pulled apart, unknotted and strung out, and then reconstituted into children's pullovers, socks and caps. The women did it on their front doorsteps, dressed in stiff, streaked aprons while their needles clicked and slipped in a way that Ursula had never quite mastered.

She had once made a scarf for Henry Springton, before the proposal, and it had been quite a joke between them at the time. It had caught on his aunt's sideboard when he was invited for dinner, and had unravelled entirely as he walked through the house, like a lost child in an enchanted forest. She thought for a moment that she might remind him of this in her next letter.

But then she shook her head quite sharply. No, she would not remind Henry Springton of the scarf. She knew that. It would be too much. It was not her style. She did not like to make claims on him, or on anyone, but especially not on him. It was easier, she found, in the long run, to keep her distance, to pretend that she hardly noticed his allusions to their past life together.

'With all dearest wishes to you and your brother,' he wrote at the end of his letter in that sprawling, careless hand of his. All flourish and no substance, George had warned her when their engagement was first announced, but she had not paid any attention. She could see it now, of course, looped into his words. *'Affectionately yours.'* But you're not, she thought. You're not mine. You never were.

She sighed and folded the letter. It had started to drizzle and the rain was running in streams down the glass. She was a fish in a bowl. She took the atlas from the bookshelf and propped it up on her lap. The previous month's copy of *The Excursionist* was slotted into it, unread and discarded between Chile and Argentina. She took the magazine out and laid it on the cushion next to her.

Ursula decided she would open the atlas and see where its pages fell, and she would take wherever it landed as a sign. She stood the atlas on its spine and let it fall, but instead of springing open at Rome or Florence as she had hoped, it fell open at the sea off the east coast of Africa and the island of Zanzibar.

This was not the sort of sign for which Ursula Bridgewater had been hoping – Dr Livingstone she was not – so she discounted Fate on this occasion, and instead picked up *The Excursionist* and flicked through its pages. '*Round the World,*' she read in a decorated caption on the second page, '*is this a dream? Can it be true that in three weeks hence we could be steering westward to circumnavigate the globe?*'

Westward, Ursula thought absently, her fingers lightly dusting the page. America.

A smile spread across her face. She thought: But why has this not occurred to me before?

She supposed she had been put off by the image of the emigrant ships portrayed in the newspapers, dirty and crowded as they sailed from the Prince's Landing Stage and out along the Mersey, past the Waterloo docks and the corn mills and the warehouses. America had not been presented as a tourist destination so much as an exile. But there were steamers now, and tourist classes. She turned to America in her atlas and looked at the size of it. It was so vast, so far away. It was just what she needed. It was more than an excursion. It was an expedition. She ran her finger over the map and traced the route detailed in the advertisement, from New York to Niagara to Detroit, Chicago,

Salt Lake City and on, down and down, to San Francisco and all its rowdiness, as Mr Thomas Cook put it. Such great distances, she thought; huge bites of land compared to the tooth mark of England.

They would be personally conducted by Mr Thomas Cook and would travel by steamer and the new Grand Central train. Ursula loved to travel by train – although she noted that, in America, they called them railroads – the countryside spreading out before her like the moving panoramic shows she had loved so much as a girl. There had once been an American moving picture show at the pavilion in New Brighton to which George had taken her when she was seven years old – it might perhaps have been set in Nevada but she could not really remember – and there had been horses and buffalo and men dressed in waistcoats and open-necked shirts. There had been music and coloured lights, and the fabric picture reel was strung across the stage. She remembered one picture of a sunburnt man in a wide-brimmed hat sternly holding up a deer skin, a desert of bright yellow sand behind him.

She and George had been wedged together at the end of the row. Ursula had leant into his shoulder to see over the crowded heads of the people in front of her, who clapped furiously whenever the music rose to a particularly dramatic crescendo. On her other side had been a patent stove, enthusiastically installed for the comfort of the audience, which had burned a hole in Ursula's stocking, and it was for this reason more than any other that Ursula suspected the Nevada desert to be unbearably hot.

There would be no music on the trains, and no coloured lights, but she looked forward to it all the same. How much grander that it should all be real!

Of course, George would not want her to go. He never

did. He did not understand her restlessness, what it was that required her to leave this carefully organised life he had made for her. Ursula resolved to ignore his objections, as she always did. She thought: I have spent too long sitting on this windowsill and contemplating the meaning of my own existence.

She smiled then, because this was exactly the sort of phrase she liked to use purely to enrage George. He found notions of existence exasperating. George preferred things to be kept simple. He considered that one was either alive or dead and that was all there was to be said on the matter. He was the same with tiredness. It irritated him to see people yawning or being listless, or moaning about being tired. George was, on principle, either awake or asleep and that was that.

Ursula decided to keep off the subject of existence when she mentioned this new trip to her brother. After all, there were plenty of other reasons why she would want to go to America. She wished for adventure, certainly, but she also suspected that America might have something to teach her. The name conjured up vague and slightly alarming pictures of men, like the ones on Josiah Wedgwood's anti-slavery medallion. She owned a set of Wedgwood crockery which had been left to her by her mother, and which demanded from every piece: 'Am I not a man and brother?' She pictured men chained and begging; ragged armies pushing through cotton plantations to free slaves; fiery revolutionaries; the topplers of Empire.

And there were the Niagara Falls to be seen. She had viewed Frederic Church's wonderful painting of the Falls when it came to Liverpool before she had even gone on her first excursion to Wales. She had stood in front of it and felt the rush of its current under her feet, the foaming, curling, flashing water rendered in a spray of luminous paint across the canvas so that it had seemed almost to move in front of her eyes, pulling her in. Then there is New York City and Boston Common and Los Angeles, the City of Angels. Horse ranches and cowboys and brown bears. Yes, she thought, I think I might like America.

She bit her lip. The tour was scheduled to depart in six weeks' time. Ursula consulted her desk calendar. It was already nearly February. She did not want to go on the whole trip, all 222 days of it, coming round from the East via Japan and India. She might have done if Miss Joy and Miss Emma had been accompanying her, but it was a long time to be just by herself, and besides, it would be too much all in one go. She might perhaps go East another time.

Ursula frowned. She hesitated for a moment, and then she sat down at her writing table and scribbled a quick note to the offices of Thomas Cook and Son in London, instructing that a Lady's ticket for the American section of the trip be held in her name, payment by banker's draft to follow.

As she folded the letter, she thought that she had never been so far in all her life, and she felt a small jump of excitement in her stomach. It was an exile – but it was also an adventure. Despair had hovered for a moment, but had lifted, forestalled by the menu of scrupulously chosen cities and sights on the tour itinerary. The place-names appeared on her atlas as venison-coloured patches of earth, distant and unimaginable.

But then she remembered Egypt, and the sensation of being all alone on top of the Great Pyramid at Giza, and for a brief moment her enthusiasm deserted her. She took out her pen and amended her note to Mr Thomas Cook – two Ladies' tickets this time, for herself and a companion – because she could not quite clear from her mind the prospect of all that wilderness.

Plans

Ursula Bridgewater had plans. She awoke early and wrote lists. There was luggage to arrange, travel details to attend to. The pile of books beside her bed grew to incorporate volumes on the history of America, the civil war and the voyage of the *Mayflower*, *Uncle Tom's Cabin* and *The Scarlet Letter*. She made notes in the margins and no longer noticed the cold, endless English winter which had so depressed her in recent months.

She did not even think of writing back to Henry Springton. She stuffed his letter into her atlas and then slotted the atlas back into its leather case, and placed it on the bottom shelf of the bookcase, and she did not take it out to read over the details of Leonard's horse as she might once have done. She told herself that it was because she did not have the time to reply, but it was not really that. It was not that at all. She did not want to write to him because she simply did not have enough energy for the task. She could not muster it up.

And there was also the question of her companion, as she had reserved the second ticket without being quite decided upon whom to ask. There were friends she could invite, she supposed, women who had expressed a passing interest in her previous travels, but she found that she did not wish to be accompanied by those women in whose drawing rooms she was obliged to smile so politely and talk so earnestly about unscientific things while she was in England. She did not wish to be trammelled by their expectations. She was tired of talking about hosiery and drapery and fashions in candlesticks, and of being patronised on the subject of men, or more precisely, of marriage. They pitied her, and they did it obviously, without any acknowledgement that she might not want to have married their pinch-cheeked, absent husbands; that she might be perfectly happy with her own arrangements.

Of course, they did not know how she felt about Henry Springton. George knew, although it remained unspoken between them, but she had not told anybody else, and it was for this reason that she found their pity discourteous. She did not patronise them when they spoke of their interests, their domestic tribulations and their holidays to cold, stone-flagged cottages in the Lake District, and it irritated her that they would not extend the same courtesy to her.

Going abroad offered a respite from all of that, where she could dress as she liked, as a Red Indian if she chose, and could walk on her own, arms swinging by her sides, without anyone trying to lead her about by the elbow.

It was unfortunate that her previous maid had so recently departed, encouraged by Ursula to set up a boarding house with an indoor bathroom for which Ursula had insisted on providing the initial capital. Mavis would have done very nicely, all things considered. America would have suited her entrepreneurial spirit. She thought of asking George, even though she knew already what he would say – that one cannot simply leave a factory to run itself – and that although he had previously consented to the suggestion of an excursion in theory, America was hardly Scarborough, was it?

She spread the word among her circle of compatriots that she required a new lady's maid, not too young, but not old either. She ought to be young enough to want to learn, to travel, but not so young as to require looking after. There would be the normal duties, of course: dressing, arranging food, taking messages; these were to be expected. But, more than that, Ursula wished for someone untrained in the social niceties of her circle. She wanted a maid who would let her do as she liked, who would not gasp at her attire or spread gossip, who was thoughtful and self-contained and had a sense of purpose such as she had sensed in Mr Thomas Cook in the Holy Land.

In the meantime, Ursula did very nicely without one. The housekeeper, Mrs Anderson, took on extra duties and Ursula thought of perhaps asking her to be a companion, but on balance Ursula reflected that she was a little too heavy-footed to be constantly present. Besides, Mrs Anderson had a family of three sons in Liverpool, and a husband in the Navy who was always about to come home but never did.

Alongside all these preparations and planning, there was still her part in her brother's tea business to attend to. She would often host the dinners held by her brother for his colleagues, and on these occasions she was not obliged to retire to the drawing room, but could remain at the table for as long as she liked. She enjoyed these evenings, sitting up and discussing politics and, occasionally, if she knew the company well enough, smoking cigars. In later years, after George's marriage to Miss Delilah Jones, an enthusiastic campaigner of whom Ursula would heartily approve ('she is so utterly, delightfully, un-charming!' she was to exclaim on the announcement of her brother's engagement), these would become louder, angrier affairs. As the work-forces unionised, George Bridgewater would become known in certain hot drink circles (not just tea, but also coffee and cocoa) as a sympathiser, but this would not be for many years yet. For now Ursula enjoyed the glimpses these dinners afforded her of a male world from which she was otherwise excluded.

Hosting aside, it also fell to Ursula to oversee a number

of deliveries and collections. The crates of tea arrived from India at the docks and were brought down to Bridgewater's Tea Factory on Crown Street to be sorted and packaged and distributed. This was not Ursula's business. She had no practical training and, although she would lament this lack of opportunity to her brother from time to time, she was also relieved to be spared such involvement. The details of it bored her. She did not like process. She liked progress.

However, on this particular occasion, a collection was being made by Mr Fisher, of Fisher's Tea Shop, New Brighton, and there was no one else available to attend to him. 'If I must,' Ursula had muttered, pulling a cape around her shoulders to take a carriage to the warehouse.

The warehouse was cobbled and cold, stacked high with exotic, pungent crates, behind which the darkness sighed and scuttled. Ursula held a sheaf of papers in her hand, order forms and contracts. Process, she thought as a carriage rolled in and a short man in a top hat stepped out and extended his hand in greeting.

'I have heard,' the man said, whilst directing a boy to load the carriage just so, with the small packets on top and the larger packets underneath, 'that you are in need of a new lady's maid.'

'Yes, indeed,' Ursula replied, slightly bemused that this unlikely client might know something about lady's maids.

'Your brother mentioned it to me.' He turned to the boy. 'No, put the smaller ones on top. No, there. On top, boy.' He shook his head, wiping imagined dust from his chubby hands. 'He said that you were thinking of taking her as a companion for your trip to America?'

'Yes,' she said. 'Although I don't know what business it is of George's. He hardly notices them when they're here, but as soon as they're off, he starts complaining.' She paused, smiled. 'Do you know someone who might be suitable?'

The man handed her a piece of paper with a name scribbled on it, and underneath that an address. An orphanage. She recognised it at once, the orphanage upon which she bestowed her many-coloured scarves and to whom she delivered the boxes of apples from her brother's orchard every autumn.

'I don't want her to be too young,' Ursula said, handing the piece of paper back to him.

'Oh, no,' the man said. 'She is not young. She is seventeen, a teacher there. I knew her family, her mother. I think she would suit you nicely. She is . . .' He paused, and then stopped. 'Well, she is just a girl but she is well-educated. And, with respect, Miss Bridgewater, I think you would like that.'

Ursula smiled at him, surprised. She supposed this information must have come from George too, and she was pleased to have this aspect of her character confirmed.

Well, thought Ursula, an orphan. Why not? She took the piece of paper and thanked Mr Fisher for his suggestion.

She wrote to the orphanage that afternoon, and asked if Miss Sally Walker might be persuaded to leave her teaching post and come to work for her as a lady's maid. The trip to America was not mentioned. She would want to meet the girl first, check her tread, the pitch of her voice, that sort of thing.

Ursula did not know that the Sally Walker of Mr Fisher's recommendation was at the centre of the commotion at the orphanage. She had heard talk of the Vision in the window, but having no truck with the miraculous, had not paid it much attention. There was now a whiff of scandal about the whole affair, of which Ursula was also ignorant, after the Vision had slumped into a willowy shadow at the bottom of its pane of glass, and this had been reported in the newspaper perused by Mr Fisher on his journey to

Crown Street. Mr Fisher had witnessed Sally's discomfort when the Vision first appeared, and this new development only deepened his concern for the girl. She was unhappy, he knew that, and he felt a responsibility for the unhappiness, seeing as it was his donation that had kept her at the orphanage when she might otherwise have left. He had thought of offering her a position at the tea shop, but he worried about the associations it might have for her.

Then, on his way to meet Ursula Bridgewater, he had remembered the conversation with her brother, George, the last time they met, and he had grasped at the prospect of bringing Sally out into the world and into the employ, the tutelage, of such a woman. He knew Miss Bridgewater to be intelligent – a reformer – and the sort of woman Elizabeth Walker might have admired.

Ursula Bridgewater's letter to the orphanage arrived on the same day as Sally Walker's photograph was removed from the chapel, and Sister Thomas took this as a sign from the Virgin Mary. Ursula received a reply from Sister Thomas the very next morning, announcing that Sally Walker would be delighted to begin her new employment as soon as convenient for Miss Bridgewater, and that perhaps Miss Bridgewater would like to send for her without delay.

What an extraordinary name for a woman, Ursula thought, and her tone is a little curt. But still, how efficient.

Three

The three stories of Mary O'Hara: an elegy

Toby O'Hara did not remember his mother. He pretended he did, but he did not. He searched for her in his dreams but he could not find her. He did not know where to look. His mother was hidden from him, obscured in his memory. There were only empty hillsides, unpeopled landscapes which stretched on and on under a cloudless sky, so that when he awoke the sheet was tangled around his legs and there was a pain behind his eyes where they had strained for her in his sleep. Why did you leave me? he wanted to ask her. How could you think I didn't need you?

He thought he remembered the shadow of her, sprinting grim-faced from the house on that final morning, her arms pumping and her knees lifting in a way he had not seen before. She had seemed suddenly urgent, muscular. He did not trust the memory. He knew it was wrong because when he pictured her, there were strips of white muslin in her hair. This was her night-time hairdo, her one vanity, and Toby knew she would not have left the house without untying the strips and unwinding the curls with her fingers, leaving delicate strands of dark brown hair caught in the wooden comb on the dressing table. He knew his memory must be wrong – he was certain of it – and yet in the recesses of his mind he remembered how she had lifted him up and held him against her, compressing his chest against her hot body, his face against her tied-up hair, before brushing Edmund O'Hara aside and hoisting herself into the flying machine.

He did not talk about this to his pop. They were alone, the two of them, in a house in which they did not belong. His pop became an immigrant once more in his habits and phrases. When Edmund spoke now of Ireland, he called it 'home' without realising he had done so, and Toby did not correct him.

They worked together in the shed, making toys for the deliveries to Boston, but there was no longer any talk of flying machines. They grew to be careful with each other, keeping their hurt neatly enclosed so that it did not snag or catch. It was in the spirit of this carefulness that they learned not to speak too often of the pretty, dark-eyed woman for whom they both ached and whom Toby struggled to remember.

On Monday mornings, they cleaned the house together, just as Mary had done. They dusted and polished and scrubbed, blackening the grate with lead and shining the candleholders on the piano with lemon quarters. They learned how to clean a rug with damp tea leaves, and how to wring the moisture out of a sheet without crumpling it. They laughed and joked while they worked – letting their mops splash over their buckets and ignoring the mildew rising on the curtains – but still it remained Mary O'Hara's house, the house of her childhood, in which she had lived and died, and in which she could no longer be found, no matter how Toby searched for her in the nooks and crannies of the kitchen, the parlour, the jasmine-sweet wardrobe of blue, pepperpot dresses. There were only those three stories of his mother's childhood which bobbed now in his memory, three small rips in that endless, shimmering surface which obscured his mother from him.

When he was little, his mother would sit at the dark wood piano in the drawing room and sing lilting songs about the glens of Scotland. She had never been to Scotland, but had learnt the songs from Mrs Moody, a tired Scottish woman with swollen fingers which cracked when she stretched them over the keyboard. When Mary O'Hara sang the songs she had learnt, 'My Love is Like a Red, Red Rose' and 'My Bonnie Moorhen', with Toby next to her on the stool and her husband snoring on the settee, she sang them in that same homesick voice. She pronounced them 'rrrose' and 'muurrhen'.

During the daytime, she would play these songs carefully, as if she had only just learnt them; but when it was dark she played them with her eyes shut, not even bothering to light the piano candles. Toby liked to watch her when she played like this, the notes and rhythms clamouring and spilling into the room, her voice exotic and soft as she sang. He liked how her fingers moved so lightly across the keys, how the veins on the backs of her hands became blue and raised when she played like this, the blood pulsing and rushing around her body.

The piano had several notes missing, even back then. Two of the keys had always been missing, but a few more had been levered out by Toby as an experiment when he was younger, and then he had lost or buried them – he could not recall which – but his mother had not been cross. She had simply played the space where the notes had once been, and had smiled at him during the gaps as if they were part of an elaborate, shared joke. He remembered the outline of her face, smiling at him through a fog.

When he sat at the piano now, alone on the stool, he felt a pain in his chest. He wished he had paid more attention to her lessons, so that he might close his eyes and hear once again Mrs Moody's songs played in the dark, with their funny gaps and silences and Scottish burrs.

In spite of the opaqueness of their narrative form, Toby regarded these songs as the first story from his mother's childhood.

The second story was about her visit to the Niagara Falls, and it was Toby's favourite of the three stories. Mary went to Niagara in the spring of her sixteenth year, when for a whole day and a whole night the water stopped falling. It was her parents who took her, travelling for five days by canal to get there, and then by horse-drawn railroad. They saw the waterfall first in the dusk, its white foam glowing red through the great sweep of mist, and they heard the roar of it from their hotel bedrooms. But then, just before dawn, the water stopped. They heard later how it had slowed first to a trickle, and then just drips, until the river below had dried up entirely so that it was possible to walk to the other side. Huge crowds swarmed to the edges of it, tentatively at first, and then more confidently. Horses paraded along the soft riverbed and girls danced quadrilles with cavalry officers. Mary O'Hara's father climbed down over the rocks to unwedge a sword, left over from the war against the British, which he tucked into his belt and brought home.

Mary would tell Toby how she had gone down to the river with her father again that evening, while her mother prayed in the church because she was convinced that God was coming. She had stood with her father in the strange, dripping silence, watching the night grow dark, and then, quite suddenly, there had been a low, faraway rumble – a tremor in the earth – and an immense spray of water as the river surged and tumbled over the ledge of rock once more, and the Falls crashed back into its habitual roar.

'It was quite magical,' she told him. Toby remembered how her eyes used to shine as she spoke, small dark pebbles in water, and for a brief moment he would be able to see her, her smile unfocused and fragile, a wisp of cloud which retreated even as he grasped for it. Really, it was the only story she ever actually *told*, and it was because of this that Toby liked it best.

The last story was about his pop coming to Holloway Creek and falling (*swooping*, his pop insisted) from the roof of the general store into the river. It was his pop who had always told this story – so it did not really count – but Toby remembered the look he used to see in his mother's eyes when his pop told it, and it was because of this that he counted it as the third story; the final act in Mary O'Hara's childhood.

Four

A list

These are the things Sally Walker knew for certain as she sat on the stone steps of the orphanage in 1872 when she was seventeen years old, waiting to be collected by Ursula Bridgewater:

She knew the earth was a sphere and that the Virgin Mary had a mournful way about her.

She knew the subjunctive was a means of indicating purpose and that silver should be polished with vinegar and hot water.

She knew it was a sign of madness to be able to draw a perfect circle and that the Holy Spirit was the leaven in the lump.

She knew that her father was the sort of man who bit his nails and that her mother had been beautiful, and she knew about Empires and steam trains and the posthumous fate of Oliver Cromwell.

She knew that George Bridgewater owned a tea factory on Crown Street and that her mother had sometimes made collections from the factory for Mr Fisher.

She suspected – to say she knew for certain would be going a little too far – that she was unlikely to experience anything extraordinary in her life, and she supposed that it was probably for the best.

Sally's expulsion, or her Fall, as it was termed by Sister Thomas of the Holy Ghost, who took great delight in any story which involved a casting-out of some variety, did not come as a great shock to Sally. She had not intended to stay at the orphanage for so long, nor had she expected to leave in this manner, out-manoeuvred by a Vision in a window, but the sensation brought on by her expulsion was so familiar as to be almost predictable. When she sat on the steps of the orphanage, thin and neat, her hair pinned up under her hat, waiting for Ursula Bridgewater, Sally did not feel sad or disappointed. She felt only that same internal giddiness she had felt for as long as she could remember.

She had received a note from Mr Fisher the previous day informing her of his acquaintance with Miss Bridgewater – *'a perfectly remarkable lady'*, he called her, but neglecting to mention her penchant for the occasional cigar which was well-known among the tea salons of Lancashire – and that he had recommended Sally as a lady's maid. *'She is a traveller,'* he wrote, *'and you may benefit from this inclination.'*

Sally had not known what he meant by this – she imagined camel leather shoes and bright drapes – but she had understood once more that here was yet another thing for which she was indebted to him, and for which she was unutterably grateful. Oh, she would thank him; she would say the words, but she would feel the inadequacy of them even as she spoke them. They would be too formal and she would not be able to look at him, then he would stutter and interrupt her a little, and it would be the same as it had always been.

His letters had become less frequent over the years, distant in a way they had not been when she was young, but appropriate and formal. He came to see her a few times a year; he would have come more often but Sally pretended to him that she was busier than she was. She did not tell him how she spent her Saturday afternoon holidays, venturing into the city or taking walks in the fields behind the orphanage, to Woolton Village and back.

When she did allow him to visit, they spoke only of inconsequential things. They did not speak of her mother, or of the matter of his donation on her behalf. Instead, she told him what she had learnt and what she was teaching, and he listened and patted her on the head at the end of each visit. It was an odd habit, but neither of them seemed to know how to stop it – he would open his arms to embrace her as he had done only once, in the Royal Infirmary on that terrible day twelve years earlier when she had pushed him away, but instead of allowing herself to be scooped towards him, she would bend her head forwards, her eyes down, willing him not to come too close, and he would pat her on the head. It was awkward, but it was also familiar; a reminder of that odd life she could barely recall when she was small and happy.

She held his latest letter in her hand as Ursula Bridgewater, tall and straight-backed with an unnaturally long tread, whirled out of the carriage and strode to the door of the orphanage. 'Sally Walker?' she asked, and then smiled quite suddenly.

Sally nodded.

'Right then,' she said. 'Come along. My brother is waiting in the carriage.'

It was quite common for Ursula Bridgewater to produce in those around her the clammy sensation of being hurried. Sally attributed this haste to the rain, not knowing that her new employer, dark-haired and brusque, only ever approached at pace. She clutched the paper package containing her belongings and followed Ursula down the steps to the carriage. The door swung open and George Bridgewater reached out and took Sally's hand as she clambered in and, just for a moment, Sally Walker was a lady in one of her mother's stories, dressed in silk and climbing into a pumpkin. When Sally was settled, George reached for Ursula's hand, but Ursula flapped him away, pulling herself into the carriage by the handle next to the door.

'Really, George,' Ursula murmured, settling herself next to the window and arranging her rain-soaked bonnet over her hair.

George grinned at his sister and dropped his hand, not appearing to be in the least offended by his sister's response. He smiled at Sally. Sally lowered her eyes. She did not wish to appear too bold in front of this elegantly-dressed man, with his neat whiskers and starched collar. He was tall like his sister, and older than Ursula, his eyes greenish-blue where hers were grey, but with the same dark hair.

'You mustn't mind my sister,' he said to Sally, and Ursula tutted at him and then patted his hand in a manner which Sally found at once disconcerting and comforting.

The rain blew more ferociously now along the streets rising up from the Mersey as the carriage rattled back towards the city, and towards Ursula and George's house in Aigburth, and Sally pressed her hand against the window. Outside, there were omnibuses topped with hunched men holding sleek, black umbrellas, returning from offices in the city centre; low brick buildings which led down to the bustle of the docks and through whose windows Sally had peered during her walks into town on Saturday afternoons. There were boys with chestnut carts sheltering under trees at the side of the road, and women clustering children into doorways, mops leant up against door jambs. She remembered

111

how she had often walked with her mother under their umbrella along the Promenade at New Brighton, and how she had liked to wriggle her hand free of her mother's to run ahead and dance in the rain.

There were droplets now on the window, and a sudden shiver of lightning.

'How topical!' exclaimed Ursula.

Sally looked up at her.

George coughed. 'Don't you mean tropical?' he asked.

'No, Georgie, I do not. I mean what I say. It is topical because I was reading about it only today. Walker . . . Shall I call you Walker? Yes, now, Walker, have you heard of Professor Hopper?'

'Bear,' George said with a sigh. 'Not now.'

Sally shook her head. She wondered at whether George had really called his sister a bear, or whether she had misheard, because Ursula Bridgewater did not look in the least bit like the sort of lady who would permit herself to be named after an animal, and a ferocious one at that.

But for the moment, there was another question in the carriage. 'Do you know what lightning is, Walker?'

Sally looked up. Ursula was peering at her over the top of the *Illustrated London News*. Sally knew, because she had been told, that lightning was a manifestation of the wrath of God, and yet she also knew, even before she opened her mouth to speak, that her answer would be wrong. Or, at least, it was not the answer Ursula Bridgewater wished to hear, a situation which Sally Walker had learnt could amount to the same thing.

'The wrath of God, ma'am,' Sally whispered, because she could not think of anything else to say.

'The wrath of God, my girl, is an irrational answer. It shows a surplus of superstition, a shameful ignorance of science, to attribute natural phenomena to the mood of a deity. It is a ruse concocted by zealots, to scare people into remaining down, down, down, always on their knees.' She paused. 'It is not your fault, of course. No blame can be attached to you. You are still young.'

Sally blushed.

George shuffled uncomfortably in his seat. 'Maybe we could discuss this later?'

'But just listen to this, George. How can she not be interested?' Ursula opened her copy of the *Illustrated London News* and spread it across her knees. 'Professor Hopper yesterday demonstrated to the Royal Institution of Science the production of a spark of lightning from an electromagnetic coil measuring precisely twenty-nine inches,' she read aloud. 'Now, how about that? Electricity.' She paused for dramatic effect. 'In the sky.'

Sally looked out of the window at the sky. She heard George sighing quietly to himself, and she thought that it was the sigh of a man who considered his sister to be slightly deranged. Sally looked at Ursula. She did not look deranged. She looked noble. She looked, Sally thought, a little like St Joan of Arc, but with more hair.

Sally was not quite right about the cause of George Bridgewater's sigh. She could not have guessed that when George sighed, it was because he was thinking that, really, the production of lightning from an electromagnetic coil was just another thread in the delicate tapestry of his sister's lack of a husband. He would not have dared to communicate such a thought to Ursula. She is such a prude, he was thinking, and yet she will not leave it alone. It is all sparks and electromagnetic rods with her. She will get a name for herself.

But Sally Walker, who had never before heard of Professor Hopper or his method of producing sparks of electricity from metal rods, and was not sure why anyone would wish for such a thing in any case, took her palm from the window and rested it on the seat next to her. She looked back at Ursula.

'But how?' Sally asked, anxious to be topical, and then nervous in case she had stuck too long on the same topic.

Ursula, sitting with her back straight in her crinoline dress, looked at her and nodded in a regal fashion. 'You see, George,' she announced. 'Of course she is interested.' She smiled at Sally before proceeding to inform her of the methods of storing electric charges in glass vials. She told her that in the last century – 'a sublime century,' Ursula remarked wistfully – an abbot in Paris had lined up two hundred of his Reverend Fathers along a mile-long wire, and then released an electric charge into the wire to show the speed at which electricity can travel. It was, Ursula explained, just as he expected. The reactions of the priests were almost simultaneous, if differing in expression. 'Quite sublime,' she concluded.

Sally held her breath as Ursula spoke. The hairs on her neck prickled. It made her shiver, this sudden static, and she felt refreshed. It was perhaps the rain, the carriage. She knew that her expulsion was meant to be a punishment, but she did not feel punished. She felt delighted to be in this small enclosure of plush upholstery, with intricate iron handles on the doors and soft curtains on the windows, listening to her straight-backed employer expounding on electrical sparks while rain dripped unnoticed from her bonnet. Later, when she knew about such things, Sally would describe the feeling as being puffed full of helium. She did not expect it to last but, for a brief moment when nobody was looking, she thought that, perhaps, it was the opposite of falling.

Five

Missing notes

As the years passed, Toby clung to the fictional version of his mother that his pop crafted for him. When he was young, his pop told him: 'You must brush your teeth before you wash your face . . . practise arpeggios, not scales . . . bake bread in the shape of a knot. That is what your mother would have wanted. She was very particular about arpeggios . . . about bread being in the shape of a knot . . . about the order in which things were best done.'

They ate jam for breakfast and for lunch. There was enough jam in that cupboard to last a full eighteen months after Mary O'Hara's death. In later years Toby would develop an allergy to it or, more strictly, an aversion, as he came to associate the stickiness of it on his fingers with that period of despair.

Edmund O'Hara kissed Toby's hair every night and ruffled it in the mornings. He smiled at him and called him 'Kiddo', but sometimes he would find Toby standing at the kitchen window, staring out across the field towards the hill in the east, and Edmund would blame himself for having grown careless, for not distracting the boy enough. He would cough from the doorway and clatter into the kitchen, as if he could, by all this noise, drown out the soft thud of his wife's absence.

When Toby went to bed, Edmund prayed all alone with his hands pressed against his eyes, his palms clammy with the self-consciousness of prayer. Forgive us our trespasses, he whispered. Give us our daily bread. He said the lines even though he did not mean them. He resorted to them because he was unused to prayer. Deliver us from evil, Edmund whispered politely, breathlessly. And then, something he did mean: Dear God, tell her I'm sorry.

At the same time, he thought: There is nothing there. There is only sky. But he did not want to think about the sky. He wondered if Toby remembered that final morning, how Mary had pulled at his sleeve in the doorway and told him he could not put the boy in the flying machine.

'He's too delicate, Edmund. He'll die.'

'No he won't. He's not delicate. He's a tough little lad.'

'That's not what I mean.'

He had called to her when she ran past him to the flying machine, but she had ignored him and climbed in. 'He's not getting in here,' she whispered when he caught up with her. 'I'll fly the damned thing myself, but that boy is not coming anywhere near it.'

Did Toby remember how she had waved to him as she left the ground, and how she had smiled then because she had kept him safe? Edmund had not understood until that moment. He had wanted his boy to fly but he had not seen the danger. He had intended it as a gift, an extravagant gesture for his son.

He no longer thought of it as a gift. Now he understood what he had not understood before, a thing which Mary had known by instinct but which he had missed until the moment he saw her small, shuddering smile from that ridiculous machine. He understood everything. He understood about the pickled vegetables, the jam, the clean linen folded in cupboards. He understood about the starching

116

of his best collar, the slippery sweep-marks on the floor. He wanted to wrap his arms around his boy, to wrap his whole body around him.

He thought: But I am too late.

Toby did remember that last day. Of course he did. It was just that he did not remember the chronology of it well enough to connect the rush and flurry of his mother's feather duster, the urgency of all that jam, to those final days in his pop's workshop when the flying machine was so close to being complete that Toby was forbidden from entering in case it spoiled the surprise.

But he knew that, now, when his pop went upstairs at night, he did not go to sleep. Toby could hear his feet padding on the floorboards, the thump of his knees and sometimes his hands. He knew his pop was praying, and he saw this as a private thing which he must not disturb. He did not know that when his pop prayed on his knees, squashed into the small space between his bed and the smouldering fireplace, what he prayed for was forgiveness.

As Toby grew older, he would sit with his pop on the porch at night, Edmund drinking whisky and Toby drinking beer, and both of them smoking thin cigarettes, and Edmund would look at his tall, brown-eyed son and bite his lip. He felt the past as a tremor, a rumbling in his conscience.

If he would only ask me outright, Edmund thought when Toby was eighteen, nineteen. If he would only just break cover and run at me straight, then maybe I could wring it out of myself and there it would be, all my fault and his mother an angel, and finally – it hurt him even to think it – the possibility of absolution.

For she was an angel, and Edmund allowed that; he

encouraged it. It became the only thing he would say about her, this man who had once talked himself breathless over the third story of Mary O'Hara's childhood. He spoke of Ireland still, and continued to make toys and dolls, but now every figure he delivered to the toyshop in Boston was small, with a thin, pepperpot build and dark brown eyes. 'She was so beautiful, so gentle,' he would say. 'She adored you.'

Toby smiled when they spoke of her. He sat with his long legs crossed, sunburned and stringy, with woollen socks rumpled around his ankles. His face was blank, except for that slight compression of the lips, that soft, careful smile which came whenever there was talk of the past. He uncrossed and crossed his legs.

When Edmund looked at his son on those occasions he felt the boy had a sense of apartness from him that he could not understand. He felt Toby watching his every gesture, treading carefully around him. He suspected that his son did not ask him about his mother because he wanted to spare him, to let him forget if he did not wish to dwell upon it. And yet Edmund ached to remove the burden of the secret from himself. After all, the truth is important.

Ask me, he thought. Ask me everything.

But Toby did not, would not, and it was because Toby would not break cover and come at him straight, that Edmund remained silent. When Edmund went to bed, Toby sat on the porch and read a little longer, books from Boston on farming and on the French fashion of hot-air ballooning ('not that,' Edmund thought when he saw them, 'please not that'), and still he did not tell him.

But it was not just because he was scared, or even because the boy did not ask. It was also because of all those jams and pickles and folded pillowcases. It was because Edmund understood. Too late, but he understood, and he would not undo his wife's final act of love by ladling such guilt onto his own son.

So he did not tell Toby how his mother had never in her life wanted to fly, that she had foreseen disasters in dreams and that he had found her once in the workshop with a broom poking at his beloved bat, his prototype. He would not tell him how the flying machine had been measured out for his own ten-year-old body. He did not want Toby to know that it was not so much a tragedy as a sacrifice.

He thought: Dear God, make him ask me. But he also thought: I must leave it alone.

And so it was left alone, and Edmund O'Hara kept his secret. He believed he was doing as his wife would have wished. He did not realise that in relieving his son of one burden, he was implanting another, although Toby O'Hara did not see it as a burden so much as a legacy. It was a purpose.

Six

A new sort of uniform

The house in Alexandra Grove was a large, red-bricked merchant's house. It had steps leading up to the front door and pillars on either side of the steps. It was grand and modern, with a gravel driveway and a turret. There were stained glass windows in the hallway which depicted watery patterns of fruits and flowers, and when Sally carried her belongings up the stairs to her small attic room, the rain-washed colours fell magically on her legs and arms.

The room was white and clean. There were no etchings of the Passion on the walls, no lurid paintings of any bleeding hearts. Sister Jude had given her a small portrait of the stoning of St Stephen to take with her ('he is my favourite of the Martyred Saints,' she told Sally), and now Sally took it from her bag and looked at it, trying to imagine what Sister Jude liked so much about this particular portrait. She saw the cuts on St Stephen's body, the torn flesh and the wild hair. But, for the first time, Sally also saw the rays of sunlight painted onto the hillside behind him, brushed white and golden, as if the heavens were opening beside him. She smiled, and propped the portrait up on the small table next to her bed.

There was a window set high into the wall of her room, and Sally moved the chest of drawers so that it was underneath the window, and she hoisted herself onto it. From there, she found that she could see across to the new park with its croquet pavilions and archery kiosks, and umbrellas bobbing along the paths between the cherry trees.

Sally had not yet been informed about the trip to America. She thought she had been engaged as a housemaid, not knowing that this position was already held by Mrs Anderson with the heavy tread. She expected to be busy, expected her hands to be cold. Carpet-cleaning and laundry and endless tiles to be scrubbed. She thought this was what Ursula Bridgewater required in a maid, that she be industrious and uncomplaining, lively but largely inconspicuous – that she be unhysterical – and this suited her perfectly.

There was a knock at the bedroom door. Sally jumped down from her perch at the window and found Ursula standing in the wood-panelled hallway, clutching swathes of fabric on quilted hangers. Ursula did not explain what they were for. She came in and laid them out on Sally's bed, and then she picked one up, a deep, crimson dress, and held it out in front of her.

'Yes, this should do you very nicely, Walker, although you might want to take the hem up a little,' she said, holding the dress against Sally's chest to assess its length and fit. 'I am a little taller than you.'

'It's lovely, ma'am,' Sally said, 'but I was expecting a uniform.'

Ursula squinted at Sally, taking in her narrow waist, her thin arms. 'Well, it is a uniform in a sense, Walker. All societies have uniforms. It may not look like one, but do not let yourself be fooled.'

Sally nodded, uncertain how to respond.

Ursula pulled out another dress, and then another and handed them to Sally. 'Take this, and this, and perhaps this one too. You will need them for our trip.'

What trip? Sally thought for a moment, but she did not ask because Ursula was now pressing the dresses into her arms. Crimson, midnight blue, primrose, white with small blue flowers. Sally wanted to cry with happiness at the prospect of so much colour.

'Thank you, ma'am,' she whispered, although at the same time she thought all sorts of other things; that she would never have an opportunity to wear such beautiful things; that she could hardly lift them; that she could not very well kneel on the floor and scrub in one of these; that they were so soft against her arms and her neck; that she might put them on and sleep in them at night; that her mother would have liked all those ribbons and loops and delicate pieces of lace.

'Oh, and the attic bathroom is entirely yours,' Ursula said, gesturing to a small door to the left of Sally's room while still holding the remaining gowns which she had judged unsuitable. 'The housemaid and cook both live out. Perhaps after lunch you might like to bathe, but not now. Mrs Anderson is expecting you in the kitchen.'

Mrs Anderson was a stocky woman with flat feet and a collection of jaunty tam o'shanters which she sported below stairs when off duty. She had a bad back, and this produced in her a tendency to approach life on the diagonal, her right shoulder dipped towards the fireplace and her hand clasping her hip for extra support while she rambled on to Sally.

'The mistress has given you some of her dresses, I believe,' Mrs Anderson began, although it was not a question. No response was sought. 'She tried to give them to Mavis but they didn't fit. Tall girl, that Mavis, much taller than you. Have you heard of her? I'm surprised you haven't been read one of them letters already. She's become quite a businesswoman, according to the mistress. Can you believe that? The mistress is so proud of her, you should hear her talk. Mavis this and Mavis that, and always reading out her letters over breakfast. Says that Mavis came on a treat while she was here. Came on a real treat, she did.'

Mrs Anderson did not pause for breath. She talked on and on, unexplained phrases, snippets of information, one after another. Conducted tours to Scotland, America, Lady's compartments, Atlantic crossings. Mavis and her guesthouse with its indoor bathroom.

Sally did not understand much of Mrs Anderson's conversation. She stood by the window and smiled until her cheeks ached. But what about me? she wanted to ask. Where am I to sit? What am I supposed to be doing? Where is my uniform? Who is Mavis and why are you telling me about her? And what do you mean, 'came on a treat'?

Mrs Anderson conducted all her relationships in this manner. She had a didactic streak and believed that her ability to never allow a lull in conversation – 'putting people at their ease,' she called it – proved that she was a good listener, for this was what Mrs Anderson believed herself to be. What she was, in fact, was a good talker. When she spoke, she inhaled noisily through her nose, hissing like a steamboat, whilst continuing to talk through the starboard side of her mouth so that there was no real opening for an interjection.

'Cup of tea with your lunch, dear?' she asked eventually, gesturing for Sally to sit down at the table.

Sally nodded. 'Yes, please.'

Mrs Anderson limped over to the kettle. 'You will be quite comfortable here,' Mrs Anderson continued. 'It is much easier to live in than to live out. It would be much better for my back if I could have that luxury but I have my boys to attend to. Three of them, stomachs like horses, the lot of them. And my husband's as bad, although he's in the Navy and not at home at the moment, but he's expected back any day now.'

Mrs Anderson wore a curtain ring on her left hand. She twisted it while she waited for the kettle to boil. She did not like her curtain ring. It took the wind out of her sails. She glared at the kettle until it hissed, then wrapped its handle in a teacloth and removed it crossly from the stove. She did not like to be reminded of the uncertain nature of Mr Anderson's whereabouts, and Sally would soon find that this was the one topic upon which Mrs Anderson could not be drawn. She would mention it several times a day, would pluck it out of nowhere, but she would not expand on it. She used exactly the same words each time, that Mr Anderson was expected back from sea any day now, and it was only after Sally had been at the house for nearly a fortnight that she found that this had been Mr Anderson's status for a number of years.

'Your duties, dear, are simply these,' Mrs Anderson rattled over lunch, her curtain ring now forgotten. 'You must keep the mistress happy. You must arrange her attire in the mornings and before dinner, arrange for her things to be cleaned and mended, but you will not be doing any cleaning or mending yourself. You just talk to me dear, and I'll help you along. You must run messages, collect journal sub-scriptions, keep fresh flowers in the drawing room. And then there is all the packing to be done. There are only a few weeks to make all the arrangements. The master is beside himself about it, but she won't take no notice of him. But anyway, that's not your concern. Miss Ursula will tell you what to pack, but it is your responsibility, both your own things and hers.'

'Packing?' Sally asked, although even as she said it she remembered now the letter from Mr Fisher, and Ursula's words in the attic. For the trip, she had said, and Sally had not asked her what she meant.

'Has she not told you?' asked Mrs Anderson, putting a soft, stout hand onto Sally's arm. 'She's taking you to America.'

Sally stood on the dark-panelled landing in the attic. She pushed the bathroom door ajar and peered in. It was clean and tiled, with a small, square window set into the ceiling. The bath tub stood in the middle of the wooden floor, in front of the swept-out grate. There was a yellow sponge next to the polished brass tap, discarded by Mavis as a remnant of the old, careful life she was leaving behind.

America, Sally thought, and for a brief moment she remembered standing on the Promenade outside the tea shop in New Brighton, holding her mother's hand, both of them looking out into that grey mist of sea which might or might not have held her father, nail-bitten and lost in all those dizzying currents. She remembered the curve of the horizon beyond which lay Ireland, and beyond that, far beyond that, beyond the sheets of ice and clustering storms, lay America.

Thou rulest the raging of the seas, she thought. Save me.

She took a deep breath and stepped into the bathroom. It was too large for her, too grand. It was surely a sin to have such luxury. And yet she had been told to bathe and she did not wish to appear ungrateful. There were three buckets of water next to the bath, and a kettle over the fireplace. There was charcoal in the grate. She must use it. She tiptoed across the floor, breathing that wonderfully sharp chemical smell which she would later learn to associate with hotel rooms and luxury but which, at the moment, reminded her only of the laundry room at the orphanage. She bent down to light the fire in the grate, waiting for the paper to catch and setting the water to boil.

The water echoed against the bath. Sally gasped as she stepped into the tub, holding the sides as she lowered her body in, and then submerged herself completely. She ran her hands over her stomach, over her chest and arms, feeling the unfamiliar smoothness of her skin. She tipped her head back until the water washed across her face and into her eyes and ears in a glorious swirl of silvery light.

No, she would not get carried away. She was being hysterical and she must stop. She must attend to her duties, whatever they were.

She sat up in the bath tub, and her hands were slippery, then soft; her fingers puckered in the wetness. Her skin glowed blue and white under the glassy sheen of water, a shimmering Vision in a window. Ridiculous, she thought, as she stood up in the tub and reached for her towel, droplets clinging to her narrow, goose-pimpled body. But for a fleeting second – it was gone almost before she had registered it – she wondered if perhaps the Virgin Mary had known exactly what she was doing after all, appearing in the window like that and getting her out of there.

Seven

Balloons

Toby started his balloon experiments when he was sixteen years old. His pop refused to help so Toby prevailed instead on the local magistrate, Judge Jake Gadston, who had known Toby's mother all his life and had never once heard her express any wish to fly.

Judge Jake Gadston was an octogenarian with no teeth and milk-bottle spectacles. He demonstrated the principles of ballooning by cutting the top off a small tin and filling it with oil. He tied a white silk bag to the tin, and strung it through with twine so that the tin hung beneath the bag. At dusk, Toby and his pop sat together on the porch while the Judge set fire to the pool of oil, holding the silk bag above the flame to catch the rising heat. Toby remembered it exactly, how the bag had billowed upwards, pulling away from the old man's fingers – a shimmering, floating lantern.

'Hey, Pop,' he whispered. 'Don't you reckon Mum would have liked that?'

His pop, sitting on the porch with his head in his hands, did not reply. He only smiled, and it was a tight, stretched smile.

Balloons were not Toby's passion. They were a starting point, a way of getting used to a new scale. To take Judge

Jake Gadston's way of putting it, they were arpeggios in C major, played fast and mixed up with some staccato in-filling, but Beethoven they were not. They were part of the legacy of Toby's childhood, but they were not his purpose. For this, Toby had something far more specific in mind.

But, for now, they were a good distraction. It was Judge Jake Gadston who oversaw the ordering of the rubber-coated silk from Boston for the large balloon skin, and his niece who made the wicker basket. His grandson collected a roll of fisherman's netting from Gloucester, Massachusetts, to enclose the balloon and secure it to the basket.

Toby saw to the mechanics of it all. He continued to read books on ballooning, combing them for details of weight and air pressure and lift. He worked on the adjustable gas valve which was to be fitted to the top of the balloon and could be opened quite easily by tugging on a rope. He filled small potato sacks with sand and attached them to the rim of the basket to act as ballast bags and he worked out a system of tethering the balloon to the ground using an arched root of an old oak tree.

The balloon made its first flight in the late afternoon when the wind was at its lowest. Judge Jake Gadston went with Toby, the old man clinging to the inside of the basket and hollering that he was dying and that they had to come down right now.

'We can't. We're going too fast,' Toby told him. 'We have to level out.'

'Goddamn,' Judge Jake Gadston moaned, looking out over the side of the basket for the first time, and seeing a crowd of faces becoming smaller and smaller, a trail of tiny people chasing them across the field below.

'It will take time,' Judge Jake Gadston had declared before the flight, 'to get used to the new perspective. It is a question of evolution.' But up in the air, with his glasses fogged up and his hands blue from the cold, Judge Jake Gadston forgot about perspective. He could only laugh, an old man's laugh at first, rusty and out-of-practice, but then becoming lighter, younger, until there was a stitch in his side and tears running down his face.

'*Never before,*' Judge Jake Gadston wrote later in the scrappy notebook he referred to as his memoirs, '*have I experienced a feeling of such absolute hilarity as I felt at that moment.*'

It was hilarity which Toby felt, but it was also something else. It was cold; a dry, freezing cold and Toby felt a burning sensation in his throat, something odd and secret he could not quite put his finger on. They rose to four hundred, six hundred, eight hundred feet, and Toby had a sense of being closer to something than he had ever been before, although he did not know exactly what. His pop would have called it a flicker of God. That was the sort of thing he had started to say as he had gotten older. Toby considered this under the chalky glare of the clouds, but decided that no, it was not God. But it was something.

'Stop stamping, boy,' Judge Jake Gadston shouted at him, gripping the balloon ropes as he giggled and guffawed. 'You're going to make us fall.'

Toby turned to him and grinned. He was not stamping. He was dancing. He was cold, and the valve was stuck, but he was happy. This is what his mother had wanted to see, he thought, this flicker of life. He crouched down and blew on the valve until he felt it give, and it was then, just before they began their descent, that he noticed the gleam of red in the sky and a crescent-shaped chink of sun bobbing up above the horizon once more, a final flourish before setting for the second time that day.

Eight

The various insights of Captain Algernon J. Gordon

Ursula was in an expansive mood. She always was on boats.
She liked action, adventure: the chugging, belching departure, the ceremony involved in the waving-off at the docks.
She had never made such a long voyage before. She and
Sally stood together on the deck, Ursula in an evergreen
dress – 'the colour of adventure,' she had told Sally that
morning while Sally was laying out Ursula's clothes on her
dressing chair – and Sally in Ursula's too-heavy gown of
dark crimson, hemmed up and taken in but still not quite
right.

They stood together, green and red, and looked for
George Bridgewater and Mr Fisher on the floating landing
stage below. There was such a jostle of people that they
could not pick them out of the crowd. There were flower-
sellers and a brass band, jugglers and people walking on
stilts. Trunks and crates were being hauled up the side of
the boat.

It was busy and unfamiliar. Sally looked out at the Pier
Head, trying to fix it in her mind so that she could recall
it later when she needed it. She had never thought of this
part of Liverpool as home before. Home was somewhere
else. It was Mr Fisher's tea shop at New Brighton, the white
lighthouse beyond Fort Perch Rock and the cold, grainy

sand on which she had once stood to watch the ships leaving for America and Australia. She had scoured the deck rails of those boats from afar, searching always for a man's hand raised aloft in recognition, perhaps a parrot on his shoulder, who would jump from the deck and swim to her. He never did, of course, although occasionally people would wave back to her, but they never jumped. Her eggshells went undelivered, and she smiled now to remember them, and to remember herself as she was then; lost and unreachable.

She lifted the bunch of white roses Mr Fisher had given her and waved them, just in case he could see her. He had come to see her off and had thrust a bouquet at her as if she, not Ursula, were the Lady Excursionist. He had embraced her before she had had time to transfer the flowers to her other hand, so the arrangement had become crushed between her chest and his arm. She felt a thorn pressing against her, threatening to break the skin that held her so tightly in, and the moment was suddenly lost, so that instead of saying all the things she longed to say to this kind man, she had lowered her eyes and thanked him too politely, as she always did.

She stood on the deck and her eyes roamed the crowd for him. The boat shuddered and a great cloud of smoke belched from the largest, middle funnel. Sally leaned out to look back at Liverpool as the boat churned past the golden ship of St Nicholas's Church which, later, would be blocked by the Royal Liver Assurance Company Buildings, but for now dominated the view from the landing stage. They passed warehouses stacked with corn, and the bright red brick of the new brewery. Bags of Lancashire cloth swung from creaking cranes onto steamers to India, to China, and broken tea crates littered the water of the harbour.

They remained outside until they had lost sight of the city, churning down to the mouth of the Mersey along the promenade where Sally had walked so many times with her mother, from Seacombe to Wallasey to New Brighton and its parade of tea shops.

Sally felt her arm being taken. She looked at Ursula, swaying slightly as she stood on the deck, a tall pine tree in a breeze. 'Shall we, Walker?' Ursula asked, gesturing for Sally to accompany her.

They went into the ladies' salon, and Sally waited while Ursula ordered a pot of tea, and led her to a table near the window. Sally felt her stomach rise and fall upon the waves, her breath pitching and surging as if caught up in a storm. The sky was a silky, aquamarine colour. It lapped against the window. She felt light, giddy. She wished she could slip away to her cabin and hide from that sickening sheet of sea, but Ursula was too excitable to be left alone. She beamed out of the window, regaling Sally with stories of her childhood which seemed so flamboyant, so colourful, that Sally found it odd that anyone would wish to run away from such memories.

'Well I was the girl, you see, so I was never allowed to go to school. I was *deprived* of Latin, Walker,' she said with a sigh.

Sally listened to all of it, the small details as well as the sweeping statements. How Ursula and George had performed plays at Christmas with their boy cousins, elaborate productions involving costumes, paints and flowers. Sally heard how George would string a flickering line of lanterns across the front of the stage, how they used packing cases for horses and sheets for ghouls and, on one occasion, the head of a real Bengal tiger for George to wear.

'He said it was allegorical, and that was why I wasn't allowed to wear it,' Ursula declared. 'But it wasn't.'

Ursula lamented how she had been given all the dullest roles with no proper lines. She was frequently obliged to tie a handkerchief around her face when pretending to be an Eastern princess. She told Sally how her cousins had taught her to swoon, to clasp things to her bosom, where her bosom was, and how to die quietly from a broken heart, not dramatically as they did, clutching swords under their armpits and muttering curses as they fell. She was just a girl, they used to tell her, and Sally tried to imagine Ursula Bridgewater as a child, dressed in a navy-and-white sailor dress, her dark hair falling in spirals from her ribbons and her foot stamping on the polished wooden floor of the nursery.

No, she could not quite imagine it. Ursula was too tall, too grown-up. It was not just her height. It was the set of her shoulders. It was her laugh, her array of neck creams, her umbrella. It was the way she spoke of her brother in that dismissive, affectionate way, which seemed almost careless to Sally who had never had a brother, and never would.

'Oh where shall I get another brother, ever?' she had once heard Ursula tease George in an exasperated tone ('It's from *Antigone*,' Ursula had enlightened her, although this did not clarify matters much) and Sally could not forget the sorrow of this line. It echoed in her. It was almost primal.

At first, she had offered consoling responses to Ursula's stories, until she realised that Ursula did not wish to be consoled. Sally's role was to be audience, admirer, follower. No reference was made to Sally's misfortunes and this was quite proper. She could not have coped with pity in any case. She liked the feeling of being absolutely taken over, instructed and amused.

Ursula would move on to more recent incidents which Sally sensed were largely for her educational benefit. One such disagreement involved a clerk at the Newhaven Telegraph Office whom Ursula had encountered on her first visit to the Continent. Sally did not notice the transition, but she sat forwards all the same, paying attention. This particular story ended, as with so many of Ursula Bridgewater's stories, with the young man getting his comeuppance.

'And that,' she announced, touching Sally on the forearm and smiling in a deliberate sort of way, 'taught him not to underestimate smart young women who wish to send telegrams to their brothers.'

'I'm sure it did, ma'am,' Sally replied, wondering what she would write in a telegram if the situation arose. She might write to Mr Fisher. '*I am on a boat to America*,' she might begin, '*Land of the Free*.' She had learnt this from Ursula. '*Yours etc.*' But she would not really do that. She did not know how. It was just an impulse. It was a message in an eggshell. She sighed and reached for the teapot.

On the first night of the three-week voyage, Ursula and Sally sat with the captain at dinner. Captain Algernon J. Gordon was famous in seafaring circles. He was the same Captain Algernon J. Gordon of the White Star Line Company who, when rescuing the crew of the sinking *Constantinople* during a storm back in 1867, had famously pulled the tiller of the lifeboat from its groove and raised it above his sou'westered head in the middle of the surging Atlantic, and threatened to brain the first man who refused to join in the rescue.

He was a tall, strong-looking fellow with a full beard and a fondness for a game of whist before bed. At the ship's concerts, he would appear on the stage before the interval to give a jovial rendition of 'I'm Afloat, I'm Afloat and the Rover is Free', and it was this tradition which cemented his reputation as having an eye for the ladies. This was not altogether true, although he allowed it to flourish as it meant he was bothered a little less by the male cabin passengers, who had a greater tendency than their feminine counterparts to approach bearing questions about the state of the weather in Newfoundland at that precise moment, or the speed of the Gulf Stream waters in June.

'How the devil would I know?' he wanted to reply when asked such things, although he seldom actually said what he thought, usually managing instead to stutter out a response whilst reaching for his gold pocket watch. He was at his happiest when marooned in his stateroom, searching for the North Star, noting the density of the air, the temperature of the sea, the exact position of the ship upon the earth.

Captain Algernon Gordon had been born in Scotland, on the banks of the Clyde, as he liked to say, although in reality he had been born a good stretch inland, near Motherwell. But he attended a school in Glasgow which had been established for the sons of Methodist missionaries, and although half the pupils were not actually the sons of missionaries, they were treated as if they were. There was a glamour in this for a small boy whose parents had never left the western coast of Scotland, to be told that his was a mighty inheritance of spreading the knowledge of the Word made Flesh, and even if this did not quite take with Algernon Gordon, he smelt the sea on it all the same, and it was this which pushed him towards the great landing stages of Glasgow.

The sea formed his natural horizon. When he left Glasgow to attend the Royal Naval College in Greenwich, he missed the west coast. His rooms looked out over the Thames where it flowed eastwards to the Continent, but he never quite took to the Thames in the way that he had taken to the Clyde. It was the Atlantic he wanted, that vast, gleaming stretch of icy water which separated the Old World from the New. He missed the natural horizon of the sea, the way his boyhood city seemed to recline against the hills of Scotland whilst gazing always outwards.

It was from these beginnings that Algernon Gordon began to believe that the act of crossing the Atlantic was a transcendent, almost spiritual experience. He had observed more than once how the traveller who made the crossing had a different way of walking when they departed from how they had walked when they approached. He saw it as a loss of innocence, in the geographical sense. The Atlantic voyage had a dignity and a romance which, say, a passage to France or even Egypt could not claim, where the ship followed the coast of Spain and never quite broke free from the safety net of land.

'Ah yes,' thought Captain Algernon Gordon as he stood at the door of his stateroom, 'it is indeed a grand and noble thing to allow such a journey into the soul!'

Sally Walker knew this sensation by its less exalted title of seasickness. She had no sea legs, Ursula informed her helpfully after Sally had vomited in the corridor outside the dining room on the first night of the voyage. She had been apologetic, and had fallen to her knees to clear up the mess with a table napkin, but Ursula had taken hold of her arm and gently pulled her back to her feet.

'Leave it, Walker. It is not your job,' Ursula had told her, and Sally had not known what to do. She had returned to the table to be greeted by Captain Algernon Gordon grinning delightedly at her.

'Sick, eh?' he asked, shaking his head and smiling at her in a manner which Sally did not know how to interpret.

He had seen it before. He had felt it himself, that first time. He recognised the symptoms. Some felt it and others did not, but it delighted him to see it, because he knew that it was something extraordinary. It was a gift. It was the sensation of really going somewhere. It was the Atlantic striking at her soul, getting its clutches into her so that never again would she be able to forget the existence of all this vastness, of all this sea and sea and sea.

'Oh, she will think it is seasickness now,' he thought, 'but one day she will know it for what it is.' And he chuckled to himself as he retreated happily to his stateroom for his bedtime game of whist.

Nine

The uses of adversity

Toby packed his bed sheets, two pairs of trousers and four poplin shirts, two blue and two white. He wedged socks and books and a small cushion into the sides of the trunk, and then wrapped his pop's fruit bat in towelling and placed it on top of his dinner plate and bowl. He advertised the piano for sale, with its black-stained wood where the candle flames had occasionally flickered in the evenings. He sold it to Mr Pedy from the village, who had just married a woman from Boston and was, Mr Pedy explained, accustomed to musical entertainments.

There was a quibble over the missing notes. 'They have always been missing,' Toby explained. 'You'll hardly notice them after a while.'

Mr Pedy sat on the piano stool and cracked his fingers over the keys. He played *Moonlight Sonata*. He played it crossly. He declared that it did make a very big difference, to be missing the low C sharp. The upper B flat was not so much of a problem for this particular piece but, he raised his finger, that is not to say it may not be so for his new wife, who might wish to transpose it, or – he considered as an afterthought – play something else.

'I'm not certain she likes Germans,' he said. 'Musically.'

Toby nodded. It was true that there was a certain emptiness to Mr Pedy's recital, but Toby considered that the crossness of the rendition had a larger impact on the piece than the missing notes. He suggested a discount to cover the cost of replacing the missing keys, which Mr Pedy grudgingly accepted.

It took four of them to move the piano, grunting sonorously in time with its echoing clunks. After it had gone, Toby sat on the floor where the piano had been. The skirting board was thick with dust, huge lumps of it that he picked up and rolled into a ball and threw out of the window. He thought of his mother playing the piano at night, laughing at the missing notes, and the sudden jumps and silences. He remembered his pop leaning forward in those later years, holding his breath, itching to say something, always itching, but never seeming to say the thing he wanted to say. He died with his mouth open and his breath caught up in his throat, and Toby pumping his chest. Too late it was then, in any case, but he had not realised until then how he and his pop had clung to the gaps and silences of their own communication. They had been too gentle with each other. Too afraid of the scratch, Toby saw now, to relieve the itch of silence.

He took his trunk to Niagara Falls, loading it carelessly onto carts and railroads and wagons, all the while tending to his other piece of luggage, his balloon, that huge piece of oiled silk, folded carefully into its basket. There were limp sandbags hanging from its sides. It attracted attention at every stop. Of course it did. It pleased him that the people he met were so incredulous.

It is a state of mind, he decided, which keeps these people rooted to the ground. They are not air-minded. They do not think of flying, and yet to look at a domestic goose you would not say such a lumbering, irritable animal would think of flying. But it does. It flies because it is air-minded.

Toby did not know how much he sounded like his pop. By the time he was old enough to really remember such things, his pop no longer spoke in such a manner.

Toby arrived in Niagara in February and took lodgings in a room on the American side of the river. The town was ugly and industrial. Where he had expected forests and meadows, he found gristmills and thick stone dams, pulp mills and lumberyards and shacks. All the viewpoints along the front were fenced in by hoteliers and entrepreneurs who charged exorbitant fees to tourists to see the Falls. Toby did not mind. He had not come to see the Falls, or at least, not specifically. He imagined it silent and trickling as his mother had described, not thundering and foaming as it was now, the mists rising in the morning so that the air was wet against his throat.

His room was cold and small. It was on the ground floor of a tall, weather-boarded house. The walls were white-washed, and set with a brick fireplace and two small windows, and there was a large table pressed up against the stove. His pop would have called it poky and told him it reminded him of 'home', by which he would have meant Ireland. This did not worry Toby. He did not need anything grand. He was twenty years old; young enough not to mind a bit of damp but old enough to keep his clothes folded in piles.

He spent his first day in Niagara designing a leaflet, and then arranging to have it printed on coloured paper – 'Fly over the Falls in O'Hara's Magnificent Tethered Balloon'. It was not a catchy name, but it was informative, and Toby knew that when a people, a nation, have not yet become air-minded, information is the key to changing their outlook.

And the balloon *was* an attraction. It was a new, more

extravagant way of seeing the Falls than all the other views on offer. It vied with the steps down to the water, the walkway behind the Falls, the *Maid of the Mist* steamer which took its passengers directly into the spray of the water. He could charge whatever sum he liked, and although he did not wish to extort money, if people chose to pay five dollars for a single flight, then it was hardly Toby's fault, was it?

This balloon, as we already know, was not Toby's passion. It was lucrative and enticing, but it was also garish. It was just a job. It was a series of arpeggios, delightful and urgent and beautifully played, but it was not a symphony. Toby's symphony was contained in his other lodging, a tumble-down cowshed three miles upriver which was just large enough, according to his measurements, to contain a flying machine in the shape of a bat.

Toby worked on this every afternoon; he left behind the bustling streets of tourists and curio shops and hustlers and walked out across the patchy battlefields of the 1812 war, still bumpy with debris and thistles, to his cowshed. He could not think about his flying machine rationally. He knew, he supposed, that it was an oddly-shaped thing, large and unwieldy, a bamboo frame strung with oiled silk, and on the days when he saw it like this, it was just a thing: a ridiculous, over-large 'thing' and he wanted to break it up with his hands, tear it and snap it and be rid of it forever.

But on other days, and these were the best days, he did not see it as a thing, but as an idea. Every nail, every plank, every lath of bamboo was beautiful to him. It was bigger than itself. It sparkled in his mind like fresh snow. It lay clean and unmarked in his imagination. It was a snowflake, an icicle; too delicate to touch. His head spun with it. He could not talk about it because he knew that some things are best left unspoken, and that to play every note can somehow diminish a song.

He worked on it in private, in the cold mornings when it was too windy for ballooning, and on Sunday afternoons while the other men walked down-river beyond the railway suspension bridge to fish and drink beer. They would invite him to join them from time to time, and occasionally he went along, but he could not match their enthusiasm, however hard he tried. It made him impatient to lose an afternoon's work. He could not enjoy it. His whole being was distracted by his flying machine.

He knew the machine was reckless. It was completely impractical. It served no purpose in the world that could not be served by bridges and horses and railroads. Sometimes, when Toby went into that old cowshed and fixed his scaffold to the walls so that he could build the frame of his machine around it, he almost fooled himself. When he measured out the wings, sawing wood and sewing oiled silk, and fastening wheels to the runners and brakes to the wheels and blades to the propeller, he almost forgot that his intentions were multi-layered. He almost convinced himself that, perhaps, he was simply an inventor after all.

But, most of the time, it was wind that Toby imagined, wind in his hair, wind against his shirt and his eyes, wind in his cuffs and in his bones, wind in all those sheets and singlets and endless billowing shirts which had hung in the yard on the day his mother crashed into the fence at the bottom of the field. He pictured the drama of it, sunlight on the oiled silk of the wings, the breeze across the tops of the trees. He remembered his mother's hand waving to him, the jars of jam stacked up in the kitchen when his pop carried her indoors. So it was not just wind he imagined. It was not just flight.

If he had only been able to express himself better, there would have been no need for all of this. 'Why did she leave us?' he might have asked his pop all those years ago on the veranda. 'How could she think we did not need her?' But since he had not, then this was how he would have to do it. Even now that it was nearly finished, as he laid the wooden launching boards over the grass, as he sanded the joints and nailed them together and filled the gaps with sand, he knew that he still could not separate his dream, the grand idea of flight which frosted and shimmered in his mind, from the sugary lift of all that jam. It was simply a way of shouting at the wind, of asking and being answered, and it was a thing he would not admit to anyone, even to himself – that his flying machine had nothing to do with flight at all. It was a means of going backwards. Of bringing her back.

Ten

An English face

Mr Thomas Cook called his touring group out onto the deck of the ship in advance of the first sighting of America. He spoke as a missionary rather than as a tour guide when he described America as 'a meadow of republican brotherhood.' He sighed, just as he had sighed on the Mount of Olives as he looked out across the holy city of Jerusalem, and wrapped his scarf a little tighter around his neck.

Ursula Bridgewater felt a tingling, pollinated sensation in her nose upon hearing this. She gave a non-committal nod. She was uncertain as to how this would present itself, practically. Besides, the coast of Newfoundland did not seem to be anything like a meadow. It was cluttered with logs, and there were small beaches of stones. There were no cranes, no warehouses, no people. She longed for something green, something dry.

She had spent the voyage sitting nobly on the window seat of the ladies' salon, reading aloud to a pair of sickly widows from the touring party whose chests were flattened by an excess of bodice under their dresses, and who had attached themselves to Ursula before the steamer had even left the Irish Sea.

'Whether I shall turn out to be the hero of my own life,' Ursula had read, with an air of resignation as she imagined the

grandeur of these words falling onto the gravelly ears of such sober and unenterprising women as the ones she saw before her, *'or whether that station will be held by anybody else . . .'*

Such wonderful sentiments, Ursula thought. To aspire to that, to being the hero of one's own life. How well put!

She was disappointed that Walker had not been there to listen. She suspected, quite rightly, that there was little opportunity for reading Dickens at the orphanage and she thought Walker would like it. As it was, the girl's head had been stuffed full of Beatitudes and letters from various Apostles, and Ursula did not see that this was enough for anyone in these modern times of Queen Victoria. It was for this reason that she had packed a series of improving books into Sally's travelling case – poetry and science – which she hoped would give the girl something to start on, but she had been too sick to read them at sea.

Over the next few days, they followed the eastern coast of America down past Boston to New York. New York was as busy and as plentiful as Ursula had imagined. They disembarked in Manhattan, where there were barrows piled high with cauliflowers and bananas, candy stores and horse-drawn omnibuses, and booths where you could have a portrait photograph taken for a dollar. Mr Cook took charge of getting all his tourists from the landing stage to the hotel, and he attempted to engage a carriage for this purpose. There ensued a general commotion over the price, with hats being waved and suitcases dropped smartly to the ground, until finally it was decided that the luggage would take its own carriage under the supervision of an elderly gentleman, and the rest of the tour members would travel by stagecoach.

Ursula, being accustomed to carriages, was delighted with the novelty of the stagecoach. They passed along wide streets of brownstone houses, between which were small restaurants with starched white tablecloths on the tables. There were parks and gas lamps which still flickered with light even though it was nearly midday. In the carriage there was a lingering smell of hay, of shirts washed in buckets and hung out to dry, of women slung with children; a rough, milky smell that Ursula wished to bottle up and keep in her drawing room at home. She thought of it as the smell of America, and although she did not find it in any other place than in that first stagecoach, it stuck.

The trials of New World transportation came up again over the first dinner taken by the touring party in the dining room of the Grand Central Hotel, New York. As Mr Cook would later report in his correspondence from America to *The Times*, anyone wishing to engage a private means of transit from one place to another in America was obliged to be, at the very least, wide awake. And this is what he announced over dinner in New York, repeating his joke until he was certain everybody had heard it.

The dining room was on the first floor of the hotel, a large, high-ceilinged room with mustard-coloured velvet curtains and red candles fixed into the walls. There were enormous dishes of meat and fish and pastries laid out in the centre of the table, huge oblong plates decorated with grapes and walnuts. There were hams and chickens and plover eggs, slices of beef in gravy and plates of pink salmon. Jugs of iced water clinked on the table.

Mr Cook sat at the head of the table and speared peas with his fork. Ursula was intrigued by him, just as she had been in Scotland and in Egypt. He ate with his elbows out and stirred his tea with the wrong end of his spoon. He was disciplined and yet he was not. He had a head for timetables, for schedules and currency exchange and biblical scenes. He wrote lists of places he would like to include on future itineraries, added notes to his guidebook and listed the details of trains going to places he would never visit. She admired his tenacity but he also frightened her a little. He was so earnest.

He was also a radical. He spoke in a manner with which she was still relatively unfamiliar, that of third-class carriages and the working man, of Factory Acts and suffrage and the Great Exhibition; of how human nature in England had been changed forever by the snows of 1870 because snow is the greatest of all levellers, and once it is gone there will always be the memory of that brief moment of equality. He did not use the word 'equality'. Of course he did not. He called it kinship, brotherhood. But it is what he meant.

Ursula felt what she had felt in Jerusalem, that it was a relief to be swept along in someone else's passion. It saved one from one's own uncertainty. It gave one direction. It is the only way, Ursula thought conversationally as she cut into a lump of cheddary cheese, of escaping fully from oneself.

Mr Cook held a piece of potato on his fork and waved it as he spoke. It dropped onto his plate but his fork continued to wave. 'Disgraceful, wouldn't you say? Twelve shillings per head for a single journey of fifteen minutes.' He addressed himself enthusiastically to Ursula in his broadest Leicestershire voice. 'I tell you, if they catch you when you're sleepy, they'd be taking you for a fool. You've got to be wide awake.'

Ursula nodded again in acknowledgement of the joke, smiling encouragingly while her thoughts migrated to the fruit bowl at the other end of the table. She did not notice the point at which Mr Cook leapt from the specific to the general, but when she next paid proper attention to his conversation, he was discussing how the extortionist tactics of the Yankee cabbies was an inevitable side-effect of capitalism, that under such a system private transit will end up being reserved for the very wealthy, and everybody else must always be huddling together.

'I expect it will be the same with the railroads,' he continued, 'huddle, huddle, huddle.'

Time passed. Ursula watched the lamplighter at work in the street below, leaving a shimmer of yellowy glass in his trail. When Mr Cook began listing the timings of the Sierra Nevada stretch of the Central Pacific Line, including scheduled rest breaks, Ursula nodded to the waiter and murmured that, on second thoughts, she would take a glass of beer with her meal. She saw Mr Cook pause as the beer approached the table. He put his hand up, palm outwards, as if he were going to push it away.

'Madam,' the waiter said, bowing slightly as he presented the foaming glass to Ursula.

Mr Cook lowered his hand. He smiled at Ursula, a strained sort of smile which did not occupy her too greatly at the time, but which she would remember on reading the cutting taken by George of the publication of Mr Cook's correspondence to *The Times* from America (in which was also mentioned the need to be wide awake), and in which Ursula found a description of herself as 'a lady with an English face' drinking a solitary glass of beer in the Grand Central Hotel, New York.

'Ha!' she would say upon recognising herself. 'English face indeed.' And she did not know whether to take it as an insult or a compliment, or merely as a statement of fact.

What a stone!

There was a letter to Henry Springton, half-written and folded in Ursula's bag. She had started it during the five days they spent in New York, detailing the highlights of the voyage and then pronouncing light-heartedly on the American character and climate. It was in the same vein as all her letters to him, witty and amusing and cynical, but whereas previously she had admired her letter-writing persona and had wished she could keep it up all the time, on this occasion she found the struggle to remain consistent towards Henry Springton, in an epistolary sense, tiring.

She had already sent postcards from New York to Miss Emma and Miss Joy, regaling them with details about the Sickly Widows on the boat and Captain Algernon J. Gordon aka The Rover. She had written to her brother from the drawing room of the hotel in New York after an evening spent skating on the frozen lake of Central Park, crowded with people and lit with calcium flares. 'I fear,' she wrote to George, 'that our Sally Walker is in danger of entering the dramatis personae of the expedition as the Resident Dormouse, but I have plans for her transformation and she may yet turn out to be a New World Traveller.'

She wondered if she might write to Mavis, and decided that she probably would, although she would wait until they were in Utah where women were allowed to vote, and she could send word to the boarding house on the nature of this progressiveness in practice.

It was only Henry Springton's letter that she had not completed. She had intended to finish it in New York and post it from the main post office so that it would arrive within the three-month time limit she usually set herself, but she had not done so. She had been distracted by the gilded and steepled rush of the city – so many lives being lived in one place, and so many ways to live them! – and there had been no time for it.

She thought she might finish the letter on the railroad to Niagara Falls but now there was the scenery to attend to, tea to drink and sandwiches to eat. Sally dozed off early, her head resting against the sliding door of the compartment and her pink-stockinged feet propped on a hat box. Ursula could have done it then, but instead of retrieving her pen from her bag, she continued to gaze out of the window. She just needed a few moments to muster up the energy required for the task. She stared out of the window until she could see only her own reflection gazing back at her out of the gathering dusk.

Ursula sighed and looked away. She took the letter from her bag and spread it out upon her knee. She took out her ink bottle and placed it on the table in front of her. Her pen hovered over the letter, and for a moment she looked up and saw her reflection in the window once more, but this time there was something about it which caught her eye. It was familiar to her – of course it was – and yet it was also unfamiliar. She stared back at herself, tipped her head to one side and then to the other. She smiled, a slightly forced smile which had an odd effect in the window glass, but it was not this which alarmed her. It was the expression in her eyes as she held the letter to Henry Springton on her lap: weary and distant and perhaps a little haughty.

It was dark when they arrived in Niagara. Ursula could hear the great roar of water as they stepped out of the carriage at their hotel, but she could not see it. There were two moonlit clouds of spray rising up above the wooden buildings which lined the front, and a tremor of earth beneath her feet. She was tired and hungry; dinner was being laid out under oil lamps in the dining room but Ursula felt a sudden surge of impatience to see that great cataract captured so magnificently in the painting at the New Brighton Pavilion, remembering the wonderful sensation of water seeming to stream beneath her feet as she gazed at the canvas.

The hotel overlooked the Falls. If she hurried, there would be time for a quick look before dinner. She ran down the stone steps and into the slippery basement of the hotel, and then out onto the path which led to the hotel's private viewing platform. She anticipated a great ocean falling from the sky. The air sparkled with spray, small stars in the night sky. Ursula walked faster. There was a high wooden fence blanketed in damp algae, and the bolt on the gate had rusted stiff. She had to reach up to draw it back and her fingers trembled as she tugged at it. The gate caught on the grass as she pushed it. It did not matter. She wished only to see this wonderful miracle of Nature.

The gate swung open. Oh, Ursula thought, standing perfectly still. It is not at all what I imagined. She felt her shoulders droop a little. The Falls were lower than she had pictured, and not quite as commanding. She had expected to feel struck but she did not. The water did not have that luminous quality she had seen on the painting, and the island was in the wrong place entirely. It was ugly, and surmounted by an odd, stone tower which perched over the Canadian Horseshoe side of the Falls.

The gong rang for dinner from inside the hotel and Ursula turned to go back in. But how can I not be moved? she wondered as she forced the gate shut. It is one of the great wonders of the world and I look upon it and I feel nothing! Her face was wet with spray. She could not go to the dining room like this. She plunged her hand into her bag in search of a handkerchief, and she found the still-unfinished letter to Henry Springton refolded and crumpled against the side of her bag.

She put it back and drew out her handkerchief to wipe her face and, as she did, she thought: What a stone I have become!

*

There was an itinerary for the following day. It was slipped beneath the doors of the hotel rooms before breakfast by Mr Cook. A group excursion to the ferry landing was to take place in the morning, led by the hotel manager. The entire party were to walk down to the river, take the ferry across to the Canadian side, and then walk along the bank until they reached the cavern behind the great sheet of water at Horseshoe Falls.

Ursula could not bear it. She had no enthusiasm for the expedition.

'You must go, Walker,' she instructed Sally, noticing the stricken look on Sally's face but deciding that, on balance, it would be good for the girl else she would never be rid of those Dormouse tendencies. 'It will be an adventure for you,' Ursula continued, 'but I do not wish to suffer such a disappointment again.'

Ursula waited until the rest of the group had departed from the lobby, and then descended from her room to take a walk through the town. There were curio shops and tea-gardens lining the road, and huge, wooden hotels with advertising boards slung up along their high fences. The day was cold and bright. Hack drivers and guides called out to her as she walked, offering boat trips and singular views. Ursula paid them no attention. Her mind was on the waterfall and her failure to respond in the way she had wished. She supposed it betrayed a lack of deep emotion, a failure to engage spiritually, and she thought that perhaps this was a side-effect of her earlier romantic disappointment.

So this, she thought as she marched along the main parade, ignoring all the fuss and bluster around her, is what I have become because one man did not want to marry me. Well, she conceded, one man who expressly did not. She acknowledged in her silent conversation with herself that there may also have been others who might not have wanted to, but had not informed her of their preference either way. It was only Henry Springton who had actually told her, had written it in a jovial letter to avoid any doubt.

It is because of him, she thought as she clipped a pebble with her heel, because of Henry Springton, that I have made myself become the way I am. I have made myself walk too fast, be too sharp, carry an umbrella even when it does not look in the least bit like rain. I cannot take pleasure in Nature's wonders. I judge everyone and everything and I cannot hide a single thought that passes into my head. Even when I like something, I like it too much. I am too enthusiastic. I gather too much detail. It puts people off. And yet, that is what I have wanted. A barrier.

Oh, Henry Springton, she sighed, and was immediately cross with herself for thinking it. I invoke him as other people invoke a deity, she thought impatiently. It is a silly habit, and I must stop it.

Still, it played on her mind as she marched past the bustling tourists and toffee-sellers who crowded along the street. It played on her mind because Henry Springton had never told her *why* he did not want to marry her. She could have borne it better if he had been specific. She would not have minded hearing it. It would have interested her, in fact. It would have been like the poem about the louse on the lady's hat – 'O wad some Power the giftie gie us, to see oursels as ithers see us!' – or like reading a horoscope.

Perhaps, she thought wistfully as she headed past a shop selling 'Indian Curiosities' – knick-knacks and nonsense, she thought – and on down to Prospect Point, perhaps she had not loved him properly. Perhaps she had not loved him enough. Or perhaps she had simply not shown it enough. She had not remonstrated with him as she might have done, had not begged him to change his mind. Perhaps he had mistaken this brokenness, this willingness to accept, to not cause a fuss, as proof that it was not enough anyway.

Yes, she had agreed quietly even though she had not agreed at all, *we were more friends than lovers anyway*.

But he had not given a reason. He had simply changed his mind, and that was all she knew. She had waited for an explanation. She had not meant to wait – it was a passive sort of waiting – but while she waited she found she had grown old. She had not noticed it happening. She did not feel old. She felt sometimes colder in her hands than she had once done, more shivery about the spine, but that was the only difference she had actually detected. She still stood just as tall, her hair dark brown and her teeth white and solid. Quite handsome, she sometimes thought. Although not quite enough. And now, at thirty-five, also quite old.

She reached a junction and turned right. She did this unconsciously, without thinking of where she was going. There was water on her arms, her face. Her dress was damp with spray. It would stain but she paid it no attention. It did not matter. She wondered if Henry Springton had perhaps seen the seeds of what she would become lurking within her even then, and he had changed his mind because he saw them lying dormant, waiting to sprout. Perhaps he was put off by them, as they now put other people off. Perhaps it was not just a question of willowiness after all.

She reached the end of the street and was surprised at how far she had come. She had only meant to wander in the vicinity of the hotel, but here she was at Prospect Point, at the very top of the American side of the Falls.

She looked down, searching for the rest of the party, thinking they might be walking along the river bank, but she could not see them. She looked over to Goat Island in the middle of the two great streams of water, separating the straight American shore from the horseshoe Canadian side. The river sparkled in the sunlight. There was such a rush of water, of clean light, that she allowed herself to stop. There was a rainbow. Of course there was – so many prisms and so much light – but beyond that, she also saw something else: an odd, round shape, bright blue and scarlet. She could not quite make it out. She squinted through the haze of water. The shape lifted up into the cool morning air, a shimmering bubble of silk, a delicious dream tied to a wicker basket. She smiled suddenly, her mood unexpectedly lifting, and she felt the spray from the water-fall falling on her lips and eyelashes like luminous paint on a canvas.

Eleven

Oliver Cromwell

Sally watched her feet, small and careful in too-big rubber boots, following the expedition up from the river and along the steep, spiral steps of Table Rock on the Canadian side of the Falls. The water thundered in her ears, a deafening roar of foam as she picked her way through the mud and entrepreneur-cut rock. She could not look at the water. It sickened her. She remembered the pictures Mr Fisher had so lovingly posted to her – those terrifying ones of Charles Blondin cooking omelettes on his tight-rope, dressed in striped trousers and a jaunty waistcoat. She felt the spray soaking her stockings. She felt it running over her knees and along her arms. She wished she could stop, turn around and go back and cover her head with her eiderdown.

The hotel manager, Mr Williams, tried to talk to her. She could not hear him, but she did not wish to, in any case. He would probably encourage her to look over the side, away from her feet and down into the rush of water.

Besides, he was American, and Sally was wary of Americans. She had grown accustomed to hearing Ursula's thoughts on the country, the condensed history of the United States according to Ursula Bridgewater. Sally had heard all about the grand rebuff of Empire delivered in the previous century. Her image of America was crowded with muskets and axes and pots and pans, with secession and cotton and Transcendentalism and lanterns lifted in white church spires to warn against the coming of the British Army. She saw the wide streets and the gleaming buildings of New York but she did not understand them. There were parks and rivers and an ingenious suspension bridge over the whirlpools of the Niagara River which Sally supposed to be real, but all of this hovered in the background, filtered through a reddish-gold haze of revolution and heresy.

America was, in Ursula's version, a land of vagabonds and preachers, of religious tolerance to a degree which in any other civilised country would be known as insanity, of witchcraft and co-operative movements and republicans, and it was as a result of this unofficial lecture series that Sally anticipated a certain amount of scruffiness, of uncouthness, to reside in its inhabitants. She expected grubby collars and rumpled socks. She imagined burnt saucepan handles and invocations of a non-conformist, white-clapboard God.

Sally did not know how this would be personified in its people. She supposed later, when she had time to think about it, that she had probably expected something along the lines of Oliver Cromwell, although she had not been able to put her finger on it at the time.

On top of this, the hotel manager was not helping himself. After crossing the river and walking to the base of the Horseshoe Falls, Mr Williams unslung the sack from over his shoulder and pressed an oiled calico cloak onto her.

'It's far too big,' she protested, but he would not listen.

'I got some stockings for you too,' he said, before turning to see to the other members of the party.

The stockings were made of blue worsted. She pulled them on under her skirt, and then tied the cloak under her chin. The hood was loose, but she pulled it over her eyes. There was a ledge ahead of them, curving behind the great curtain of water as it fell. They were not at the top of the Falls, but nor were they at the bottom. There was a distance of perhaps seventy feet below them. The other members of the party were ahead of her, stepping into the narrow cave behind the water. She saw Mr Cook step forwards onto the ledge. No, no, no, she thought, clutching at her chest. She saw the spray glancing off his shoulder, white, foaming fingers of water pulling softly at him while the gulf yawned below. I cannot go, she thought.

'Come along,' Mr Williams said.

Sally stood still. Her hood had fallen back and water was trickling down her neck. The cave was shadowed by stone and water. There was moss growing on the edges of the rocks, but it was not so much green as brown. It was a place without light, without hope. There was only water, drumming on and on into the great precipice. She could not see, could not breathe. No, no, no, she thought again, although this time the words shrieked in her mind, and she stepped away, turning as she did so to find the path which led back to the ferry and, once she began to run, she did not look back.

*

'Your hair is wet, Walker,' Ursula observed, tilting her head to inspect Sally's appearance and balancing her teacup on the arm of her chair. 'You are utterly bedraggled.'

'Yes, ma'am,' Sally agreed, although she had changed her dress before coming down to tea, and had tried to comb her hair so that it did not frizz and knot. She was damp, yes, but she was not, she did not think, utterly bedraggled.

'Tell me, how was the expedition?'

Sally hesitated. 'It was very pleasurable, ma'am. I think you would have liked it.'

Her demeanour displayed none of the fear she had felt at the entrance to the cave. It disappointed her that she had been unable to go in, and yet she had known that she would not. Ursula would have gone in. She would have put up her umbrella and stepped forwards onto the ledge. She would have put out her arm to touch the falling water, and she would have declared it wondrous, hypnotic, transcendental. She would have considered it an adventure.

Sally sighed, and then shivered. She wore two bodices and a scarf but still she could not get warm. She picked up her teacup and held it in both hands.

'Now, I have a surprise for you, Walker,' Ursula announced, placing a scone onto her plate and smiling delightedly at Sally.

Sally pushed her eyebrows up, attempting to imply interest rather than alarm at this announcement.

'I have arranged with Mr Cook that, rather than take the steamboat with the rest of the tour this evening' – here she leant forward in a conspiratorial manner and added in a stage whisper, 'the rest of the riff-raff – you and I shall instead fly over the Falls.' She clapped her hands onto her legs. 'What do you think of that?'

'Fly?' Sally asked numbly, whereupon Charles Blondin came trundling into her mind, pushing a wheelbarrow. She thought suddenly that Ursula wished for the pair of them to walk the high wire and that this is what she meant by 'flying'. Sally put down her cup of tea. Her head felt unbearably cold.

'Yes, fly,' Miss Bridgewater said, handing Sally a napkin to mop up her spilt tea, 'in a tethered balloon.'

'Oh,' said Sally, although she felt even as she said it that it was an inadequate response. 'Tethered,' she echoed uncertainly, in an attempt to reassure herself. She had not counted on flying. She had been prepared for the Falls – she had not wished to see it, that terrible rush of falling water, but she had accepted that she must, and now that she had seen it she did not wish to see it again – but she had not anticipated balloons.

'You'll need your gloves, Walker,' Ursula said, raising her cup of tea to her lips with a smile. 'And your adventurous spirit.'

Sally nodded. But I don't have one, she thought. I don't know where to find it. I am not you. I am me. But I don't want to be me any longer. I want to say the things you say. I want to laugh loudly and have sea legs and not run away when I am scared. I want a brother and an umbrella and a scientific bent. I want to know about the Pyramids and the Highlands and what to wear in the Alps. I want to tell Mr Fisher how grateful I am. I want to make you look at me and say: Sally Walker, how adventurous you are, how proud I am, and haven't you come on a treat?

But Sally did not say any of this. Of course she did not. She said only, 'Gloves, ma'am?'

That evening, Sally walked slowly towards the waterfall with Ursula. The air was sharp and clear; it stung her cheek. She was a coward. She was Samson without his hair. She reached up and fixed a stray curl of hair back into its clip.

She whispered Psalm 121 in her head, running the words together in a frenzy of half-conscious prayer. The words fused drunkenly in her mind. She remembered Sister Thomas's voice, the sweep of her arm, her habit of pronouncing on which passages ought to be learnt by heart and which ought not, how she preferred the Beatitudes of Matthew to those of Luke, how hymns needed to be taken with a pinch of salt as they had a tendency to stretch the truth for the sake of a rhyme, how one should turn to the psalms in times of need.

I should tell her I will not go, she thought. Then she thought: I must go. I should not be so scared all the time.

Ursula pointed out the balloon on the field, lifted her arm and waved her umbrella at the young man.

Such confidence, Sally thought.

The balloon was red and blue, huge blocks of coloured silk expanding and rising above a roaring flame and, below that, a mass of ropes and sandbags and wicker. A small crowd had gathered to watch, men in suits with stomachs protruding over their belts; women in aprons, their hair piled up onto their heads in plaits; small children gathered in groups, nudging and jostling and laughing.

Sally thought: Dear God.

Ursula Bridgewater was already aboard the basket. The Falls roared behind her, endless and deafening. *Blessed are the meek,* Sally thought, and then she shook the phrase from her head as she imagined Ursula might deem it unscientific. And it was, she supposed. It was unscientific and it was unlikely. Perhaps it was unscientific because it was unlikely, and for a brief moment she smiled because she thought that was exactly the sort of thing Ursula might say.

At first, Sally did not see the young man standing next to the balloon and holding his hand out to her. Later, she would imagine that she had. She would draw him into her memory, sketch him in amongst the crowds. She would see his dark brown eyes searching for her as they walked towards the balloon, his maple syrup hair. He was wearing a bearskin hat and a blue shirt with a black jacket. She would remember the cigarette he kept tucked behind his ear, and that wide crooked-teeth smile; a freckle on his earlobe.

161

But, really, she had not noticed him any more than she had noticed anyone else. It was only as she stepped into the basket and felt his hand landing lightly on her arm that she looked up and saw him. She felt a blush rising to her cheeks. Her crinoline cage snagged and caught and she felt a sudden rage with herself for her own clumsiness. She shook the dress loose. It was impractical and uncomfortable. She could not get used to it, and yet she must be grateful for it.

He smiled at her, his face golden in the afternoon light.

Oh, she thought suddenly, and she smoothed her dress over her waist and hips. She stepped into the basket and held her breath while the young man strapped a harness around her waist. The bright balloon billowed above them, the basket ropes straining as it gusted and flapped; great swathes of blue and red dancing giddily upwards into the infinite waste of sky.

Twelve

But did she sneeze loudly or softly?

Toby O'Hara did not normally offer afternoon trips, but the air was calm that day, and there had been something about the lady with the umbrella who had come to find him when he returned from his morning flight – the way in which she held her head as if she were peering over something, the unguarded laugh – which had prompted him to allow a four o'clock excursion.

She was older than him, and had that same sense of pent-up energy he remembered from his mother's hands when she played the piano, blood pulsing under her skin. And there was her accent: soft, with traces of his pop in it. It was not the same – he knew she was not from 'home', that unimaginable place to which his pop's mind had retreated as he grew older and less steady on his feet – but he thought she might be from somewhere close or, at least, closer than he had ever been.

She told him her name as she stepped into the basket. 'Miss Ursula Bridgewater,' she said, smiling at him as if she were going to start laughing again, 'Ursula, like a bear.' She pointed at his hat with her umbrella as she spoke, and then swung the umbrella down under her arm and held it there, as if she thought it might be of some use in a storm.

'Welcome aboard,' he said.

'Well,' Miss Bridgewater declared, looking up at the balloon, 'it is just like a giant toy.'

Toby nodded in surprise at the accuracy of the observation. He noticed the plumpness of this woman's lips, the lines on her face which he had at first thought of as age, or even of past disappointments, but which now seemed to deepen into a smile, so that her whole face smiled, her nose and her eyelids rather than just her mouth. How Pop would have liked this woman, he thought.

'And this is my companion,' Ursula announced, turning around and holding out her arm towards a girl who was walking slowly towards the balloon, her hands clasped in front of her chest as if in prayer. 'Miss Sally Walker.'

Toby saw the whiteness of Sally's knuckles, her lips moving almost imperceptibly. The word 'perishable' came to him, and he thought no, that is not quite right. She is just timid, no more perishable than anybody else. But even as he thought this, Sally Walker lifted her eyes and looked straight into his, and for a brief second he did not know what to think.

It was always the same. Every time the balloon gasped him upwards into the sky, Toby thought of his mother. He looked for her in the retreating fields, the endless, aching skies. Had she imagined how this would feel when she was younger? Had she dreamt about it when he was no more than a weight in her stomach, holding her down? Or was she surprised to find that there is not so much noise once you have left the ground, that it comes as a shock to see the world continuing below without you and hardly even noticing your departure. So small, it seems, from above.

She cannot have seen it as he did now: ploughed earth and flattened fields, mills billowing black smoke over dugout roads and channelled water. There would not have been enough time for her to see it, not enough height. But perhaps she had sensed how it would be. Hands waving, faces uplifted, smaller and smaller, until everything below blends into nothing more than a vast shrug of land. Hills, really, but from the sky they are easily mistaken. Dust and ashes and no way of telling between them.

It was the wrong sort of flying, Toby knew that. It was slower, higher. It was not the extravagant gift his pop had made for his mother, and towards which she had sprinted in the dawn, brushing Edmund aside as she climbed into the machine. He tried to remember her face, her expression. What was it? Delight? Anticipation? He pictured her as he had always done, stern, almost angry as she ran across the field with the white strips of muslin in her curled hair, and he shook the image from his mind. He knew his memory to be wrong. It was not like that. It could not have been. It was a gift, a present.

Perhaps she had not realised that she might crash. She had thought she would come back. He remembered how she had picked him up and pressed his face into her hair, how she had waved at him from the side of the flying machine as she left the ground.

But how could you leave me? he thought. How could you think I didn't need you?

She was wrong, of course, Mary O'Hara. Toby thought this as he adjusted the valve, watching Miss Bridgewater lean out to wave at the people who had come to see the balloon rise from the ground. I did need her, he thought. We both needed her. Did she not see that?

It worried him that he could not remember her. Yes, he could remember her hands as she played the piano, her eyes shining at the memory of Niagara Falls. But that was all. And it was not enough.

His pop had rarely mentioned her in those years after her death, and Toby had not liked to ask. But what was she really *like*? Toby had wanted to ask him. What made her laugh? What did she like to eat? Did she talk loudly, quietly, quickly? Did she sneeze noisily, or did she have one of those soft, internal sneezes? Did she squint at distances, grind her teeth, snore, sleep on her back, her front, her side? Could she keep a secret? What was her favourite thing in all the world?

'You,' Edmund O'Hara would tell him. 'She adored you,' and Toby would grin at his pop, such a wide grin that it was almost possible to misread it, to mishear the key and think it was plain old F major, no notes missing, no gaps or silences.

Perhaps, he thought. Perhaps she did adore me. But she still got into that flying machine. She still leant out to wave her arm in – what was it? – exhilaration, excitement, as the machine lifted from the ground. She still left me. So perhaps she did adore me. But maybe not quite enough.

'Walker! Come and look at this!' Ursula Bridgewater sprang from one side of the basket to the other. Toby noticed how the girl did not follow her – not really – and did not look out at the waterfall, the horizon, the people watching from below. The girl's face was flushed, and her eyes were bright blue. A pepperpot, his pop might have said: smooth and ceramic. She stood in the basket and gripped the side and she did not look down. He saw her lips moving softly. Toby thought of poetry. He watched her from the corner of his eye and he thought of all sorts of things, but he did not suspect the Beatitudes.

Toby could not guess at the relationship between the two women. They were not mother and daughter, he was certain of that. My companion, the older woman had called her, and there was no resemblance at all, physically. He saw how the younger woman was careful of Miss Bridgewater, how she listened and deferred. But he also saw that when she spoke, nodding and answering in that reserved, polite manner of hers, the words which came out were not the same ones she mouthed when she thought nobody was watching.

But *I* am watching you, he thought.

At his mother's funeral, the Reverend had stood at the pulpit with his hands raised and asked the Lord to bless Mary O'Hara who was pitched from this world into eternity on the seventh day of September in the Year of our Lord 1862. Toby never forgot that phrase. He had seen the violence of it. Pitched into eternity. As if eternity were the next field along, where the stream twists through the dips in the grass and there are buttercups in summer, and where his pop's flying machine lay ripped and tangled against the fence.

He had seen her arm move. His pop had run, had cried out, but Toby had been frozen to the porch step, his mouth open and his feet tight. By the time his pop reached the bottom of the field and hollered to him for a blanket, his mother's arm was no longer moving.

There were cows in the next field, Toby remembered. He had run inside to drag the cover from his bed, and when he came outside again his pop was holding Mary O'Hara's twisted body in his arms. Toby had had to look at the cows because he could not look at his mother. 'I'm sorry,' Edmund O'Hara had whispered as he wrapped his wife in the blanket, 'I'm sorry I'm sorry I'm sorry.'

He carried her up to the house, into the living room, the dining room, the parlour, the bedroom, the kitchen with its rows of pickled vegetables and sugared fruit. He did not put her down, accidentally knocking her feet against doorframes as he walked from one room to another, whispering and turning, while Toby sat on the stairs with his knees pulled up into his small chest and listened to his pop's breathless remorse.

'I'm sorry I'm sorry I'm sorry.'

The sun was setting. Toby knew that it would be freezing soon, and his arms had already goose-pimpled under his jacket. Droplets of sunlight were spread out across the sky, fading into the distant, gathering clouds. They floated above the bustling streets and ugly factories which belched black smoke from tall, carbon-smudged chimneys. He was interrupted by Ursula, turning suddenly to look at him.

'But how can you be certain,' Ursula began, 'that it will always work?'

He looked at her. He smiled. He knew that it would always work because it was science. The balloon became lighter than air, and that was why it flew. There were numbers and measurements involved. He did not say this because he preferred to maintain an aura of mystique when talking about his balloon. It was business. He told her what he told his other passengers. He said, 'It's all a question of faith.'

There was a pause. The girl opened her eyes and looked at him, and for a brief moment he saw a flicker of a smile on her lips.

Ursula nodded thoughtfully. 'But I don't believe in faith,' she said after a short pause. 'I believe in engineering and in the principle of hot air rising. I believe in the theory of aerodynamics, although I'm not altogether sure it is relevant to balloons. It may be. It is not my area. But I do not believe in faith.'

She thought he was talking about God. No, he thought in

response to her silent accusation. No, I do not believe in God either. But faith and God are not the same thing at all.

He bent forward, reaching for the valve, but then hesitated for a moment. He remembered his first flight with Judge Jake Gadston. It was reckless, he knew that, but he could not stop himself. He could not explain it exactly. It was the sudden thought that there is more to faith than God. It was the memory of his pop and his talk of pepperpots on the porch at night. (But did she sneeze loudly or softly? Could she keep a secret?) It was the thought that it would be a wonderful gift to give to this woman who knows that a balloon is just a toy, and to a girl whose head is full of poetry.

He looked up at the two women and grinned. 'I want to show you something,' he said, and instead of pushing the valve in to make the balloon descend as he should have done, he pulled it out so that there was a jump in the basket, a startling upwards tug.

They went up until they could see the sun edging above the horizon once more and, for a brief moment, he glanced at Sally as the sun burst from the darkened earth, reclaimed for the second time that day.

A question of faith

Later, Sally would write to Mr Fisher and attempt to describe the sensation of rising above the Falls in the balloon, the *roar* of it: 'Like the ocean in one of those gigantic seashells in the tea shop window,' she would write, although this did not convey exactly what she meant. There was the quivering of the basket, the cold air on her face, the terrible prospect of being so very high.

'Miss Bridgewater declared it overwhelming but, Mr Fisher, I found it not so much overwhelming as immensely fearful,' she would later write, and then would immediately cross this sentence out, judging it too dramatic. Instead she would write: 'Miss Bridgewater was immensely happy,' because she did not want him to think her ungrateful.

And it was true. In the balloon, Ursula Bridgewater *was* immensely happy, not just with the mechanics of the valve system and with the sky – 'Look, Walker, if you stretch out your hand you can *touch* this little cloud' – but also with herself for having 'discovered' Toby, this wonderful American whom she enjoyed interrogating about the workings of the balloon.

Sally did not wish to touch any clouds. It was just fog, she thought, and she was well-acquainted with fog. She remembered it clinging to the waterfront at New Brighton, sagging over the fields to the south of the city. She felt homesick for it, for the grey stone of the orphanage, for the pillars and porticoes by the train station and the square windows of the new warehouses at the dockyards.

Here, there was fog, but it was not the same sort of fog. It was wet and bright. The sky was a deep red, laid out across the earth, and the sun was golden on the horizon. There were no cobbles, no dirt; the roads down below were thin ribbons of pale earth. Sally felt a tingling in her neck. She knew that the earth was a sphere – 'an oblate spheroid,' Ursula had corrected her on the boat to New York, 'which is quite different' – and yet now the curve of it astonished her. It made her feel dizzy.

There was a wobble, a drift of wind against the balloon. The ropes of the basket strained and creaked. Sally glanced down at her feet, at her mother's soft-leather shoes which Mr Fisher had presented to her in a decorated box when she left the orphanage. She wished she could feel brave, but she knew she was not. She felt quite sick. The young man said something but she could not concentrate on his words. She held the sides of the basket, running her hands along the lines of wicker. She was grounding her hands, tricking them into thinking they were on solid ground, that nothing had changed. Look, she was telling them, it is only a basket, and baskets do not fly.

The fields below were cut into rectangles, with paths following the curves of the hills. There were furrowed ridges and trees, their leaves spread to catch the light. It was unbearable. She could not look down. Ursula held out her arms so that her cloak billowed, and she hopped from one side of the balloon to the other. Please, Sally thought. Please stay still.

Ursula did not stay still. She trotted first to Sally and then to Toby. She craned over the sides. She bent down to inspect the valve and tipped her head back to observe the blur of hot air rising up into the great silk shadow above their heads. She waved her hands up and down as if shaking out a huge white sheet.

Sally found all this movement unbearable and yet she would not let it show. She did not wish to cause a fuss. Her arms shivered. She wanted so much to enjoy it but she could not. She had no umbrella, no brother, no scientific bent; she was just herself and she wished to be standing on the ground.

Ursula proclaimed it to be quite remarkable that they did not fall.

She declared the balloon to be a triumph of science over nature.

She pronounced upon the infallibility of gravity and that, by all calculations, they must fall eventually.

She said it was quite magical.

She declared she did not believe in magic.

Sally wrung her hands around and around each other. She was wearing her new lilac gloves, a gift from Ursula before they departed. They were fur-lined and soft. She did not notice. Her head ached. She felt that familiar gush of sea-sickness overtake her, a weakness in her knees. She was afraid of falling – of course she was – but she also feared something else, something which rose inside her: the idea that she might jump, not to die, but for the sensation of it, because she thought it might be quite exhilarating. But then she thought: No, I will do no such thing.

'But how can you be certain that it will always work?' Ursula had insisted, and Toby had looked up at her. Sally did not wish to hear his answer. She wished to block it out, and yet she could not because as he spoke he looked at her; a small, soft glimpse of something unexpected. 'It's all a question of faith,' he said.

Sally saw the look on Ursula's face, surprise first, and then delight at the prospect of enlightened argument.

'But I do not believe in faith,' Ursula announced.

Sally closed her eyes. She remembered the Virgin Mary appearing in the window of the orphanage, that odd prop-erty of cylinder sheet glass which had, just for a moment, seemed like something more than it was. And perhaps it was, she thought, as she had done several times since.

'I want to show you something,' Toby had said then, and Sally had felt the balloon jolt beneath them. The sky was dark now and they should have been going down, but as they rose up, further and further from the earth, there was a lightness growing on the horizon, and then all of a sudden she saw the sun once more, golden and distant, hovering above the curve of the earth.

Toby looked at Ursula and grinned, and then he looked at Sally. 'But look at the sun now,' he had said.

'Oh, is it not quite beautiful?' Ursula exclaimed. 'Look,

Walker,' she said, grasping Sally's hand and turning her so that she was obliged to look out of the balloon, down across the patchwork of fields and the tiny grist mills, and the silver stream of water which flowed over the Falls and under the miniature railway bridge.

Sally should not have looked. She was not brave enough. She was not Ursula. She was only herself. She recognised the familiar wash of nausea sweeping through her. She forgot the orphanage window, that brief shimmer of possibility. 'Yes, ma'am,' she gasped. And then she wiped the back of her glove across her hot cheeks and felt her eyes tighten as her knees buckled beneath her and she fell to the floor of the balloon's basket.

Thirteen

Eternity

Unless you are quite well-versed in the philanthropic projects of Liverpool merchants in the early nineteenth century, you may not have heard of Mr Joseph Williamson and his network of tunnels under the city. In Ursula Bridgewater's time and social circles, he was often spoken of as a bit of a madman, a genius, a kind and generous fellow given to flashes of rage at his tenants. It was thought by some that the construction of the tunnels was a way of creating employment, of training men in brickwork and construction, and that it was an extravagantly worthy project. It was thought by others that the man was simply crazy and had, in effect, done nothing more than create a huge cesspit under the city into which broken pots and slop buckets would be emptied until the tunnels began to fill up once more.

Whatever his reasons, the result of this project was that Mr Joseph Williamson trained an army of unemployed sailors, demobbed and demoralised following the end of the Napoleonic wars, in tunnel-building. In the first cave beneath his house they inserted a fireplace, in front of which Mr Williamson placed his favourite armchair. He ordered the construction of a banqueting hall with a wine cellar and small brick holders for gaslights. He demanded that miles and miles of earth under Liverpool be tunnelled through, and he insisted that these tunnels be set with arched ceilings and finished in elaborate brickwork.

The problem was that Joseph Williamson left no record of his intentions, having ordered all his diaries and letters to be burned before he died and destroying all other documentary evidence. He ripped up the plans to the tunnels so that it was no longer possible to say which parts of the city now lay over solid earth and which hid a vast hole, and it was this absence of paperwork – and anybody wishing to leave any form of architectural legacy should take note – which led the tunnel project to be viewed as a sign of possible madness.

By the time the men came to work on the railway, the project was largely forgotten. The tunnels were left half-built, ending abruptly in walls of earth. The men who built the railway from Liverpool Lime Street Station to Edge Hill were not the same men who tunnelled through the earth for Joseph Williamson. They came from the Lancashire countryside, from North Wales and Cheshire. They were career railwaymen, blasting lines through the countryside for the iron tracks. They had not heard of the network of tunnels that spread under the rows of tightly-packed houses in Edge Hill.

When they exploded dynamite into the hillside above a warren of tunnels, they expected to blast into rock. It became almost myth-like, the story of the man from Lancashire who lowered himself into the gap after the explosion with his oil lamp slung over his shoulder. He had done it hundreds of times before, but when he saw only this endless, tunnelled blackness, he screamed and tugged at his harness to be lifted out, because he thought he had blasted right through the earth's crust and into Eternity itself.

It was this which came to Ursula Bridgewater's mind as

she sat at Sally's bedside with a bowl of cold water and a flannel. There were fresh flowers on the table next to the bed. She had picked them that morning from the hotel garden, small bursts of colour which she had gathered up in her arms from behind the high-boarded fence.

'Are they for your daughter?' the receptionist had asked as Ursula came in, and Ursula had nodded. She told herself that she had nodded because she was in a hurry, because there was no need to pander to every single person who might wish to know her business, and that it did not matter who the flowers were for.

But she knew this was not really why she had nodded. She had not corrected the receptionist because she had not wanted to. She had liked the idea of being a mother, distracted and concerned and utterly inhabited. Now you really are being ridiculous, she told herself crossly. You must stop this.

She was busy during those three days of Sally's illness, not just with sponging the girl's forehead and keeping the room aired, but with arranging things. Ursula had forgotten how much time it took to layer chemises, bodices, stays, drawers, petticoats, when there was only one person to do it all. It took such a concentration of energy, such a huge amount of fussing and smoothing to get it all done as it should be.

And yet she did not mind, because all the while she fussed and smoothed, she was keeping an eye on Sally. She felt responsible. If the towels brought up by the house-keeper were not thick enough, she marched them back to the linen press and demanded an exchange. She required terry cotton. Well, why did they not have terry cotton? Then she would simply have to buy them herself. There would be a shop in the town, surely, which stocked proper towels. She made mugs of warm cocoa which she fed to

Sally with a spoon. She sponged the girl's head with cold water, and warmed the thick new towels on the stove before wrapping them around Sally's feet. She felt wild and generous.

I have flown through the sky! she thought. In a balloon!

From the room she could hear the incessant rush of falling water. The memory of that first viewing of Niagara Falls had shrunk entirely. Now, she could hardly believe she had ever thought them devoid of beauty; crass and squat and not much to speak of. She understood that it was not the Falls themselves which were lacking. It had simply been a case of misrepresentation. The Falls were too wide to be grand, too accessible to be terrifying. They did not fall from the mountains into a great wilderness as she had expected, but surged out of a great plain of land surrounded by mills. They were not terrifying or splendid. They were simply beautiful. They were a pearl in the ocean of all this grist, shimmering and magnificent, great torrents of ice-cold water which, even as it fell, seemed to rise in a joyous cloud of frost.

On each of the three nights of Sally's illness, Ursula slept in an armchair next to Sally's bed, her knees covered with a blanket and her head resting on a small cushion. On the first two nights, she slept with her hands fitted together on her lap, as she might have sat in England, in all those drawing rooms where she was obliged to eat endless, floury scones and exchange pleasantries. It was on the third night that the change in her occurred. She did not notice the moment when she tapped through her shell, splintering the layer she had previously thought of as solid. It was an impulse, that was all, and yet it was as strong a thing as she had ever felt. It was the notion of Eternity as a deep hole, hovering just beyond the thin crust of life. She reached out and took Sally's hand in her own – she did not think about what she was doing – and she did not let it go.

In the morning, when the worst of Sally's fever had passed and light was once more permitted to break through the cocoon of curtain and eiderdown, Ursula removed her hand from Sally's. She leant forwards and brushed a strand of Sally's hair away from her eyes. She did it unthinkingly, softly.

If she had been less ill, Sally might have flinched, not understanding that the extended arm was part of this new tip of the scales. She did not know what had caused it. Her memory held only the sensation of heat, sticky and close, of the curtained darkness and the burning sensation in her throat. Under the eiderdown, she crossed her arms across her body. It was confusing and yet it was also comforting.

Nothing was said. There was no need. Things would go back to the way they were before. There were roles to be adopted and they would do so. But it was also true that, in that moment, the relationship between them had shifted a little, had metamorphosed into a light, pretty thing, and – anyone with even the slightest knowledge of biology will know this to be true – once changed, it could not be put back.

Such hands!

The rest of the party left for Detroit the following day, but Ursula stayed behind with Sally. Before he left, Mr Cook spoke with Ursula, as he put it, man-to-man. 'You must catch us up as soon as you are able,' he instructed her, handing her a scrap of paper. 'Here is the itinerary, and I have circled the connecting trains.'

Ursula nodded in her most efficient manner whilst inspecting Mr Cook's instructions. He ran his finger along the train schedules as he talked. 'You must take Pullman's drawing-room car along the Delaware River, the Great Western line to Detroit, the Michigan Central line to Chicago, the Burlington Route to Omaha, crossing the Mississippi and the Missouri.' His eyes were shining, animated by the prospect of such elaborate timetables. 'Then you must take the Union Pacific line to Ogden, and there deviate to Salt Lake City, and then finally the Central Pacific line down to San Francisco.'

'Righty-ho,' Ursula said.

Mr Cook looked at her, concerned that she had not been paying sufficient attention. 'I would stay with you,' he said, 'if things were not as they are, but I have to go on with the group.'

'Quite,' Ursula reassured him. 'I am perfectly capable of dealing with trains . . . I mean,' she corrected herself, 'with railroads.'

Mr Cook nodded. 'I know,' he said, and Ursula beamed at him.

Together, Ursula and Mr Cook arranged for the hotel coupons for Detroit and Chicago to be exchanged for Niagara Falls hotel coupons; she said she would wire a message to him in Salt Lake City to inform him of their progress. It was thus arranged that they would catch up with the group as soon as the doctor agreed that Sally was well enough to travel.

'I'm afraid Niagara is not the *real* America,' Mr Cook murmured apologetically over dinner that evening, and Ursula had nodded out of politeness, remembering how she had felt upon first seeing the Falls.

'No,' she had said, in agreement, although she no longer believed this to be true. Oh no. Where else could she rise through the air in a balloon and run her hand through a wisp of cloud? Where else could she wander so easily through the streets on her own without feeling looked-at, pitied?

She had walked up to Prospect Point to sketch the Falls the previous morning but the result had been unsatisfactory. The pencil had been pressed too hard against the paper – she had never been able to draw lightly – and she had not captured at all the movement of the water, the icy sparkle of it, colourless and bright. But even if she could not draw it, she could still feel it. She could see it, could describe it in words; the million flashes of rainbows in the droplets of spray; the frosted cloud of mist like the cloak of an angel; the bubbling foam of water as it crashed into the rocks. She had sat on the Point, her discarded sketch-book slowly saturating beside her, and she had gazed upon the tumbling water for hours, and she had felt only delight.

And the town was not as distasteful as she had first thought. She had grown to like its ugly rowdiness. Yes, it was commercial, glitzy, crowded with old, barn-like hotels and Indian shops selling shoddy moccasins and scrappy beads. Everything was counted in dollars. Hack drivers punched each other's noses over the scramble for customers. There were posters advertising bridge walks, whirlpools, battlegrounds, daredevil shows. It was a swindle, a trick. But it was also alive. The roar of water formed the natural backdrop to the town. It surged and spilt, on and on, and Ursula felt that lovely, light-headed sensation of utter carelessness which she imagined had inspired the Romantic poets. It was hypnotic, triumphant.

Then there was the doctor, Dr Duncan Leigh of Niagara Falls, a tall man in his early forties. He was the sort of doctor who had an odd habit of seeming to flatter his patients by emphasising the severity of their condition, whilst at the same time suggesting that no condition was

180

so severe that it could not be cured. He tended to look away when asked about the progress of a patient, of lowering his eyelids to suggest a compassion he did not fully feel and which had the benefit of showing off his eyelashes which he knew were longer than average. He had been told this by a number of ladies in his younger, courting days. He wore a watch with a silver chain in his waistcoat pocket and, when describing a patient's condition, he used its Latin name when an English one would have done just as well. He did this for effect, but there was a professional reason as well. He found it could be beneficial to the patient if others thought their illness more serious than it actually was. So the reasoning behind all this Latin, which some might call pretentious, was also medical.

Dr Leigh's face was tanned and freckled, his eyes brightly hazel, his teeth white and large, but it was his hands which caught Ursula's attention first. He spread them in front of him as he spoke. Ursula could not take her eyes from them. She had never seen such hands, such elegant fingers. The effect of them was more pronounced because of the length of his arms, and they were so large, so safe-looking, that she could not help but wonder if the recommendations she had received – 'Oh, there is no one like Dr Leigh' – had more to do with his hands than with any sort of medical expertise he might have.

For a moment, Ursula Bridgewater was quite struck by him. Certainly, he had an attractive face which, although it was not handsome in itself, had an expression of such intensity that it could be said, and often was, that there was a magnetism about him. She thought that perhaps it was the atmosphere of the town, its sense of drama, of danger, but still she knew herself to be struck. Here is a man, she thought recklessly, with whom I might forget myself.

181

Dr Leigh folded the thermometer into a cloth and placed it into his bag. 'I have always admired the English for their attitude to illness,' he said. It was part of his routine, to conclude an appointment with a small distraction. 'It does not suit the American psyche to be ill. They are culturally unsuited to illness, or to any sort of tragedy. It is geographical. They,' he caught himself, 'I mean *we*, like everything to be just great.'

Ursula smiled. This, she felt, was an example of wittiness being displayed purely for the sake of wittiness, and this was one of the things she professed to dislike, and yet she was not immune to the allure of this man.

'Then it is perhaps the English who are the least suited for it, because we do not have the requisite optimism to recover,' she declared, a cup of tea perched on the arm of her chair.

He looked at her with amusement. 'Are you a pessimist, Miss Bridgewater?'

'I would not say that I was either an optimist or a pessimist. I would say, if I were obliged to pigeon-hole myself in such a manner, that I am a realist.'

Dr Duncan Leigh laughed and snapped his bag shut. The fastening was gold and shiny. 'Well, it amounts to the same thing.'

Ursula looked at him. No, she thought, it does not. One is one thing, and the other is another. How obvious that sounds. He is teasing me but I must not appear impatient. One must be patient if one is to be charming. I must make more of an effort.

Dr Leigh saw that Miss Bridgewater's face had changed in some way, somewhere around the eyes. He had not intended to upset her and yet he had done so without noticing how or why. He smiled at her, intending to placate her, and she hesitated for just a moment before she remembered that sensation of being quite struck. She smiled at him and clapped her hands as she stood up in a back-to-business sort of manner.

Ice

Each morning, Toby O'Hara called at the hotel to enquire after Miss Walker's health and was received by Ursula in the parlour on the first floor. The room was large and decorated in yellow and white, and there were exotic birds in a tall cage next to the window which looked out over the main street of Niagara Falls. There was a rattle of stage-coaches and wagons, and a rabble of tourists streaming towards the Falls.

'Walker is still not at all well,' Ursula declared on the second day of Sally's illness, 'although Dr Leigh tells me she will recover, and that is a great relief to me. He claims it is a chill from going behind the Falls, but it is my own fault really. I should not have encouraged her to lean out of the balloon like that when she is not . . . What was your word? She is not air-minded. She has no sea legs.'

Toby shook his head. Walker, he thought. How odd that this woman should call her that. It seemed oddly abrupt and inappropriate. 'Oh no,' he protested, 'I should not have taken you up so far. It was careless of me.'

'Not at all,' Ursula interrupted. She leant forwards in her chair and beamed at him. 'How many people can have seen such a thing? To see the sun set and then be made to rise again, well, it was really quite wonderful.'

Toby smiled. It was more of a grin than a smile. He remembered how he had liked her on that first day, how she had pranced about the basket, loud and unreserved, and how she had seen the balloon for what it was – a huge toy. 'It was, wasn't it?'

He pressed himself into the leather armchair, sinking down into it so that he could no longer see out of the hotel window. He sipped the tea Ursula had poured for him. He did not like this view, all these people with their holiday bonnets and sketchpads. He had come to Niagara for its tourist possibilities – there were other reasons too – and while he knew that there was no place for a balloon flight business in Holloway Creek, he also knew that he did not like his new home as much as he had hoped.

When he first arrived, he had found the waterfall both mesmerising and comforting, but now, as the day on which he would finish his flying machine grew close, he found the torrent discomforting. The water ticked in his mind, unstoppable, impossible to turn back. The town was, on the surface, friendly and enterprising. The spray glittered as it fell, but after a time he had found that there was a dampness about the place. There was competition among the business people, defamation of stallholders, insurance fires and damaged fences. There was talk of a rival balloon company beginning on the Canadian side of the Falls. Toby felt water seeping into his skin, drenching him. He could escape it in his balloon, floating up above the waterfall, but even this was tainted by the presence of tourists, of profit. There was only the cowshed which remained unblemished, with its stream of sunlight lacing through the small window in the west wall, its carpet of sawdust and cut silk making him homesick for his pop's workshop in Holloway Creek.

He sat now in the hotel. It was not the grandest hotel in the town, but nor was it the worst. It had a veranda and a ballroom with a chandelier, and although this was no longer much used for dancing – the age of Southern tourists spending entire summers in Niagara having passed with the Civil War – it added a glamour which set it a little above some of the newer establishments.

He had been into this particular hotel once before, but had never taken tea in the parlour. There was a fireplace with small hand-painted tiles, miniatures of women holding flowers and books and, in one case, a chicken. There was an iron kindling basket and brass instruments lined up next to the grate. Toby sat by the fireplace and ate two slices of sultana cake while Ursula gestured with her hands as she spoke. She told him about their planned itinerary, of how they were to see the Great Lakes of Michigan and Illinois, the salt plains of Utah where the women were entitled to vote (such progressiveness!), and the Clay Street Hill cable car in San Francisco.

'It will be quite marvellous,' she told him.

'I have always wanted to see England,' Toby told her suddenly, although the prospect had not occurred to him before. He had thought of moving to Boston, or even New York, but he had not truly thought of seeing England. It was, he supposed, the traces of his pop he heard in Ursula's voice which had prompted him to say such a thing. It was not calculated. 'My pop was in Liverpool once.'

'Why then,' Ursula said delightedly, 'you must come to Liverpool and stay with me and my brother.'

On his next visit, Toby brought a small box of chocolates as a gift for Sally, and on this occasion Ursula invited him to take tea in their suite.

'It will be perfectly improper,' she declared, 'but I'm sure it will do Sally . . . I mean, of course, Walker . . . it will do Walker good to have some more youthful company than mine.'

Sally was not asleep, but was propped up in bed, swathed

in a hot lump of blankets, her hair falling over her shoulders and a white sheet pulled up under her chin. 'I'm sorry,' she whispered, when he presented her with the chocolates. 'I'm afraid I have no sea legs.'

Toby nodded. 'So I hear,' he said.

'Oh Walker,' Ursula interrupted, 'will you please stop apologising.'

The chocolates were in a pink box, tied with a red ribbon. They looked like a love token. Toby was embarrassed. He felt suddenly that the box suggested an invitation to intimacy which he had not intended, but which, now that it had occurred to him, caused him to clear his throat and look away.

'Mr O'Hara, can we offer you some tea?' Ursula asked, gesturing for him to follow her through to the sitting room which connected the two ladies' rooms. 'We don't want to tire Walker out,' Ursula said.

Toby followed her towards the sitting room, pausing at the door to look out of the window.

'I have been thinking about your balloon,' Ursula announced, ringing the bell for tea as she did so. She sat down on the side of the settee and dusted her knees. 'Have you a patent for it?'

He smiled. 'There's no point. It is nothing new,' he said. He leaned against the doorframe, facing Ursula and with his back to Sally, and plunged his hand deep into the pocket of his trousers. 'Besides, a balloon is just air. It is not proper flying. It is, as you said, just a toy.'

'Then what is proper flying?' she asked, tilting forward so that the tendons tightened in her neck.

Toby looked away from her. He remembered her enthusiasm in the balloon, and he wondered if perhaps he might trust her with his secret. 'I think you might be able to guess,' he said, and in his mind the bat-shaped structure in the cowshed took on the appearance of something light and luminous.

'Oh, I cannot possibly,' she said.

Toby was wearing a bright blue tie. It was the exact colour of the sky through the window. He twirled it in his fingers. His cheeks flushed. 'Try.'

'But I am uneducated in such things,' she said, her face animated by this extraordinary boy, whose enthusiasm reminded her suddenly of George as a boy, producing the head of the Bengal tiger in the Christmas pantomimes of their childhood. When she spoke again – she could not help it – there was a light flutter of sarcasm in her voice, although the sarcasm was for herself rather than for Toby. 'I am just a woman, after all.'

Toby bit down upon his lip. He thought of his mother, smiling as she waved at him from the air. He heard the sarcasm but he did not understand it. 'No, no, no,' he said crossly, more irritably than he intended.

Miss Bridgewater put her hand to her mouth. 'Oh no,' she said, 'You misunderstand me. I did not mean to offend you.'

'No,' he said. 'It is not me that you offend.'

She paused, confused. 'Then whom do I offend?'

Toby's mouth opened a little. The teeth no longer bit at the lip. He tilted his head as he looked at her, and he smiled, a great white smile. 'I suspect you offend yourself.'

It was a challenge. It was not a challenge. It was a gift. It was a sudden recognition of that strong, defiant part of Ursula Bridgewater which had stood in the nursery in a blue-and-white sailor suit and patent leather shoes and stamped its foot on the oak floorboards while George went to school. It was the part of her that was bored of never being allowed to deliver the good lines in plays, of being made to swoon and clutch at her bosom, always the bosom;

of having to learn the passive voice second-hand and geography from apples. There was a bubbling in her chest. In her bosom, she thought.

She gave a small chuckle, and her face as she laughed took on that bright carelessness of youth in which you could see, if you looked closely, the girl she had once been before anyone had expressly told her they did not want to marry her.

'Besides,' Toby continued, 'you cannot be educated in a thing which has not yet been invented.' He paused. 'Or at least, has not yet been tested.'

'Mr O'Hara,' Ursula stopped chuckling. Her eyebrows lifted and her grey eyes grew suddenly very large. 'Mr O'Hara,' she said again, her lip curling upwards. 'I do believe you have built something more than a balloon. Something that is not *just air*, as you describe it.'

'Well, yes,' he said. 'Although I don't know if it will fly. It isn't yet finished.'

'Oh dear,' she said. 'How marvellous!'

'Perhaps,' Toby suggested, propped still against the door and gesturing to Sally, 'if Miss Walker is sufficiently improved, I could take you both to see it.'

'Now?' she asked.

'No, no, no. Not here. Not now. It is too big. It is ...' He stopped, unable to speak, unable to describe his wonderful invention in case it became small and heavy in the telling.

Sally stirred in the room behind him, and he turned around to look at her. She smiled at him. He smiled back and, for a brief moment, their gaze met across the sun-shot room.

Ursula Bridgewater clasped her hands together. 'But tell me, is it costly to make?' she asked, thinking suddenly of the expense of the Liverpool to Manchester railway, mixed with the prospect of offering such a thing to the mass market. Such purpose! Such progress!

Toby frowned. He was not thinking of market forces. He thought it was an offer, but he was not brave enough to tell her outright that he did not want the money he thought she was offering. Yes, he had spent his entire inheritance, which was not insubstantial, on building his machine, but he did not need more. He had all the materials, and it was finished, or near enough. And besides, he earned more than he needed from the balloon rides.

But it was because of this, because he felt suddenly hurried and because he misunderstood the expression on Ursula's face for one of charity rather than of entrepreneurship, that Toby O'Hara stood in the doorway between the bedroom and the sitting room and told Ursula the other story, the true story. He did it to set her mind at rest, to clear himself of all suspicion, to remove the taint of profit from his vision of flight.

He did not tell her everything, of course. He did not tell her that he had not run to his mother as he might have done when he saw his pop's flying machine come down at the end of the field. He did not tell her that he could not eat jam because the taste of it brought up such a sickly rush of grief that he could not bear it. He did not tell her that he knew only three stories from his mother's childhood or about the conversations with his pop on the porch.

He told her simply this: that his mother died when she fell from the sky and that he, now, was building a machine like hers.

'How wonderful!' Ursula exclaimed. 'To think you may have solved the mystery of flight for mankind!'

And when she said this Toby laughed. 'Oh, I have not done that,' he said. 'I did it because . . .' He faltered.

'Yes?'

He could not express it. He stood back, his arms folded. 'Do you know how it feels,' he asked, his voice suddenly quiet, 'to need to know something?'

What an odd question, Ursula thought. She hesitated and then nodded. It was just a few seconds, but it confused her because she had thought they were talking about the flying machine but, for that moment, it seemed that he was talking about something else entirely.

Smoke

Sally felt the fever clinging to her, swamping her. She felt the heat of her hands and her body and the pulsing of blood in her head. There were other things too; the smell of tobacco in her room (did Ursula smoke?), the sucking noise of inhalation, the crackle of dried leaves, the flushed faces, two of them now, huddled together at the end of the bed; noise, heat, laughter, sunlight falling in a stream across her face.

She heard Ursula's voice, and then a man answering her. She recognised it from the balloon. 'It's all a question of faith,' Mr O'Hara had said, as if he had known how much she had longed for it herself, how she had searched for it in all the poetry of the psalms, in the carved, blood-stained feet of Christ on the Cross, but had never been able to find it.

When she was a child, she had prayed for her mother. She had not spoken about her, had not uttered a single word, not even to kind Mr Fisher with his folded newspaper cuttings and his outings to the Punch and Judy stand in St George's Square, but she had lit candles for her in the side chapel. She had knelt in front of the Virgin Mary until her toes tingled and her knees were numb. She did not remember exactly what it was she had prayed for; for her mother's immortal soul, dove-like and wispy; for sleep to come peacefully, free from those terrifying images of the Christian martyrs which adorned the vast walls of the orphanage, free from thoughts of King Herod, of snakes and spiders and woodlice; for an escape from her endless, jolting dreams of falling.

It had not worked. Neither habit nor repetition dulled the clarity of those dreams, that dreadful, clawing sensation, the rush of air on her face. She had prayed on her knees but had felt nothing.

But then, a face in the window. No, she murmured deliriously to herself, pushing the memory of the Vision out of her head. I must try to be more scientific.

She was unnerved by having caused such a disruption. From the moment she entered the orphanage, she had practised being invisible, holding her solitude around her like a shield. But now it had been stripped away. She felt it as a raw sensation in her arms as Ursula leant over her, her hand resting attentively on Sally's shoulder.

She stirred. She tried to sit up. She could not lift her head.

'Sally,' Ursula exclaimed. 'How are you feeling? Is the sun too bright?'

Sally opened her eyes. The room tumbled before her, hazy and hot. The light hurt her eyes. She forced her mouth to smile, torn as she was between the perpetual horror of causing a fuss and the fear of appearing impolite.

'Oh no,' she whispered, 'not too bright at all. I'm much better, thank you.'

How many days had it been? Three? Surely they would have to leave soon, pack their dresses into their trunks and haul them out into the corridor. She would have to get up.

'We have a visitor,' Ursula whispered, stepping back and gesturing towards Toby.

Sally smiled, embarrassed, her face red and gleaming

191

with feverish sweat. 'I'm sorry,' she whispered. 'I'm afraid I have no sea legs.'

He laughed. Sally did not understand why. Nothing was as she remembered it. Ursula patted her arm and told her she really must stop apologising. It was said snappily, but there was something different about her tone, as if Sally had said something very witty.

Am I coming on a treat? Sally wondered hopefully. Then she thought: No, of course not. How can I be? I am not adventurous enough. I collapse in balloons and run away from waterfalls. I am not in the least bit interested in aerodynamics or valve systems.

But still, she felt her spirit skip a little before realising that this state of affairs could not be expected to last. She would have to get up soon, and resume her duties, else she might be deserted in this terrible place with its falling water and flying baskets, and an ocean swilling between her and the only home she had ever known. She had to become well again. The pillow was soft beneath her head. There were more whispers, more laughter.

'Perhaps, if Miss Walker is sufficiently improved, I could take you both to see it?' Sally suddenly heard Toby say. She saw him across the room, talking to Ursula while standing in the doorway of her bedroom.

See what? she wondered briefly. She closed her eyes and heard him pause, and then she heard him tell Ursula about the flying machine, about his mother, the crash, about how she had longed to fly, and had died for the love of it. A subdued S-shape. He did not describe this, but he did not need to. Sally lay perfectly still, as if she were Charles Blondin himself, laid out flat along a high wire strung across Niagara Falls.

And then Toby's question, his voice soft: 'But do you know how it feels,' he asked, 'to need to know something?'

Ursula did not answer. Perhaps she nodded.

But Sally knew. She did not move. She did not dare. There was a stabbing pain in her throat and she felt hot and shivery all at once. Yes, she thought. I know exactly how that feels.

Fourteen

Celia and Georgia

Dr Duncan Leigh considered himself to be a good doctor. If he did not know how best to treat an ailment, he made a point of finding out. The periodicals which arrived for him from New York were not for show. Their pages were thumbed, their corners turned down. He prided himself on his thoroughness, on being up-to-date. This was not for the purpose of garnering testimonials – although if they were offered to him, he did not like to be rude – but because he cared about his patients and he liked to see them recover.

He had grown up in a one-room house with a porch all around it and a curtain down the centre. He was not ashamed, but he did not speak of it if he could avoid doing so. He was raised by his two grandmothers who kept canaries and cockatoos and fed him on Danish puffs and kelp pickles. They taught him not to be afraid of thunder, and how to make baked beans. They called each other 'pardner' in Mid-west accents and whistled in the mornings. He was happy then, although he did not think about it much at the time. It was only later that it really occurred to him how much effort those two women had made on his behalf.

His parents were buried in the churchyard, one on top of the other. He did not remember them. *Be not afraid*, the stone tablet read, *for I will come again*. When Duncan was small, no more than five or six, he did not know about epitaphs. He thought his mum and dad intended to haunt him. The gravestone had sunk on one side, as if being pulled under from beneath. He imagined bony white fingers and long wrists. A man and a woman. He clung to his grandmothers' skirts and slept in a cot at their feet until his legs dangled over the wooden bar at the end of it, and then he was given a bed of his own behind a curtain.

The beds were set along the west wall, opposite a fireplace and a cupboard for storing bowls and saucepans. There was a table and three chairs, and a thick, unchopped log protruding from the fireplace which his grandmothers lit at one end and then pushed into the grate as it smouldered down. It was easier on the shoulders that way, they said.

It was from these two women that Duncan learned the uses of witch-hazel and iodine, of stewed nettles and quinine tonics and black cohosh for hot flushes, and his passion for Latin names and leather attaché cases can probably be dated from this era. He made a name for himself, medically, at the age of seven, when Grandma C suffered a stroke in the house and Duncan climbed onto the roof to hoist a pair of Grandma G's bloomers onto the chimney to alert her to the emergency. She had come home, red-nosed and distressed by the sight of her undergarments fluttering in the breeze, only to find Duncan singing to Grandma C as she lay on the floor by the log fire because he did not know what else to do.

The C stood for Celia. He knew this because Grandma G said it when she was cross. Grandma C never got cross, and so it was only when he was older that he learnt Grandma G's name was Georgia, an odd, stately name for such a small woman, named after the place of her birth.

It was these two women who encouraged Duncan to go to medical school in Boston, who told him that he could do anything he liked as long as he worked hard enough.

And he had worked hard. He had honed his craft, not just aspects of diagnosis, but also his demeanour. It was this which had turned out to be the greatest impediment to his happiness. He wished to marry but he had no time for the pleasantries required for courting. He knew that, while he was generally considered handsome, he was also regarded as aloof and standoffish, but he did not see how he could be otherwise and still maintain the standards he had set for himself. It was not personal, but professional, although this differentiation was often not made sufficiently clear, and most women eventually became offended with him in some way or other which he did not intend.

Dr Duncan Leigh considered Ursula Bridgewater to be what his grandmothers would have called, in their habit of not quite getting a handle on expressions, a flat-headed girl with no nonsense about her. He liked this about her. Nonsense, as he called it, scared him. He liked the fact that she was brusque with him, that she rolled her eyes when things took too long and did not pretend to be infuriatingly dainty like other women of his acquaintance. Even her sketchpad amused him. It was mottled with damp, full of bold line drawings, some of them crossed through with dismissive sweeps of pencil, but mostly drawn with an exactitude he admired. Leaves did not float from trees, but lay flat, trodden into the ground, and he admired that exacting quality in her, suggesting an aloofness to match his own.

He stood in the lobby of the hotel. It was midday. He wore a white waistcoat and a dark grey frock coat. He did not look anything like the boy he had once been, growing up in a house of women and cockatoos and canaries. He had money of his own, a townhouse with velveteen wallpaper in the hallway and a wood-panelled library. He had published articles on tropical diseases. He spoke of his patients with a gentle, possessive tone which he had developed expressly for this purpose. He leant against the mantelpiece and looked at himself in the mirror. He was posing, and yet at the same time it was not a pretence. It was, after all, his arm, his elbow. They were attached to his body. He drummed his fingers. He saw them move in the mirror. It was just that, sometimes, he did not recognise himself.

He took a cheroot from his jacket pocket and lit it. Perhaps he would wait a little longer. After all, the girl was still too ill to travel. He would insist that they stay a few more nights, for medical reasons, and then he might put his offer to Miss Bridgewater. That way, he could take a bit more time to decide if it was the right thing. He could steel himself. He could practise how he would put it.

Dr Leigh had once thought himself a pure science man, not one for poetry or music or splashes of paint upon canvases, but there was one poem that had created complications. He had found it in a collection lent to him by Miss Amelia Thompson, one of the young ladies with whom society had occasionally linked him because of her delicate education and serious blue eyes. When he first read the words of this particular poet, a G. Peterson (of whom he had never heard anything more), he had been moved. And not just moved: the poem had shocked him with its delicacy of sentiment and he had felt awed, helpless, just as he had when attending his first dissection at medical school and had held in the palm of his hand that tangle of arteries and flesh which made up the human heart.

That such emotions could be aroused in him by simple words had been a surprise, and it was indeed fatal to the prospects of any relationship he might have developed with Miss Thompson, as he knew that she, in the flesh (he had imagined this as well), could not move him in the way the words on the page of her book had. It was a plea for love, a hungry, beating sonnet, and he had copied the poem into his notebook and consigned it to memory.

He had taken to poetry after that. Not in a noticeable way, but he had read Whitman, Emerson and Poe, although he had not always liked them. He considered that they could occasionally be deliberately abstruse, and this put him off. He preferred the natural simplicity of style adopted by this G. Peterson, whose words had tugged so delicately at the chambers of Dr Duncan Leigh's heart that he was left quite unsuitable for any ordinary, practical marriage.

Yes, he thought, that is how I will approach the topic. I will read the poem to Miss Bridgewater. After all, the iambic pentameter is – the fact is surely indisputable – the correct rhythm for a declaration of love. He blew out a cloud of smoke and smiled.

'Why, there you are, Doctor.'

Dr Leigh blinked and looked up. Ursula was standing next to Sally at the foot of the stairs, her boots shining and her hair pinned up under her hat.

'We are going on an expedition,' Ursula announced. 'To take some air.'

The doctor wafted his hand in front of his face to clear the smoke. He watched Ursula while she secured her umbrella with a bow. He thought of his grandmother's bloomers and felt his neck grow suddenly hot.

'Perhaps I might accompany you?' he asked.

'How nice,' Ursula said, smiling at him but not taking his arm as he had hoped but reaching instead for Sally's. He saw, in this gesture, a flicker of the mother she might have been, softer than her spine suggested, and he reached forward to extinguish his cheroot in the ashtray on the mantelpiece.

He followed the two women out of the hotel and they walked together along the street. The air was white and hazy. There were Irishwomen selling linen cloths at the side of the road. The afternoon would be warm, but for now it was a perfect temperature, fresh and sharp. Dr Duncan Leigh did not notice the weather. His mind was distracted by the question of when exactly he might approach the subject of marriage with this fine woman, and for a moment his thoughts were so taken up with the future that he did not realise he had lost his companions.

He turned around to look for them and saw that Ursula and Sally had stopped outside the haberdashers and were both looking up at the sky. He thought first of the spray, of the rainbow over the Falls. But no, he decided, it could not be this as they were not looking in the right direction.

He heard the eagles before he saw them, a muffled, flapping sound, only just audible over the torrent of water. They emerged from behind an oak tree, rising and falling, chasing each other as they cartwheeled upwards into the sky. He had seen this once before, but only once, when he was a boy and Grandma G had explained it to him in her stately manner, this display of congress in the sky.

'What are they doing?' Sally whispered.

Dr Leigh coughed. He gave it its Latin name, his face deliberately earnest, almost scholarly, so that they would not be made to feel embarrassed. He noticed – he could not help it – the neatness of Ursula Bridgewater's teeth as he spoke, perfectly rectangular; her smooth, dignified nose. Quite handsome, he thought. Even, perhaps, quite pretty.

He described the process as it happened, how it began with an ascent, both birds circling each other, spinning and dancing as they soared upwards. The birds grew smaller, darkened by the brightness of the sunlight. The delicate tendons of Ursula's neck stood out as she squinted up at the sky.

'Then,' he said, 'they lock talons, and that is the beginning of the mating process, and as they mate they fall,' ('oh how they fall,' he thought remembering Whitman, *in tumbling, turning, clustering loops*') 'until they come so close to the earth that their wings brush against it and, when they are finished, the birds pull apart and soar upwards once more.'

Ursula frowned. It seemed that she was thinking, and she would not move until she had thought. 'But, Doctor,' she said slowly, looking at him quite intently, 'what happens to the birds if they don't, well . . .' she hesitated while she searched for an appropriate word, '*finish* in time?'

Duncan Leigh coughed. He felt his neck redden. He was not thinking of eagles. 'Then they die,' he said abruptly.

Ursula hugged her arms across her chest. 'How romantic it must be,' she exclaimed wistfully, and Duncan Leigh felt a small fluttering sensation in his stomach as he watched her, 'to die for love!'

*

Of course, Ursula Bridgewater did not really mean what she said. She knew this about herself even as she said it. She knew she could not mean it because when she had found herself in the role of spurned lover, had she not given up too easily? Had she not failed to sacrifice herself for love when called upon to do so? Had she written to Henry Springton, begged him to change his mind, knelt at his feet and torn at her breast over the sorrow of it?

No, she had not. Of course she had not. She had accepted it. She had continued to reply to his letters and to send

Christmas puddings in December, and she had never once betrayed to him how great a bite it was he had taken out of her.

It was because of this display of immaculate self-control that Ursula knew she did not mean what she said. *Yes,* she would have agreed meekly if she were a bald-headed eagle, halting mid-flight to discuss the future as the ground approached, *we had better stop, untangle ourselves from each other's bodies. We were, indeed, more friends than lovers anyway.*

But, in Niagara Falls, while Dr Leigh described avian copulation in Latin using the passive voice and gesturing upwards with those wonderful hands of his, Ursula did not wish to expose her preference for self-preservation. She was playing a part, frivolous and romantic, because she had been quite struck by the doctor when she first met him, and she liked the idea that she might be enticing him. She was doing what was expected of her, and this was why she let it go, the fact that the whole process seemed entirely counter to the notion of survival espoused by Charles Darwin, and to which she had attached herself so readily when the situation arose.

She did not say: but there are so many other things to *do* in this life!

She did not say: how impractical! or how ridiculous! or any of the other things she might have said if she were in different, female company.

She said only: how romantic!

She had forgotten about the unfinished letter to Henry Springton, half-written and still folded in her bag. It had slipped from her mind without a trace and now it came back to her with a jolt, and it surprised her that she had forgotten it so easily.

She took it out when they returned to the hotel and read

over the incidents she had already detailed. She chuckled to herself. Yes, she thought, it is rather amusing, even if I do say so myself.

She took up her pen to continue the letter. It could be finished that evening and then it would be done. There would be no need to be concerned with Henry Springton for the rest of the trip.

She read over what she had written once more to ensure fluidity of style, but this time she did not chuckle. The writer of the letter, whilst recognizable to her, seemed somehow distant, tired. It was her, but it was also not her. It was a reflection of her, detached and a little haughty. There was nothing true in the entire letter, which is not to say that there were any untruths, but she had not written a single word she really meant. There were only details, incidents; amusing perhaps, but external events rather than internal.

She wanted to write about the trip in the balloon, but she wanted to tell the truth. It had been so lonely up there, so cold and yet, at the same time, it had been immensely bright and colourful. And then there was Sally's illness, during which she had taken the girl's hand in her own and had felt a sudden longing in the depths of her stomach she had never felt before, and which she supposed was the yearning other women meant when they spoke of biology even though they did not know the first thing about fossil-hunting. It had passed, but she had understood, and it pleased her to have felt it.

She wanted to write about Thomas Cook and the train schedules, about Dr Leigh and the copulating eagles, but she could not write any of this to Henry Springton. It would give too much away. It would demand a proper response, and she realised it was this that she feared, although not exactly this. It was not that she feared he would notice her vulnerability. It was that he would not. She suspected there would be a letter awaiting her in the drawing room upon her return and it would be just as it always was, light and jolly and full of news but nothing real, nothing true, and it would disappoint her. 'All flourish and no substance,' George had said of Henry Springton when he and Ursula had announced their engagement, and he had been right.

Ursula Bridgewater allowed her pen to hover. For a moment she thought of crumpling up the letter and throwing it into the wastepaper basket beside the writing desk, but it seemed a shame to waste such an amusing account, and besides, she might like to have a record of the trip for later. She could send it to George. He would like it, she thought, and she picked up her pen and crossed out Henry's name at the top of the page and wrote instead: 'Dear Georgie'.

It gave the impression of scrappiness, but George would not mind. He would probably be pleased to receive it, even if he did not say so. He would not say so, of course, almost certainly. He did not talk about such things, but he noticed when she was feeling particularly restless; and he would sometimes put his hand on her arm and pat it, and it was comforting to Ursula that she could find herself seen through so gently.

So she wrote instead to her brother, even though she had sent him a telegram only the day before. She told him about the balloon, about Toby and the doctor with the splendid hands, and about Sally. 'She is not so much of a dormouse as I had originally thought,' she wrote, 'for I am certain that she thinks more than she says.'

She wrote that she had been gadding about Niagara Falls like a Red Indian. George would think she was teasing him, and she was a little, but she supposed she had been gadding. Three times she had taken tea with Toby O'Hara in the hotel parlour when Sally was too ill to accompany her, and once she had drunk beer with him over supper, unchaperoned. He had come up to their suite and they had smoked cigarettes at the end of Sally's bed. She did not mention this to George. There was nothing improper about it, after all. It was not romantic.

She wrote instead of Toby's flying machine, about the mechanics of it, the materials. 'I have seen into the future,' she declared, 'and it is made of bamboo and silk.' She found that the sensation of describing the machine to her brother was delightful, exquisite. She announced her intention to assist Mr O'Hara in the development of a more practical machine, perhaps with a steam engine. 'There are patents to apply for and designs to register,' she wrote, 'but I am quite capable of arranging paperwork.' And what a thing it would be to leave a legacy of flight! Toby O'Hara would be famous. Of course, she did not care for fame herself – oh no – but she desired it on Toby's behalf.

She imagined George's response. At first, she supposed he would be intrigued. He had attended the exhibition of the Royal Aeronautical Society at the Crystal Palace some years before when he had been visiting London on tea business, and he had been quite taken with the idea of it. There had been no actual flight at this event, except in the clockwork toy section, but it had seemed so close, almost graspable, that he would not be entirely against the prospect of investing in it.

But there was no comparison between the Crystal Palace Aeronautical Exhibition and Toby O'Hara – 'I suspect you offend yourself, ma'am' (how marvellous he was to say so!) – and his wonderful invention. Surely George would see that.

But then she remembered the dining room in Alexandra Grove, the streams of rain against the glass, and she imagined that her brother would probably just sigh as he read her letter over breakfast, shake his head at the prospect of all this gadding about, all this relentless enthusiasm, which she knew, she *knew*, he would attribute to the fact that she remained untouched by man. She ought to rein herself in, he had told her, if she wished to receive any further proposals, and she had nodded when he said this because she too had always assumed that she wanted a husband.

And yet, at the same time, she had also pondered: but is there a man, is there anybody at all, who will let me be just as I am?

Ursula sat at the writing desk in the International Hotel in Niagara Falls. She held her head erect and planted her feet firmly on the carpet. She read over the letter. It was a little messy, a little fevered. She supposed she could start it again, and it would not have the same alarming effect on her dear brother. But it was nearly time for dinner, and in any case she did not want to write it again. She was hungry, and she was thinking of the long, thin glass of golden beer she would order to go with her meat course. She folded the letter into quarters and neatly addressed the envelope, and as she did she smiled a wide, indecorous smile.

After all, she thought, I am Ursula Bridgewater. I can do what I like.

Speaking of Galilee

Like Dr Duncan Leigh, Sally had also been surprised by Ursula. 'How romantic it must be', she had exclaimed, 'to die for love!' Sally had puzzled at this dramatic streak in Ursula Bridgewater of which she had been previously unaware. She did not know that Ursula did not really mean what she said. What Sally did know, however, was that such an exclamation did not suit her. It seemed somehow incompatible. They did not seem to be the words of a woman who read Royal Society reports and attended lectures on German philosophy, and who knew that lightning had nothing to do with the wrath of God.

But it was not only this that had surprised Sally. It was also the fact that, for the first time since meeting Ursula Bridgewater, she had not entirely agreed with her. She had stood in the road with her arm clasped in Ursula's and she had thought: 'But is it?'

She had not said this. It was not her place. But she thought it now, as they sat together in the dining room of the hotel and Ursula ordered a drink with her dinner.

They sat opposite each other at a marble-topped table, small and round with gleaming cutlery. There was a large table in the middle of the room for a new touring party which had arrived earlier that day, and whose participants were to dine later after their evening steamboat trip to the bottom of the Falls. There were only seven other diners in the restaurant and there was no music as the band was booked to perform during the late sitting. But there were enough people to allow the possibility of a lull when Ursula's beer was delivered to the table.

'Would you like one, Walker?' Ursula asked, seeing how Sally's attention was taken by it.

'Oh no,' Sally said, even though it intrigued her. She liked the warmth of the liquid, the way it was the colour of toasted-wheat, but she could not drink it. Or more precisely, she would not. She would not want all these people to look at her with hovering forks and wry smiles.

'Are you sure? It is not wine but it is made from hops, and I am almost certain I saw hops growing in Galilee,' Ursula announced.

'Oh I could not, ma'am,' Sally whispered.

206

'Suit yourself,' Ursula said, and then paused. 'Now, speaking of Galilee, have I ever told you anything of my trip to Palestine?'

Sally cut her meat into squares. She listened as Ursula described the caravan across the desert, the tents and the tinned sardines and the robbery by vagabonds in the middle of the night on the outskirts of Jerusalem. She smiled attentively whilst trying to block the words out. She did not wish to imagine the site of the Crucifixion. There were wild roses and poppies all along the path Jesus had walked, Ursula told her, but Sally could not add this into the picture of Golgotha she already had in her mind. She had seen it in her dreams at the orphanage: the hill, the dark thunderclouds. She had seen the water pouring from the wound in Jesus's side, blood in his crown of thorns. She remembered the pictures on the walls of the orphanage, Jesus tearing at his breast, pointing mournfully at his bleeding heart. She sipped her water.

Ursula talked on and on. 'And of course, if you should go . . .' (But when? thought Sally. When would *I* ever go?) '. . . if you should go, you must remember to wear a white scarf over your face to stop the sand from stinging,' Ursula continued. 'You must observe how they face Mecca when they pray, and that their holy day is Friday. You must always carry a compass, but keep it away from iron. You must bring tinned sardines to eat in the desert, magnesium strips for looking at tombs, dried prunes for your bowel. These are the important things to remember.'

Sally picked at the food on her plate. She ate some cold salmon, a small white potato. She pressed her back against the chair and tried to concentrate. She wondered if Mavis, that previous lady's maid of whom Ursula was so proud, who had come on such a treat, had been given so much information. Could she remember it all? And did it scare her, Sally wondered, to hear such stories? Was she, too, afraid of the dark, of spiders and snakes and woodlice, of King Herod and the Passion, of falling? Probably not, Sally thought unhappily.

But later, as she lay in bed and watched the moonlight gathering in the corner of her room, Sally remembered the bald eagles, how they had tumbled and fallen from the sky. She remembered Ursula's outburst – 'How romantic, to die for love!' – and for a moment she thought that perhaps there was, after all, one thing she knew which Ursula Bridgewater did not. For back then Sally Walker knew, had always known, that dying for love was, in the end, just another way of dying, and there was nothing so romantic about that.

Fifteen

The Spellbinder

The concept of air-mindedness was an idea Toby O'Hara would return to years later during his business partnership with Ursula and George Bridgewater. It would become the driving principle behind his groundbreaking design of the Spellbinder Flying Machine, a pleasure ride, and the first of its kind in the world.

The Spellbinder would be installed in 1892 next to the helter-skelter between the promenade pier and the ferry landing stage at New Brighton beach, opposite Mr Fisher's tea shop. It would consist of a metal pole with twelve arms radiating from the top of it. From each arm would hang a small boat, each fitted with wings and propellers. When the pole spun around, fired by the two electric motors supplied by Messrs Sullivan and Droit of Southport, the boats would rise up and circle outwards at such a speed that their passengers, six in each boat, would be wedged against each other, wind-blown and immovable. There would be no seatbelts, no safety harnesses or bars, just a rotational force pinioning the pleasure-seekers of New Brighton to the outer edge of their boats and giving them the exhilarating sensation of flight.

It would make the people of England, as Toby would declare

in his speech at the opening of the machine, air-minded. It would be a masterpiece of its time, of any time.

However, this is jumping ahead a little. At the age of twenty, Toby O'Hara did not intend to become famous; he did not wish, as Ursula did on his behalf, for such things. He was air-minded, but only in the literal sense. He had yet to learn its figurative benefits. It would be a number of years before Toby understood Ursula's enthusiasm, and realised that it was, in fact, a legacy worth leaving, this hint of the possibility of flight.

Toby would indeed go with Ursula and Sally to Liverpool, but he would not go in order to become famous. He would go because George replied to his sister's telegram, suggesting that Toby might take a job in the tea factory, and design a more efficient tea-packaging machine. And Toby would accept because he would think that at least it would keep his feet on the ground. Although there would also be another reason.

Once across the Atlantic, Toby would go to Ireland to visit his pop's family, that sprawling, maple-syrup-haired heritage of whom he had heard so much when he was a child. He would expect to feel quite at home, and did not expect it to be so cramped, so small. He was tall, he knew that, but so too had his pop been tall. And so too were his pop's younger brothers, the ones he had left behind when he went to America, who had left Ireland as soon as they were old enough and gone instead to Liverpool and to Paisley, and had not returned. They were all tall, according to the aunts and children who remained. But the ones who would welcome him into their homes like the returning Prodigal Son, who would ruffle his hair and tell him he looked just like his pop and feed him on stew, bowls and bowls of it even though it was Lent, were not even as high as his shoulder.

He would tell them about his balloon and Niagara Falls,

about the salt plains of Utah and the steamships of the Atlantic, and they would look at him as if he had stepped out of a picture book. He would describe the balloon for them, and make a miniature version out of thin paper, rigged up over a cut-off tin as Judge Jake Gadston had once done on his pop's porch when Toby was sixteen years old. He would pour oil into the tin and set it on fire, and tell them to watch as the paper lantern took off, floating up and up until the edges of the paper caught fire, and it fell from the damp sky; a tumbling ball of light over the fields of Ulster.

A fallen archangel, his auntie would call it.

No, Toby would think, it is not. It is a balloon, a toy.

He would not stay in Ireland long. It would not be what he had imagined. He had thought all these people would be like his pop but they were not. Instead he would find himself longing to get back to his workshop in the factory and his tea-packaging designs.

It would, however, be whilst Toby was in Ireland that he would begin to develop the idea for the Spellbinder. There would be twin girls in the house where he would stay – cousins, or perhaps second cousins, Toby could not remember which – who would follow him everywhere. They were perhaps six or seven with long hair tied up in plaits, and they would cling to him, one on each arm, and shout at him to lift them higher, higher. This is how it would begin. Instead of lifting them, he would spin them, holding their two hands in one of his and lifting his arms out and turning his body until he could hold them almost horizontally, and it would feel as if he was making barely any effort at all.

'It's just like flying!' they would squeal dizzily.

Later, he would describe this process to Ursula, and he would draw a sketchy design of how it could be implemented by a machine. Whereas Toby would see that this method had the practical benefit of offering speed and exhilaration whilst also remaining effectively in the same place, Ursula would see its possibilities in terms of mass appeal. Such an experience could surely be offered to the industrial population of the north-west of England for the price of a train ticket between Liverpool and New Brighton. It would require only one piece of equipment and, once constructed, it need not be expensive to maintain. It would allow people to *do* something with their lives, even if they had only sixpence and half a day's holiday every three weeks. In short, it would provide the sensation of flying without the expense and the risks of engaging in actual flight, and it would be this which would, one day, become Toby O'Hara's legacy to the world.

It would be Ursula Bridgewater who would first urge him to make the Spellbinder, and later still it would become useful in Ursula Bridgewater's adopted cause of voting rights for women, both literally and figuratively, but this point is merely of historical interest. For Toby, the Spellbinder would be a job. The idea originated in a design, pure and simple, and it was because of this emotional detachment that, in Toby's mind, it would lack the urgency of his earlier cowshed construction. He would not feel anxious about it in the way that he now felt anxious about his flying machine. It would be a thing of great promise, of extraordinary engineering, but he would not worry about it, nor would he dream about it. He would show the designs to friends, arrange publicity for the opening day, and he would not mind. It would not be that he did not care, but that he would be able to see it for what it was in a way that he was unable to do for the flying machine in the cowshed: that intricate, delicate design into which he had poured all his energy, all his ambition, from the moment he had seen his mother fall from the sky.

So it would be an entirely different thing that Toby would invent one day, and which would give him the acclaim and riches that Ursula Bridgewater hoped for on his behalf. At the opening, he would dedicate it to his wife even though she would refuse to fly in it.

'I have flown twice in my life,' she would tell him, 'and that is quite enough for me.'

'Just once more,' he would plead, but she would fold her arms and refuse to be persuaded into one of the hanging metal boats.

But all this would come much later. The main thing to note at this stage is that Toby O'Hara would, indeed, one day be famous for flight, although not in the way Ursula anticipated in her letter to George.

Sixteen

A trot

It was on Dr Duncan Leigh's instructions that Toby O'Hara hired a carriage with a velvet seat for their excursion. The day was bright and crisp with a faint gust of wind. He had arranged to meet Sally and Ursula outside the International Hotel. They were going for a trot, he told Mr Watling, the young man whose job it was to hold the door for guests and assist them with their luggage. Mr Watling nodded. He rearranged his feet on the blue carpet, now a little threadbare in parts, and bowed in the manner required by the hotel manager.

This sudden formality made Toby nervous. He rubbed his hands together. The expedition was reckless. He knew that. His flying machine was a thing he had not thought to share with anybody until now. He had intended to build it alone, unwatched. He hardly understood the impulse which had led him to ask these two women to see it.

He looked up and saw Sally and Ursula walking towards him, Ursula leading at pace, as was her habit, with her umbrella tucked under her arm. She took Toby's proffered arm, and when he reached out to take her umbrella, she did not stiffen as she might when her brother attempted such courtesies in England, but handed it to him quite naturally. She seemed surprised to see it, as if she had not realised she had brought it, and she allowed it to be slotted out of the way under the velvet seat next to the picnic basket.

Sally's hand was warm in his as she stepped into the carriage behind Ursula. There was a sense of celebration in the air, of cakes and oranges and potatoes roasting in tins. Toby sat in the driver's seat at the front of the carriage and smiled at the two women, a too-broad smile, and the air around him seemed oddly fragrant.

Once they had left the town, the fields by the roadside became sprouting and sappy, dark green against brown earth. Toby turned around at intervals, pointing out landmarks and good fishing spots. He told them of the time he had found a brown bear in the woods behind his house when he was just twelve years old and had hit it on the nose with his fishing rod. He smiled when he said this, but the reason for his smile was complicated. It was not just the memory of the bear which was, now he thought about it, mildly terrifying, but also the way Sally was looking at him: wide-eyed and admiring.

They turned off the track and into a long, sloping field. The cowshed stood at the top of the ridge on the far side. Toby's hands trembled as he steered the carriage towards it. In his mind, it was – there was no other word for it – majestic. It was a gleaming stable for his wondrous invention.

But now, as they approached, he felt his stomach lurch to look at it. He saw, as he had not observed before, how the shed slanted in the sunlight, its white-washed walls discoloured and sun-dried. It had a corrugated iron roof, untidy with rust and nails, and there was a bird's nest in the gutter. The paint on the door was flaky and mottled, which gave an impression of dreariness, of a common shed with dirt on the floor and a smell of damp straw.

In that moment, he no longer saw it as a reflection of

his own resourcefulness, mirrored in the perfect slotting system of the wings, in the nifty rudder function, in the neat and meticulous graphs showing upward drift on the x-axis and air resistance on the y. He forgot with what delight he had fixed the propeller to the front of the machine, how he had breathed upon it, waxed it with his hot breath, before polishing it with a dishcloth. He saw none of that now, only a huge door with rusted hinges which he would have to open by standing with his back to it and kicking backwards like a horse; and behind that, a heavy, ridiculous clump of machinery.

They drew nearer, trundling across the field in the carriage. There were thistles in the field with small white flowers. Toby wished to speak, to cover the sudden quiet of anticipation. He might have mentioned the farmer's habit of letting the field lie fallow for a year, or the sheep who sometimes wandered in to feed, but he did not trust his own voice. He unbuttoned his collar and tugged at the scarf around his neck. There were two eagles circling above them, their huge wings spread and their beaks curved. Toby did not notice them. He pulled on the reins to stop the horses.

'Have we arrived, Mr O'Hara?' Ursula asked from the back of the carriage.

'Yes,' he said. 'Yes, this is it. You will think it ridiculous, I'm afraid.' And he was afraid. He had not expected to be so, but now that he was, he did not know what he should do. It was a terrible effort to talk. The carriage clattered beneath him. There was a stumping of hooves, defiant and awkward. They will be leaving soon, he thought. It does not matter what they think.

And yet it did matter, because he had built it up in his mind. He wanted to be able to square up in his usual manner but he could not find the energy. He stepped down and gestured towards the cowshed, but his arms were heavy, as if the air had condensed and thickened, and he was moving them now through water. He kicked backwards against the door to loosen the latch, and then dragged it open through the grass so that there would be enough light for them to see. He stood back and sighed. He leant his head against the door.

'Here it is,' he said.

'But Mr O'Hara,' Ursula gasped, 'it's the most wonderful thing I have ever seen.'

'It's not finished yet,' he mumbled.

'But it's perfect. It's so elegant.' Ursula walked up to the nose and touched it. She ran her hand along the bamboo frame, pushed the propeller through a quarter-turn. 'It is ingenious,' she said.

He shuffled his feet in the grass. 'Do you really think so?'

Sally stood back from the machine and her expression was inscrutable, curious. He could not place it.

Ursula fixed him with a look, her neck held perfectly straight. 'Mr O'Hara,' she said loudly, almost insistently, 'I am not in the habit of pretending to be impressed by things that do not impress me. So yes, I really do think so.'

Toby smiled. He took a step closer to the machine. There was a faint gust of wind, a rustling of leaves outside, and a patch of light falling on the tip of the propeller so that the front of the machine looked suddenly grand, as if it were illuminated from within. It was not so bad, in fact. He walked around it thoughtfully.

'Perhaps,' suggested Ursula, 'we might see it in the daylight?'

Toby looked at her and nodded. He pulled the door open and wedged it ajar with a stone, and then he wheeled the machine out onto the field. There were clumps of grass

217

which caught under its wheels, but he pushed harder and soon there was a glistening track in the late-morning dew.

'This is the lever for adjusting the wings,' he explained, as he bumped and jostled the machine into the field so that there would be room to attach the wings. His voice sounded eager once more, almost booming in his ears. 'They are fixed planes but they must be adjusted so that they face into the wind. And this is where I will affix the tail, when I have completed it.'

He explained every detail as he remembered his pop explaining it to him. Not just the mechanics of it, but also the principles. He described his method. He felt the wind rise and fall against his bare arms where he had rolled up his sleeves. He told them it was a sublime piece of audacity, and then he laughed because he now knew what it meant, and it was, it was. But so, also, was this: the way he allowed his hand to brush against Sally's arm as he pointed out the different features of the machine, the way she leant in so close he could smell the milk-white sweetness of her skin.

'But tell me, if you anticipate overcoming the total weight of the machine simply by achieving a certain speed,' Ursula asked, taking out a small notepad and pen, 'what speed will you need to achieve to overcome gravity?'

Toby looked at her. He frowned. 'There is also upward drift,' he said, 'which helps. If the wind blows directly this way,' he stopped and pointed uphill, 'and I take off down-hill into the east, then the wind should catch beneath the wings and it will lift quite easily. It is not all gravity and resistance.'

He looked at Sally and smiled.

Sally smiled back. Her face was flushed and agitated. She lifted her hand and pressed it to her forehead.

'Are you unwell?' Toby asked suddenly.

'Oh no,' Sally said. 'I am not at all unwell.'

'Then what is it?' He saw a flicker of panic in her eyes before she hid them from him once more, turning away so that when she spoke, her voice was so quiet that he had to lean forwards to hear her. He thought of his pop bending down to talk to his mother, his hands on his knees.

'It is just that I think I would not be brave enough to fly such a machine,' she confessed. 'I am not even envious – I wish I were for then there would be some hope – but I am not.'

Toby looked at her. Her words, so light, so soft, seemed to press into him. Cold crept up his arms. He saw that she had been biting at her lower lip so that her lips had become red and swollen, and he felt, for a brief, inexplicable moment, suddenly scared of what he was going to do.

'No,' he said, shaking his head a little too hard, as if dislodging bathwater from his ears. 'It is quite safe. There is the parachute.'

Sally nodded. 'Of course,' she said. 'The parachute.'

'That reminds me,' Ursula interrupted, looking up from her notebook, 'I have been thinking about it and I have come to the conclusion that you should register the patent of your parachute design under a separate patent from the flying machine.'

He hesitated. 'But the flying machine is not my invention,' he said. 'It is my pop's.'

'But is it the same?' she asked.

Toby looked at it. He tilted his head to one side. He squinted and then closed his eyes. When he did, he saw his pop sanding a bamboo frame in his workshop, the bat dangling from the ceiling, and he saw his mother waving at him from the air. Mist, he thought, there was mist on that morning, and he pulled it down in his memory like a white silk curtain might be pulled across a stage to give the impression of fog. 'No,' he said, walking back into the shed to collect the wings from where they were propped up against the wall. 'I have tried to make it the same – I have used the same prototype,' here he gestured towards the stuffed bat, balanced on the windowsill of the cowshed so that it stared outwards, 'but it is not exact.'

Ursula did not look at the bat. She stopped, frowned, wrote something in her notebook.

Sally, however, did look. The bat was tilted to one side, its stripped wing facing out into the room. Its eyes were bright red. She shuddered, and took a step away from it.

Toby saw the shudder. He was not well-versed in images of the Devil – he had not grown up with oil paintings of the martyred saints surrounding his bed, nor had he been obliged to attend chapel every morning before sunrise and watch the dawn break through stained glass portrayals of the flickering coals of hell – but he knew the reason for the shudder. He had often felt it too, a shivery stillness in the air around the bat, a dense, oxygenless vacuum which he had taught himself to ignore. But this was not the cause of Sally's shudder. It could not be.

'In what sense,' Ursula chimed into the silence, 'is it different?'

Toby shrugged. 'I cannot be sure, but I think the wings are a little longer. And there is the parachute.'

'And your pop,' Ursula said, 'did he register a patent?'

Toby looked at her. 'I don't know,' he said. 'I never asked.'

Ursula nodded. She made a note of this in her notebook. Edmund O'Hara, Holloway Creek, 1862. 'Perhaps, if it's not too presumptuous, you might let me see your designs. I have some experience in the arena of patents and I should like to be of assistance.'

Toby shrugged. He did not mind. If she wanted to see the drawings, then he would give them to her.

'You are too modest,' she told him. 'It is a grand talent you have. You must not hide your light under a bushel.'

Toby smiled at her. He knew she was wrong. The sun was suddenly bright, immense in the morning sky. He squinted and looked away. It is not a talent, he thought. It is a legacy.

But now, in the company of these two women, Toby did not wish to admit to such a thing. He walked back to the shed to fetch the wings, and then he attached them to the machine, propping them up with firewood so that they would not sag. He put stones in front of the wheels to prevent the machine from slipping forwards. He demonstrated how the parachute would be nailed to the junction of the tail with the pilot's board, so that if the machine flew too high he could simply jump off. He slotted and wiped and adjusted everything to perfection so that it matched exactly the bat he had inherited from his pop. At the top of the field, he looked down upon its long slope of grass, at the nailed-together boards of wood which formed a smooth stretch of solid ground for launching.

Sally and Ursula stood next to him, one on each side, their long dresses ruffling in the breeze. Sally reached out her hand and placed it for a brief moment on his arm, and he felt a tingle along his spine. He felt the anticipation (of what? of flight? of something else?) as a glittering sharpness in his stomach. Ursula shook her head and murmured that it was quite wonderful.

No, thought Toby, it is not wonderful. It is just necessary. That is all.

It was almost complete. It needed only a tail and then it would be finished. He had built the frame of the tail already. It was a box, three feet wide and four feet deep. The oiled silk had been cut to size and he would sew it the following day. Toby licked his finger and held it up to the breeze.

The weather vane on the roof was pointing mostly towards the west, but still flickering northwards. He looked up at it.

'Is it blowing in the right direction?' Sally asked.

'No,' he said. 'Not quite. But almost.'

So, water

Sally was alone in the hotel room. The shutters were flung back to reveal a cold, bright Sunday afternoon and there were bells ringing in the distance. It had snowed overnight; a late, unseasonal fall which had melted on the roads but still clung thickly to the roofs of the buildings in decorative caps of shimmering ice.

Ursula had gone to a service at the local Baptist church because she wished to write something on religion in her journal. 'I suspect it will be lengthy, Walker,' Ursula had said, and Sally had assumed she meant the journal entry rather than the service, but now she did not know. This service would later form the basis for Ursula's paper submitted to the Royal Society on the influence of the Republic on American theology, and which was returned to her unpublished when she sent it under her own name, and was accepted with a handsome payment when she resubmitted it, without her brother's knowledge, under the name of George Bridgewater.

'Should it truly be the case,' she would write in a letter to *The Times* when detailing this turn of events, 'that words on a page can change their value according to the gender of the person holding the pen?'

This incident would also prompt the creation of the Liverpool Movement for Women's Suffrage, headed by Ursula and supported by George. It would be the trigger, although the seed had been planted long before that. In her memoirs, she would cite the incident with the head of the Bengal tiger in the annual Christmas play, but really, it was not until she came to America that she began to think seriously about the vote as a means for change. In Niagara Falls, these thoughts were at a formative stage in Ursula's consciousness. They were still mixed in with those earlier thoughts of witchcraft and muskets and burnt saucepan handles, but were soon to be thinned out so that they could take root and flourish unhindered.

Sally, meanwhile, was instructed to rest. 'It will be good for your head, Walker,' Ursula had announced as she whirled out of the room, leaving *Robinson Crusoe* on the table next to the bed for Sally to read if she liked, even though it was the Sabbath.

Sally picked it up and opened it. She knew she should not. She remembered Sunday afternoons at the orphanage, where silence was to be observed while the girls read the Bible or, occasionally, if Sister Jude was on supervisory duty, the exotic tales of the Missionary Willie Anderson of Calabar.

A sheaf of papers fell from the book onto her lap. She did not recognise them at first. There was an envelope amongst them addressed to Ursula Bridgewater, and marked from the United States Patent Office. It was already open – it could do no harm, Sally thought, just to peep – and she took the letter from the envelope. Ah-ha, Sally thought. The patent was confirmed as registered in 1862 by Edmund O'Hara of Holloway Creek, New England. According to the office records, a further application had been made to withdraw the patent in 1863, but no return address had been given. Perhaps, it was suggested, the respondent knew of the applicant in which case the patent application might be returned forthwith?

Sally looked at the papers on her knee. She closed them back into *Robinson Crusoe* and sat down heavily in the armchair. She did not want to look at them. She did not want to see how Toby's pop had plotted and constructed the too-heavy thing which would take his wife from him and tear at his son's heart as it fell. It was a gift to her, Toby had said, and she must have wished for it. She would not have planned for it to crash, of course. But she should have known.

There was a short pause. Slowly, Sally opened the book once more. She unfolded the drawings and laid them out on the table. Her head was hot. There were people talking in the corridor outside her room. She could hear their voices rising and falling, shrill with sudden laughter.

There were drawings and charts. She could not make them out. There was a picture of the bat, beautifully sketched in faint pencil so that there was very little resemblance between this man's vision of it and the horrid, mangy creature she had seen in the cowshed. There were outlines of the wings, although they were perhaps, as Toby had said, a little shorter, and there was a plan of the tail. There were numbers and symbols. There were scribblings on air resistance and upward drift and friction. The equations were long and spidery. She read them aloud, and it was while she did this that she became aware of the fact that there was a constant in the equations which she could not place. 'T', she read and continued on, hardly noticing it. 'T', she read again, and this time she did notice it, but she did not stop. There it was, in every equation.

She turned to the final drawing, an exquisite sketch of a flying machine in the shape of a bat with a short-haired figure on board. It was the finished version. It was marked as *Figure 10*, but this was not how she knew it to be the finished version. She knew this because Edmund O'Hara had drawn a huge exclamation mark along the side of the paper, all the way down. She looked more closely. The sketch of the figure was quite detailed. It was smiling and its arms were outstretched in delight. There were wisps of pencil in his hair, suggesting wind, flight. And it was labelled 'T'.

'Toby!' she cried out loud to the hotel room as she would not have done if there had been anyone to hear her. She pushed back her chair and went to the window, pressing her head against the glass, her teeth biting at her lip, picking, peeling. A dusting of snow whirled gently from the trees, falling on the road and on the deserted stalls of the peanut-sellers and on the women's bonnets as they returned from church. She heard the water battering the rocks as it fell. Her throat was thick with the dust of fever. She gulped some water, and put the glass down sharply on the table, a smart, practical noise amongst all this mess, and then she swept the papers into *Robinson Crusoe* and, tucking it into her walking cape, she stepped out into the corridor.

*

He was in the garden of his lodgings when Sally arrived. The snow was shovelled into heaps along the sides of the paths. There was no wind at all, just the soft crunch of feet and the slow drip of melting snow. He was making a snowman, one big oblong of ice on top of another, as high as his shoulder. The snowman was bright white, with small black twigs and frozen leaves rolled into its compacted body. Toby had smoothed its joints into a thick, finger-printed neck, and given him buttons for eyes and a stick for a mouth.

'Here,' he said, handing her a small apple. 'Will you hold this? It's for the nose.'

She took the apple and watched as he scooped out a hollow for it in the middle of the snowman's face. She felt breathless. She could not concentrate on snowmen. She put the apple into the pocket of her cape.

She thought: this is none of my business. And then: Perhaps he knows already? 'I have to show you something,' she said. 'Could we perhaps sit down?'

She walked towards a bench in the garden. It was still wet with snow and Toby stopped her, taking out a handkerchief to wipe the seat. He gestured for her to sit down and she did; not in the section he had wiped, but in the wet. It seeped into the seat of her dress but she did not notice. She held the drawings close to her chest, pressed still into Ursula's book. Toby sat down next to her. Nothing was said for a moment. They looked at each other, nervous, expectant: a boy and a girl; and the snowman smiled at them, a twiggy, noseless smile.

'No,' he said when she handed the drawings to him, pressed them onto him so that he could see for himself. 'It was my mother who flew. My pop drew them but he drew them for her. It was a gift. It's just a mistake.'

And when he said this, he truly believed it. It must have been a mistake. He was too certain of it, he had placed too much upon it, for his belief to simply fade. He pressed his palms against his eyelids, as if by pressing hard enough he might be able to force this new knowledge back into the blackness so that he would not have to think about it.

It would not go.

He remembered, as he had not done for years, the fuss caused by the arrival of the bat in the cardboard box, and his pop carrying it down to the workshop after it was banished from the house. He pictured his mother simmering at the kitchen window, standing next to the potato pot on the stove, while his pop hammered in the shed until it was too dark to see.

He remembered the jam she had made in huge saucepans at the end of that last summer, her face small and cross and her mouth sticky with anger. She had piled the furniture into corners and hung the rugs from the trees, and he and his mother had laughed as they beat the rugs with sticks, dust billowing out in puffs of air. There was the smell of sawdust; that warm, childish smell his pop had carried around with him beneath his fingernails and in the cracks of his skin.

Then a memory of another pair of hands, his mother running to him in the dawn, picking him up and hugging him to her, her thumbs sharp under his arms, dragging him away from the machine. And then later, those same hands waving at him from the air.

'I'm sorry I'm sorry I'm sorry,' his pop had said.

Toby sat on the bench next to Sally and pressed his hands into his eyes. He rubbed at them, until he saw sparks of white in the blackness, and it was only then, when he opened his eyes and found the pale patches of white still imprinted on his eyes from where he had rubbed them, that he knew it was all true.

He stood up and walked away from her, patting her shoulder awkwardly as he turned from her so that she would not think him rude. She watched him trudge into his lodgings, his snowy feet trailing ice across the mat. The door swung behind him but it did not quite shut. Sally stood up and followed him to the house. She knocked on the door, too timidly, so that he would not have heard anyway, and then she pushed the door open.

His lodgings were small with a sloping roof. There was

a rug on the stone flags of the floor and a bed pressed up against the wall, its sheets white and smooth. Toby was standing at the window with his back to her. Next to him on the shelf were plates and jugs and pots which she would have expected to be dusty but which were not. They were bright ceramic, aquamarine and lavender. There was an oak table in the centre of the room and three chairs which did not match, and there was a knotted loaf laid out on a square of muslin.

Toby did not turn his head. Outside, the sky was yellow and bright. The room glowed as the light washed across it, but he stood at the window and did not turn. Sally did not know what to do. Please, she thought. Please what? She clasped her hands together. She laced and unlaced her fingers.

Toby sniffed.

Sally looked up at the sound. She knew its cause, saw his neck, his lovely shoulders drooping. She did not know what to do and yet she stepped forward. She smelt snow on him, white and cold. She touched his arm. He turned. His face was confused, crumpled, and his eyes were wet with tears. So, she thought. Water.

Standing on her tiptoes, she reached out her finger and wiped it gently along the bottom of his eyes, as if the tears were her own, and then she folded her hand around her finger so that she could feel his tears against her skin, a shimmering wetness in the palm of her hand.

Her worried lips

In Genesis it was written that God created a firmament in the midst of waters to divide the waters from the waters. And He created fowl to fly above the earth in the firmament of heaven, and creatures to creep upon the earth and whales to live in the sea.

But his mother had waved to him from the air and her face had fogged in his memory.

His pop had hung a fruit bat from the ceiling and told him it was a sublime piece of audacity.

And Toby had strung a basket to a balloon and he had floated above the creeping earth, rising through the firmament from one water to another, and he had seen the sun set twice in one day.

He thought: you fool.

Sally had left his lodgings not thirty minutes earlier, and he hurried now along the slushy street, past the cobbled yards and rows of lodging houses. It did not matter that he could stand and look at the machine he had made and know that it would fly. He was certain that it would. Or at least, there was no reason why it would not. This was not the problem. The problem was that he no longer cared.

He carried his designs under his arm, rolled up into a tube and tied with string to present to Ursula Bridgewater. There were charts and graphs and drawings, carefully drawn, meticulously plotted. He wanted nothing more to do with them. They were just like the drawings his pop had sent to the Patent Office, returned now to Ursula. They were astonishingly alike, in fact, except for the parachute. (Why had his pop not thought of that?) There were differences in their methods, certainly, but he saw in his pop's drawings the same blinkered passion he saw in his own.

He suddenly felt very tired. He had wasted so much time, so much energy in building a machine just like his mother's so that he could know, finally, why she had done it. And he had thought that maybe, if he could only find the answer to that one small question, he would be able to forget that terrible sound, that wave of her hand, that pitch into eternity.

But he had been wrong. It had not been her dream after all. It had been his pop's, and his pop had been building it for him. Why didn't you tell me? he thought.

He walked faster now, turning down the main street with its gaudy postcard-sellers and toffee-apple stands. It was not a real place. He felt this strongly, as he had always done. It was glitzy, artificial. Even the waterfall was too extravagant, too loud. There was such a rush of water. It drew the crowds and they stood with their mouths wet and open, their eyes glazed with the showiness of it all – but it was of no real use to anyone. It was an inflated balloon of bright silk, insubstantial and weightless.

He walked up the steps of the hotel with the tube of drawings in his hand, tapping them against his palm. He paced the lobby with nervous, too-wide steps. He would burn the machine. He should burn the drawings too. He wound his fingers through his hair, curling it and then smoothing it out. No, he would give them to Ursula as she had asked. He had no need of them for himself but he had heard of this English craving for progress, for inventions, and he wanted to do her a kindness. A maid led him up the stairs to the second floor and along the corridor.

Sally opened the door. 'Oh,' she said, her eyes widening in surprise.

'Is that our Mr O'Hara?' Ursula called from the dressing room, where she was preparing to go out. Dr Duncan Leigh had invited her to take tea at his house, and she had already changed her dress three times that afternoon, and was still not quite satisfied with her appearance. 'Has he brought his designs?'

'Yes, I have,' Toby called back, lifting the tube of drawings and handing them to Sally. 'All of them.'

'I'll be ready in just a moment. I have something wonderful to show you which arrived yesterday from the Patent Office.'

Sally looked up at him. He noticed that there was an odd colour in her cheeks. 'Have you not told her that you brought them to me?' he asked.

She shook her head.

'Well, it is of no consequence,' he whispered, pushing the envelope towards her. 'I have no need for them. Miss Bridgewater may keep them if she wishes.'

'But I thought you might want to have them,' she said.

Toby looked at her and shook his head. 'Oh no, I am done with flying machines.'

There was a pause. Sally looked down at the drawings in her hand. 'But your machine?' she asked. 'It's ready. It's finished.'

'It is ready to fly, yes. It would fly. But it's not going to. I cannot do it.' He paused and looked away from her.

'But you have put so much work into it,' she said.

Oh how ridiculous she was! She was practically willing him to fly. Why? Why, when she had run to show him the drawings so that he would not get into that stupid machine which would surely kill him, did she now wish to persuade him against giving it up?

'Yes,' he said. 'But that doesn't matter. The work was not a struggle.'

Sally looked at him. She thought: it is a stupid machine anyway. It is not a grand and noble thing. You will break both your legs. You will die like your mother and it will all have been a waste. She lowered her eyes. 'I should not have shown you the drawings.'

'Oh no,' Toby said, shaking his head, smiling. 'I'm glad. But I'm not going to fly it. I will burn it instead.'

He heard Ursula drawing back the curtains of the

dressing room, the sound of a window being opened. 'The snow is melting,' she called out. 'You can hear it dripping.'

Toby leant towards Sally. 'Please, do not mention this to Miss Bridgewater. She will try to dissuade me and I do not wish to be dissuaded.' He took a breath and called through to Ursula once more. 'Miss Bridgewater, I have an appointment to attend. I shall leave the drawings with Miss Walker.'

'Oh, but I must see it once more, to check the measurements for the patent,' Ursula called out from the dressing room.

'Oh,' he said. 'Must you really?'

'Yes, yes. Perhaps tomorrow? Did you finish the tail?'

'Yes,' he said. 'Tomorrow then.'

He looked at Sally and she looked back at him, and then she nodded. He ran his hands up his arms and stepped back from the door into the corridor. His fingers were blue. He tilted his head to one side. 'Thank you,' he whispered, and then he turned to walk down the corridor.

Sally closed the door. She stood with her hand on the doorknob, waiting. It is a stupid machine, she thought again. It is dangerous. It is reckless, and Ursula is entirely wrong about it, just as she was wrong about the eagles. He would only die like his mother and I could not bear it.

But then she remembered his face when she showed him the drawings, that droplet of saltwater glistening in the palm of her hand. She closed her eyes. She thought of her mother holding her hand on the promenade, and then of that terrible day, horses' hooves stamping on the pavement; a soft, white arm, and lovely fingers reaching for her.

She felt a great sob of hysteria rising up inside her, wet and unbearable; a huge great wave threatening to swamp her in its own vertiginous depths. She thought of how she had knelt at the feet of the Virgin Mary in the chapel of the orphanage and watched the flickering candles against those tiny blue feet, willing herself not to cry, not to hit her pillow with her fists, not to cling to Mr Fisher's waist, not to remember.

Ursula was humming a nursery rhyme in the dressing room. Quite suddenly, Sally opened the bedroom door and began to run along the corridor, then down the stairs and out into the street. 'Wait,' she called. He did not hear her. Her voice was too quiet, too timid. She took a deep breath and closed her eyes. She tipped her head back and then she said it again, louder this time, almost a shout, and was immediately embarrassed. She hunched her shoulders against the excruciating echo of her own voice coming back to her. 'Wait!'

He heard her this time and he did wait, turning in the hotel garden. Sally walked up to him, casually, as if she had not just shouted at him, had not thrown her head back like a fishwife at the docks and hallooed at him. I must say what I think, she thought, trying to rid herself of the sense of rising panic. Why should I not? She crossed her arms across her chest.

The garden was a maze of snow-frosted privet hedges, of tangled arches and soft shoots curling around high stone walls. Sally walked past him to the side of the hotel. He would follow her. She knew that, and yet she did not quite expect it. She heard his footsteps on the path behind her.

'Don't burn it,' she said suddenly, halting by the wall of the hotel.

He turned away from her and looked at the ground, but his foot no longer tapped, and she noticed this now, the absence of noise, of movement. He shook his head. 'I have to. It's foolish.'

Yes, she thought, it is, but it is no more foolish than this: that I have never done anything in my life until now; that Mr Fisher used to talk to me about my mother and I would not listen; that he arranged all this for me and I could not thank him, I could not even look at him, because I refused to be reminded of her. I covered my ears and my eyes and I would not think about any of it, and I pretended it was because I am practical. But it is not that. It is because I am afraid. I am afraid of my own giddiness.

'No,' she said. 'It isn't.'

Toby watched her. He saw the flush of her cheeks, the new brightness of her eyes. He tried to make his voice sound lighter than he felt. 'I cannot fly it now. I will show it to Miss Bridgewater, but then I will burn it.'

Sally uncrossed her arms and crossed them again. The hem of her dress was wet where it brushed the snow. She did not understand her own agitation. Perhaps I love him, she thought, but the thought was hazy in her mind. She heard the roar of the Falls behind her and she forgot for a moment where she was, and put her hand to her forehead because she thought the noise was coming from inside her head. Toby leant forward and gently caught hold of Sally's hand.

Look, she thought deliriously, *I see the heavens opened.*

Toby stepped closer and took her in his arms, bending down as if he was going to kiss her cheek. He brushed his cheek against hers, and then his lips against her cheek. He caught the edge of her worried lips with his. She felt her spine slacken, felt his hands on her back. He hesitated, and then he kissed her again, this time directly on the lips. He ran his hands up her body, into the smooth softness of her waist, her neck, her hair.

He stopped, moved his head away from hers, touched her neck with his fingers. Sally did not move. She knew she should but she could not. She felt blood creeping up her neck, into her cheeks, her lips. She closed her eyes. She thought of her mother's bright white blouse against the cobblestones. She thought of Mr Fisher and Sister Jude and the Virgin Mary appearing to her in a window.

She pressed her hands into Toby's back. He kissed her again and this time she kissed him back. She knew it was wrong and yet she could not help it. She bit at him, tugged at his lips, and she could not stop. She did not understand it. She felt dizzy. Her head was light, and she felt that familiar whirling sensation of falling, and it was for this reason more than any other that she did what she did. It was entirely involuntary. She lifted both her hands and placed them flat against his chest, and she pushed him away.

A breath of snow

Dr Leigh was sitting in the lobby of the hotel when Sally returned. He noticed the small furrow between her eyebrows, the redness of her lips, the odd heat in her neck. He watched her stop, place her hands on the desk, and ask if there were any messages for Miss Bridgewater. The girl was distracted. He saw it in her manner. Her cheeks had taken on a feverish flush which seemed to come and go as she waited for the telegram to be folded and handed over to her, the colour never quite reaching the surface but coming in waves under her pale skin. Dr Leigh had not, until this moment, noticed how pretty she was. He had not noticed her eyes, large and sad, and made even more attractive by this new colour. It was not illness, he could see that. He had seen it in women before, this sense of fluctuating, of coming and going internally.

He did not call out to her but remained seated in the armchair next to the fire, his newspaper resting on his lap while he waited for Miss Bridgewater. He had resolved to

235

ask her today. It was all planned. He would point out the cherry tree in the garden, mention the brickwork around the door, and suggest a slice of stem ginger cake which he had made himself. He would woo her with his home, and then she would be unable to refuse.

Sally did not see him. She walked through the lobby and up the hallway, her hand pressed against her cheek. She felt breathless. Her throat hurt terribly and her palms ached where she had pushed Toby away. She had not meant to. She had pressed her body into his and had kissed his lips while she plucked his white cotton shirt from his trousers until she could feel the goose bumps on his skin.

Had they been spotted? If Ursula knew, perhaps she might send her away, back across the Atlantic to the orphanage and all those long miserable days, each one the same as the one before. Sent *home*, she thought, although she no longer knew where that was. Her mind remained blank, and although she could still summon the image of the orphanage, of the landing stage, of the beach at New Brighton, none of these quite fitted the word.

Ursula was preparing to go out when Sally entered the room. She was wearing her green shawl and holding her umbrella. Long drafts of cold sunshine blew into the room, and the pale carpet glistened in the light. The plans Toby had left for Ursula to inspect were on the writing desk, thin rolls of creamy paper, covered in pencil marks. Ursula stood in front of the mirror, adjusting a white fur hat which she wore high on the very top of her head.

'There you are!' Ursula exclaimed. 'What do you think? They told me it was wolf skin!'

Sally nodded, widening her eyes and sticking out her lip a little to suggest considered approval. 'There was a message for you at the desk, ma'am.'

'Ah-ha,' Ursula said, opening it and holding it out in

front of her. She smiled as she read it. 'It's from my brother. He wishes you a speedy recovery, dear.'

'That's very kind of him, ma'am,' Sally murmured.

'And he wants to meet our Mr O'Hara. I suggested in my last telegram that we should invest in this machine of his.'

Sally looked at her. She had not known Ursula had even suggested such a thing. But of course she had – all that interest in his plans, his calculations, it all made sense. But surely now he would not wish to go to Liverpool. He had not created his machine for money or fame or for showing to Englishmen. He had made it for himself. He had made it for his mother. But Sally had ruined it for him.

'Ma'am,' Sally began tentatively, 'do you think it will fly?'

Ursula looked at her. She saw the frown in the girl's forehead, a small wishbone mark between her eyebrows. She smiled at her, and lowered the telegram. She gestured towards the plans, the pencil markings which Sally might once have seen as brave and clever, but which were now pointless because they were built on an untruth. No, not an untruth exactly. A mistruth.

'Walker, I have studied those plans. In the normal course of events, I would say that man was not put on this earth to fly. But our Mr O'Hara is different. There are some people in this world who do not have to obey the normal rules to which everybody else is obliged to adhere. We, by which I mean you and I and everybody else, are obliged by gravity to walk with our two feet on the ground. Not both at once, of course. That would be impractical. But in general we must adhere, both in theory and in practice. But Mr O'Hara is different.'

'Yes ma'am,' Sally said, while Ursula paused for dramatic effect.

'So to answer your question, no, I do not *think* it will fly. I *know* it will. I am certain of it. There is no reason why it should not. All the figures add up. The materials are light and well put-together. It is perfect. And he believes in it. And isn't it wonderful, that he will have done such a thing, that he will have taught the rest of us such a thing? How many people can say as much, and at such a young age?'

Sally nodded. She tried to smile but she could not quite do it.

'I have always said,' Ursula concluded with an expansive sweep of her arm, 'that one must *do* something with one's life. And he has.'

Sally thought: but it isn't perfect, because it is all wrong. He thought he was building something else, and now it is only a flying machine. It is not what he intended. It is simply the shell of it.

('Do you know how it feels,' he had asked, 'to need to know something?')

She could not focus her eyes. The carpet swayed in front of her. She sat down and took a deep breath. She had promised she would not tell and she had thought she would not. He was right, Ursula would be disappointed, and she would try to persuade him to fly it.

Sally was quite used to secrets, to dealing with things alone. Had she cried when her mother died? Had she knelt at Mr Fisher's feet and begged him, on her birthday, at Christmas, to take her away from the orphanage because she was unhappy? Had she ever so much as sighed, stamped her small foot, uttered a single word of need to all those nuns, telling them that she was so lonely and could they please, please, just once, pick her up and hold her? No. She had not. She had been perfectly quiet, perfectly calm. She had kept it all to herself and she had not been hysterical about it.

She took a deep breath. It was ridiculous, she knew – it was not her secret after all – but she could not carry it along with her own. It was too much for her. She knew he would be making a mistake to burn it. She was unaccustomed to such judgements, but she knew she was right. She saw it in him more easily than she saw it in herself, and it was because of this, because she could not bear to see him cast aside his beautiful bamboo-and-silk-dream, that she decided to confess.

'He will not fly it, ma'am.'

'Of course he will.'

'He will not.'

'But why?'

'There were some drawings.'

'These, I know. They are right here, on the table.' Ursula pointed at them with her umbrella.

'No, I mean the other ones. The ones from the Patent Office. I found them.'

'Oh?'

Sally paused. She felt her stomach contract a little. 'I showed them to him.'

'And?'

'He thought his father . . .'

'His pawp,' Miss Bridgewater corrected, her voice taking on an American drawl.

'Yes, his pop. He thought his pop built it for his mother. But he didn't. It was meant for Toby. His mother flew it instead.'

'Oh.' Ursula paused for a moment. 'I see.'

Sally nodded. 'I showed him the pictures. He will not fly it now. He is quite set upon it.'

'Have you tried, Walker?'

Sally nodded. She did not trust herself to look directly at Ursula. Her skin burned. 'Yes ma'am,' she whispered.

'Indeed,' said Ursula. She looked at Sally, and noticed for the first time the flush of the girl's cheeks. The umbrella swung thoughtfully. Ursula paused, smiled, grinned. 'Then it is perfectly simple. Someone must fly it for him.'

'I beg your pardon, ma'am?'

'You, Walker, must fly it for him.'

'Oh I cannot, ma'am,' Sally said quickly. 'I don't know how. I will fall.'

'Of course you can,' Ursula said.

But I can't, thought Sally. I can't I can't I can't.

Ursula rubbed her hands together. 'Of course, I don't mean you should actually fly, Walker. There is only one parachute, for a start. I just mean get the thing started.'

'Oh, ma'am?' Sally asked.

'You were there, were you not,' Ursula continued, 'when he showed us the wings, and where it should be launched from? You pick things up quickly. I have noticed that about you. So you will prepare everything, and when he sees you, he will get on that machine too, because he won't be able to bear it flying without him, and then you will jump off. You will be quite safe. You won't even leave the ground.'

'How do you know he will get on too?'

'Human nature, my dear. He won't be able to help himself.'

Sally nodded. She wondered if Ursula was, in fact, a little bit mad. 'But what if it crashes?' she asked.

'It does not matter if he is going to burn it anyway. Here,' Ursula said, pushing the designs towards her encouragingly, 'perhaps you should study these while I am out with Dr Leigh.'

And so Sally was left alone. There was tea in the pot. It smelt of Mr Fisher's arms, his barrel-chest. Toby's plans lay untouched on the sideboard. For a long time Sally did not move. She sat at the writing table with her hands pressed together, and she looked out of the window at the snow-lightened sky. There was a gap in the clouds where the sun fell in streams on the hillside, just as it had during the stoning of St Stephen. She remembered the open wound of the Bleeding Heart on the walls of the orphanage; torn flesh and a bright light.

She shuddered. No, she thought. I cannot do this.

She sat down and, as she did, she felt a lump in her pocket. It was Toby's apple, the snowman's nose. She had forgotten to give it back to him when she left his lodgings. She put it on the table in front of her, a fine cedar table with a glass top. It was reflected in the glass, a fuzzy, earthy shape. She picked it up and turned it over in her hand. She put it back. She picked it up again.

She remembered Sister Thomas of the Holy Ghost declaring it a sin (of what? Sally thought now. Of the flesh? Of gluttony?) to eat apples whole. She thought of the Vision in the window, the Virgin Mary coming to save her. She smiled and picked up the apple. She was seventeen years old and, on the Virgin Mary's advice, had still not bitten into an apple whole since those careless, pre-orphanage years. She cupped the apple in her hand. It was a perfect fit.

She went to the window and lifted the apple to her lips. There was a low rumble of sky above her. Thunder, she thought, although the clouds were white and wispy, and there was not even a hint of rain. She opened her mouth and bit into the apple. She felt the skin of it under her teeth, and then its flesh, pale and exposed and delightful to the tongue, and not at all the sort of thing of which the Virgin Mary would approve.

She bit down and, as the apple fell apart in her mouth, there was another rumble, louder now, more of a crack. And this time Sally looked up and saw the snow breaking

241

and tumbling from the roof of the hotel, a curdling flurry of white which sparkled as it fell past her face at the window and onto the road below, landing with a deep thud in an explosion of snowflakes.

Sally dropped the apple to the floor and spat her mouthful into her cupped hand.

It was at that moment that Sally Walker began to suspect that faith has a sort of power in it. Ridiculous, she thought, you are being ridiculous, but she sank to her knees all the same. It was terrifying, but it was also wonderful. The fear of God, Sister Thomas of the Holy Ghost would have called it, that woman who had lifted her up in the mortuary over the wrong body, who had stamped her foot like a horse when she thought herself alone in front of the Vision in the window.

Perhaps, Sally thought, but if the fear of God is a breath of snow, then it is not so very fearful a thing as the Old Testament would have us believe. It was not God – or, at least, Sally did not *think* so – but it was something. She felt it in her knees, rising up through her legs. She pushed her shoulders back and straightened her spine until she felt the skin on her body grow taut, and she felt – she did not know what she felt. Excitement, anticipation? No, it was not that. She felt jubilant. She would fly that machine and she would not be afraid, and then wouldn't Ursula Bridgewater be proud of her? Wouldn't she have come on a treat? And wouldn't that be something to have really *done* with her life?

Seventeen

A conversion

'Ah, Miss Bridgewater,' Dr Leigh said as they stepped out of the hotel for a stroll, Ursula's gloved hand looped around his arm. It was an irritating habit he had, the way he placed his hand over her wrist as they walked, and strolled now too fast, now too slow. He seemed unusually talkative. He kept stopping and starting, slowing down in the middle of a sentence and picking up again if she tried to interject. He talked about the climate in Canada, the life expectancy of bees, the likelihood of surviving a jump over the Niagara Falls.

Ursula would have said he was nervous, but she did not know what there was to be nervous about. She did not say anything, not wishing to cause offence, but all the same she could not help but wonder why it was that so many men of her acquaintance frequently failed to see that a monologue does not pass for conversation.

Perhaps I might have something to say, she thought, if I could get a word in. Perhaps I might wish to talk about the Baptist movement, republicanism, Toby O'Hara's pioneer spirit. Or perhaps about Sally, whether I am pushing her too hard, whether I am being too much, too restless and fidgety, whether I should not be encouraging her quite so much because she does not have my advantages.

They walked down the main street, stopping to look at ribbons and candy and the book store.

But if she does not have my advantages, Ursula continued with her internal argument, then surely it is my *duty* to push her. It is an obligation. And if she is in love with him – why should she not be? He is an inventor, and quite different from those awful young men of Mavis's – then I must encourage her.

She listened while Dr Leigh talked, leading her across the road and down a side street.

'Now,' he said when they reached his house, rubbing his hands together to warm them up, 'won't you come in for tea?'

Ursula followed him up the path and into the warmth of the drawing room, whereupon he produced a cake tin and a teapot. He insisted that Ursula serve the cake while he made up the fire. Ursula saw the certificates arranged carefully on the wall behind the doctor's desk, the lamp lit in the corner of the room to lighten the effect of the dark wooden-panelling. She admired the size of the room, the heavy furniture, the smart floorboards, the cornicing on the ceiling. She saw his pleasure at her compliments, and her praise was not insincere. The room was very nice, but it was cluttered in a fussy, precise sort of way. And she knew that it suited Dr Leigh in a manner that it did not suit her.

She pulled at the fingers of her gloves to loosen them and then sank back into the soft leather of the armchair, thinking how dignified it was to be sitting in a doctor's drawing room in America, unchaperoned but quite at ease. In England, she would have been obliged to sit up straight with her legs pressed together like a puritan. In America, she sat with her knees slightly apart, and she smiled a wide, open smile.

She laid her gloves over the arm of her chair and picked up her plate. The cake was perfectly made, stem ginger with a hint of lemon. It was, she told him, quite possibly the nicest cake she had ever tasted.

He beamed. 'I made it myself,' he said. 'It is my grandmother's recipe.'

She looked at him, surprised. 'Then you have no housekeeper?' she asked.

'Oh yes,' he said. 'But Sunday is her day off, and I wished,' here he paused and looked at her most intently, 'to make this cake for you.'

Ursula smiled. Oh Lordy, she thought. She felt her neck redden. She lifted the cake to her lips and bit into it. It really was very moist. Say something, she thought.

Dr Leigh looked at her and hesitated. 'Might I read something to you?' he asked.

'If you like.'

He took a notebook from his bookcase and opened it very deliberately at the first page. He began to read a sonnet, his hands trembling slightly. He did not need to read it. He could have recited it with his eyes shut. He knew every word, every cadence. Oh, it was exquisite. He did not look up when he had finished, but held the notebook in his fingers and closed it with such delicacy, such reverence, that its pages might have been made of silk.

'There,' he said. 'I have said it now, better than I could have done on my own.'

There was a silence. Ursula's face wore a perfectly neutral expression. She pressed her legs together.

Duncan Leigh reached forward and took hold of her hand. 'Will you, Miss Bridgewater, Ursula, do me the honour . . .'

'Do you mean,' Ursula interrupted, her defences faltering at last, 'are you trying to say that you wish to marry me?'

'Yes,' he whispered.

'But why?' Her eyes were wide and incredulous. It was almost an accusation.

Dr Leigh had not expected his proposal to be met with a question. He was perplexed. He had anticipated a certain mood to have come about because of the beauty of the poem. He had expected elation, passion perhaps, but instead he felt only a nervous tightness across his chest. She was looking at him in that unfathomable way of hers, her head tilted and her eyes bright, the plate of stem ginger cake resting on her lap. He watched as she picked it up and placed it on a small table next to her armchair.

Ursula Bridgewater stood up and walked to the window. She supposed that this would be her last chance. She would no longer be excluded from those dining rooms which required that she be accompanied by a man with whom she must dance after dinner. She confessed to herself that she, too, had entertained the idea of marrying Duncan Leigh in a mild, unlikely manner in her head, but now, when confronted with the reality of such a prospect, it seemed utterly ridiculous. She felt a sudden longing for the simplicity of her life at home. Yes, she conceded, she had thought she wanted a husband, but a fine pair of hands and a tolerable grasp of Latin are not, or at least should not be, enough. Besides, there is so much I need to accomplish, she thought.

She picked up a small pewter ashtray and inspected it absently. There were other knick-knacks in the room which she had not expected to find there. She did not know that Duncan Leigh's grandmothers had been collectors of porcelain and that their grandson had grown accustomed to having small decorations on his surfaces, and that, while he might not have chosen them for himself, he quite liked them.

Dr Leigh imagined that Ursula's thoughts were on the practicalities of it all, her brother, her home. He could not have known her thoughts were full of dancing.

Not a single foxtrot in ten years, she thought, and now this! She replaced the ashtray on the sideboard. She caught a reflection of herself in the window as she turned back to him, and it was in this brief moment of complicity between her real self and her reflected image that she was able to order her thoughts quite properly. Dr Leigh was perfectly suitable, more than suitable in fact, yet she knew she did not want him.

And then she thought: it is because I am happy as I am.

She did not know when this had happened. It had taken her by surprise, creeping up on her when she was not looking out for it. There must have been a moment, she supposed, when she tipped from one state to another, from boredom to happiness, but she had not noticed it at the time. She imagined religious conversions worked in the same way. They may appear sudden to the onlooker but that is because only the outward hints are visible, where really all conversions are the result of a lifetime's accumulation of disappointments and boredoms and quarterly letters, countered now with trips and excursions and future plans, which one day amount to this remarkable feeling. Happiness.

It is because I have a purpose, Ursula thought. It is no longer for me to sit in drawing rooms and drum my fingers on tabletops while I wait for England to change to accommodate me. We have a Queen after all. People listen to her, and she is a woman. If the women of Utah are entitled to vote, why not the women of England?

She smiled. It was almost a grin. She supposed it was Toby who had put the idea into her head with his talk of making the people of America air-minded. 'It is a state of mind,' he had said, 'which keeps these people rooted to the ground.' And it is the same principle, Ursula had thought at the time, which keeps me chaperoned about the streets, keeps me sitting in that drawing room with all those dull, endless tales of fabrics and housekeepers. And always women, only women. Except, she supposed, for George, but he did not really count.

She felt giddy with this new, sudden happiness, although not in the way that Dr Leigh had intended. She thought: I have been converted without even noticing that it has happened. I am happy that I can walk on my own down the streets of Niagara Falls, that I can fly through the air in a balloon, that I can dress myself and wash my own stays and petticoats in the bathtub, that I can bring warm towels up from the linen press to hold against the girl's forehead and that it pleases me to do so.

She collected her shawl and apologised to Dr Leigh. 'It was very nice of you to ask,' she told him, 'but I cannot marry you'. And, as she walked out into the American sun, she tipped her head back and closed her eyes so that the whole sense of it could wash over her. She smiled a wide, delighted smile, just as Mr Thomas Cook had done when he bathed with the Lord in the muddy waters of Jordan.

Eighteen

Stillness

It was on Ursula Bridgewater's advice that Sally Walker wore her best dress on the allotted morning, the one with a white lace collar and little blue flowers. Ursula had procured a carriage to take her as far as the edge of the field, from where Sally could walk to the cowshed, and the carriage was then further engaged to return to the hotel to collect Ursula and take her back to the same spot.

'Now here it is. Remember, I will bring Dr Leigh when he has finished attending to Mrs Keegan, provided that he has not changed his mind and decided to become offended with me.'

'Yes, ma'am.'

'I have sent a note to Mr O'Hara confirming that I will meet him at the field at eleven o'clock to finalise the patent. He is giving a morning balloon ride to some American tourists whom I met earlier – frightful people, very meek – and he will come directly after that. I am quite certain he does not suspect a thing.'

'Yes, ma'am.'

'So you must be ready by then. But not too soon, else he will see you from the balloon. Of course, you know that, I think. We have discussed it already, have we not?'

'Yes, ma'am.'

Ursula paused and clasped her hands together. She leant forward and put her hand on Sally's arm. 'I am so proud of you, Walker,' she said.

'Thank you, ma'am,' she whispered.

'Yes, yes,' flustered Ursula. 'Now mind your fingers and don't forget to jump off.' She closed the door of the carriage and, lifting her skirts from the floor, took the steps of the hotel two at a time. She turned in the doorway and beamed at Sally, who waved nervously back at her from the carriage window.

The field was green and soft underfoot. The sky was a deep blue, and Sally felt a light breeze against her neck as she drew back the bolt on the wooden door of the shed. The weathervane on the roof pointed directly west. It was exactly as it should be.

The inside of the shed was dark. The wings were stacked up against the wall, as they had been on that first visit when Toby explained the mechanics of how they slotted into the sides of the machine. She saw the bat perched on the windowsill, but this time she did not step away from it as she had done before, but reached out her hand and picked it up. Its skin was wrinkled and dry and its eyes were red. She held it out in front of her, and then, quite suddenly, she felt an urge – it was almost childlike – to *swoop* it through the air, and for a brief exhilarating moment she saw it as Toby's pop must have seen it when he sketched it so lovingly all those years before. She put it back on the windowsill and looked around.

She wished Ursula were with her. ('I would be of no use to you!' Ursula had cried when she had voiced this wish. 'Besides, it must be you, and you alone,' she had added conspiratorially, and Sally had not known what she meant.)

But, all the same, she wished she were there. She wished for Ursula's faith, her conviction. Of course, Ursula would not have called it faith ('I do not believe in faith,' she had insisted in the hot air balloon), but she had tapped the dressing table with her fingernail and told Sally that it was perfectly simple, that she must fly the machine for him, and what is that, Sally thought, if not faith?

Sally walked around the machine. In the shed, it seemed simple, innocent. The floor of the shed was flaked with sawdust. The tail bobbed in the air, newly attached. There was a pile of sawn wood in one corner. Outside, there were maple trees, pink with blossom curled against the lingering snow. She thought of home, of the sprawling docks and shining stone, of the cracked skin of the dockers who rolled up from the river into the taverns in sack-like trousers and grimy jackets, and who had never seen such a grand and wonderful thing as the Niagara Falls. She thought of the band-stands in Sefton Park, shaped like pagodas, where the women played croquet nearby and the boys practised shooting at trees with bows and arrows, and of the rows of tea in glass jars lined up on Mr Fisher's dark, wooden shelves.

She took a deep breath. It was time. She must take the flying machine out onto the field and turn it to face directly east. She must slot the wings into the sockets and support them with blocks of wood, and she must prepare the brakes for release.

And then what? She did not know. Her intentions were not entirely clear, even to her. It was not one thing she intended, but many.

That she show herself to be brave even though she was not.

That she give to Toby something she desired so much for herself – an acknowledgement of that vast, internal

251

emptiness, because yes, she did know exactly how it felt to need to know something.

That he would see she was sorry, that she had not meant to push him like that, so hard and with both hands, and that he might try again, might bend down and press his lips against hers once more and that this time she might overcome the dizziness and feel the warmth of another body, his body, against her own, just as she had longed for when she was small.

That he would not burn his flying machine before he had even tried it, for what a marvellous thing it would be – Ursula had told her – to show the world that it is really possible to fly.

That she might do something extraordinary in her life, something brave and unexpected and, she thought timidly, perhaps even mildly hysterical.

The machine was heavier than it looked. It was unwieldy. Sally's arms ached from holding the body up at the required angle for it to pass through the doorway. The wheels caught on tufts of thistles. The distance to the launching track was perhaps twenty feet. It was not far, and yet she could not make herself go in a straight line. She pushed with both hands against the back of the machine. That such a thing might fly seemed unimaginable. It was, by its very nature, contradictory, that so much weight was required to lift another weight.

The sun was already high. It was taking too long. He would be here before she was ready. She did not consider the possibility that he might not come. Of course he would.

She ran back to the shed and lifted the propeller onto a wheelbarrow and then fixed it to the front of the flying machine. The wings were fitted last. They slotted into the body of the machine, and there were wedges to hold them in place. She remembered how Toby had demonstrated the hinge and the bolt. It was a jigsaw of bamboo and silk. It was so delicate, so intricate; a huge shimmering skeleton. She stepped back to look at it, her hot, dirty hands clasped in front of her. It was beautiful. It was terrifying. It was a sublime piece of audacity.

She walked slowly around the machine. She removed the stones from in front of the wheels. She climbed up onto the pilot's board and crouched behind the propeller. She felt sweat breaking out across her neck.

She did not have to wait long. She saw him in the distance, running towards her, and she felt her chest grow tight. In a moment, there would be noise, the chaotic sound of wheels rushing over the launch pad, of Toby's voice shouting at her to jump, of birds flying upwards from the trees in a flap of leaves and feathers. But in the small reflection of time, when Sally Walker crouched all alone on the machine with dirt streaked lightly across her face and an ache in her lower back from where she had dragged and pushed the machine out to the field, in that moment, there was a second of utter and perfect stillness.

She thought: Dear God, save me.

Yet at the same time she wanted to shout: 'Look at me!'

Nineteen

Falling

To look at that part of town now, you wouldn't think it was anything much. There is a mall where the field once was, a hamburger bar and a hairdresser and a greengrocers, decorated with neon signs strung across their darkened windows. There is a bank and a post office, and an old school building converted into tourist apartments, and a new supermarket with gleaming cars parked in rows.

Niagara is concrete-grey and noisy with casinos and huge-windowed hotels, and the Falls are lit up at night in hot pinks and purples. There is a new railway bridge, and even the site of the great cataract itself has changed, retreating backwards by the length of a football pitch since the days when Toby O'Hara flew his balloon over the water. There is a derelict power plant and a whole suburb following the path of a new canal, all the houses now emptied and boarded up, with no sign of flight in the cracks of the pavement or along the weatherboards of the buildings, not so much as a single feather to record the longest flight in aviation history before the Wright Brothers came along and invented the airplane.

The incident did not go unnoticed. It was still a small town back then, smaller than it is now. It became known locally as the Great Flight Hoax after an investigation into the reported sightings of a flying machine in the woods behind the gristmills and workshops on the American side of the Falls. It was reported by the local press and, for a short while, the alleged location of the launching track became a minor tourist attraction, until the public's attention was diverted by a woman surviving a jump over the Falls in a barrel, and after this it was rather forgotten.

But there is a record.

For one thing, there was the Spellbinder at New Brighton beach, dismantled and melted down into Spitfires during the Second World War, but famous in its day: the outlandish machine in which Ursula Bridgewater invested her entire fortune, and that made all four of the Spellbinder shareholders rich.

There is a photograph of the opening of the ride in 1890. There is a tall man in a waistcoat and top hat standing next to a seagull. He has his left arm around the shoulders of a small woman in full skirts. Next to them, there is another woman dressed in a cycling costume, her head tipped back in a burst of sudden laughter, her neck long and straight. And there is an older man looking on from a distance, his whiskery expression bemused and indulgent. And, in the background, there is an advertising billboard for a tea shop on the Parade, beside which stands a white-haired man in an apron, resting on his walking stick.

Then there is the trust set up anonymously by the four Spellbinder shareholders – anonymous but just about traceable if you know where to look – which established a library and technical school for the benefit in perpetuity of the religiously unaffiliated orphans of Liverpool, and also provided funds to the Liverpool Movement for Women's Suffrage until 1914 when the funds were donated instead to the rehabilitation of wounded soldiers.

There are obituaries too, of George and Toby and Ursula:

scraps of yellowed paper in library archives. None of them mention a flying machine in Niagara Falls in 1872. George Bridgewater's is about tea and socialism and there is no mention of his involvement in the patenting of the flying machine, and this is quite fitting. He would not have wished to take any credit. Toby's obituary is shorter, glancing over his earlier experiments in ballooning and tea-packaging designs before mentioning the Spellbinder and his various philanthropic projects. These were to be continued under the sole supervision of his wife, who was acknowledged as having been the principal administrator in any case. Ursula's obituary is the longest. She wrote most of it herself before she died and instructed George to send it to *The Times Daily Register* after her death, which he dutifully did, and it was published almost exactly as she had written it. It reflected her main interests at the point of writing, principally the question of women's suffrage and the new craze of bicycling, so there is no mention of that first, early flight. But that is how Toby wanted it anyway. He did not want any fuss. He wanted to burn the machine, and that would be the end of it.

But that is not how it happened. Because there is one other record.

*

These are the things Sally Walker knew for certain as she sat on the flying machine while it shuddered and sprang down that long, sloping field in 1872:

She knew how to swing an umbrella and how to approach at pace.

She knew that Ursula had tapped her nail on the dressing table and told her it was perfectly simple, that she must fly the machine herself.

She knew Toby's hand was hot in her own and that there was a pain in her shoulder when she dragged him up onto the machine.

She knew she could no longer feel the bump of the field, and that her eyes were watering from the rush of all that air.

She knew that Isaac Newton had once bounced an apple thoughtfully in his palm, and that each time he had thrown it up, it had fallen back towards the very centre of the earth.

She knew that Toby was trying to tell her something important but she could not hear him.

She knew there was such a thing as gravitational pull, and that a penny and a feather would fall at the same speed in a vacuum.

She knew there was more to faith than God.

She knew she had no idea how to land.

She knew that dying for love was no different from any other sort of dying and that there was still time for her to jump to the ground and be safe.

She knew all of this. And yet she clung on.

*

Toby O'Hara no longer cared about flying. His machine had already melted in his mind. It was ridiculous, useless. It had no purpose. It might fly, he supposed, but it would not land. And even if it did, what then?

He had spent a long, sleepless night resigning himself to the fact that he had made a perfect fool of himself. The sun no longer seemed warm but harsh and too bright. He squinted at it. The birds screeched in the trees and his jacket was uncomfortable on his shoulders. He looked down at his sleeves, at the way his wrists protruded from the material, and thought how funny it was that this jacket he had once thought of as elegant now seemed so shabby.

He would burn the machine. There was no reason to wait. He cursed himself for what he had done, that sudden reckless embrace. He remembered how Sally had smiled at him in the balloon, how she had arrived at his house with the drawings clasped against her chest, how she had sat beside him in the snow and had not noticed the seeping cold. Perhaps she loves me, he had thought then.

Had she said so?

No, he supposed not. But she had pushed open his kitchen door and wiped his tear away with her finger. And, when he kissed her, she had pressed her body into his and he had felt the sweetness of it before she pushed him away.

But why then had she pushed him away?

Because she did not love him.

He walked over a small wooden bridge and along the side of a field. There were cherry blossoms in the trees and dandelions in the ditch beside the road. There were magnolia trees bursting with bright colour. He did not notice them.

Later, when he looked back, he would remember how it appeared when he first saw it, a huge bird sitting on a hill. But it was not a bird. He saw the edges of it, fragile and delicate and shimmering in front of him. His vision blurred as he approached.

He thought: perhaps I am asleep and this is a dream, and he put his hand to his forehead and closed his eyes because it is one thing to dream about a lost mother, but another to be haunted by her.

But, he thought as he got closer, it is not a dream. It is my machine. It is my machine exactly. It has my hinges, my wheels. He saw the wings he had strung so carefully across the bamboo frame, the propeller spinning slowly in the breeze as he reached the edge of the field. He started to run.

He thought: it looks too delicate to fly. I should have made it more robust. And at the same time he thought: I should burn it.

There was a flash of white cotton, of pale skin and small blue flowers.

And then he thought: Sally. He felt his heart thump under his skin.

She loved him!

No, she did not. She had pushed him away when he kissed her, both hands on his chest.

So why now, if she did not love him, were the wings slotted so carefully into the body of the machine. Why, if she did not love him, did she crouch on the pilot's board and call to him to run, run? Why did she not jump when he told her to, while she still could? Why did she hold out her hand and pull him up, and why then did she keep hold of his hand and laugh with him as they rattled down the field into the rush of air?

He did not know. But as they floated higher and higher above the ground, he found that he was laughing too. He could not help it. He had not expected the machine to go so high and so fast. They were the perfect weight, the two of them, the perfect ballast for the lightness of the wings. It was ingenious. His pop would have loved it. He would have stood on the veranda and danced.

He thought this for just a moment before he noticed the dip of the left wing and the shudder of the machine. He remembered his pop's flying boats which he made from paper when Toby was a boy, how they would fly straight when you first threw them but how their equilibrium, once lost, was lost entirely. They would plunge and spiral. He pulled the parachute from the nail above his head and he strapped Sally into it. It would not hold them both but it did not matter. He put his arms around her small body and scooped her up into his chest. They would jump together and he would release the parachute, and then he would let go and he would fall and Sally would float. He held her tightly against him. The machine began to tip.

'Don't be scared,' he shouted.

It was too late in any case. He did not hear her reply as they jumped from the side of the machine, their bodies pressed into each other, but he felt the movement of her lips against his neck, her warm breath on his skin, before he let go.

'I'm not.'

*

Toby could not move his leg. He did not try. He could not sit up. He lay in the green earth and saw the silhouettes of trees growing taller and rounder, until all he could see was darkness, and then he closed his eyes and dreamed he was flying.

He saw his mother sitting at the piano, her fingers moving lightly across the ivory keys which stuck to her fingers, and when he floated closer he saw that they were not piano keys at all but small, white labels, sticky with jam and pickle.

He dreamed of fluffy white clouds in big blue skies, of his father dressed in his uniform with gold-braided edges, jumping from the roof of the house in Holloway Creek and flying on and on to Ontario, over the Bridal Veil Falls and Goat Island and the Horseshoe Falls.

He dreamed of silk bags floating into the dusk, of bats and feather dusters, and of his mother pressing her finger into the bridge of her nose to hold back a sneeze, her other hand flapping because it was coming, it was coming, and when it came he felt the jolt of it in his dream, a bump of consciousness, and he felt his eyelids flicker, just for a second.

He dreamed of a carriage bumping over a track next to the Niagara Falls, voices calling and feet running and in the midst of it all, Ursula Bridgewater leaning straight-backed from the window with her umbrella thrust out in front of her like Boudicca's spear, and he dozed in and out of its galloping, comforting rhythm.

He dreamed of his machine, broken and tangled against the trees, and he felt a lightness in his body, a billowing, sugary softness.

He dreamed he saw a face floating above him in the dappled green light, of hands holding his head, stroking his face.

But it is only a dream, he thought.

*

In the letter Mr Fisher received from America, he read a good deal about Ursula Bridgewater. He read about New York and Central Park and a balloon over Niagara Falls, and he read about Toby O'Hara. The postmark was from San Francisco. He knew the handwriting but he did not recognise the style. It was so open, so exuberant. He read parts of it aloud to his new assistant in the tea shop – 'she is my ward,' he explained, even though this was not quite accurate – and he could not stop smiling.

He read about Dr Duncan Leigh (although there was no mention of the sonnet) who promised to take care of every-thing, to dismantle the shed and to keep the bat safe for Toby in Niagara. He read that Ursula Bridgewater had burnt the flying machine right there in the field, and that they had left Niagara Falls the next day, travelling by railroad along the course of the Delaware River to Detroit, and then to Chicago, a city of ashes after the great fire of the previous year, and up along the eastern slope of the Rocky Mountains with all its prairie fires and wolves and Indians. He read about Utah (so progressive!), and how one might climb onto the roof of the great Tabernacle in Salt Lake City to witness the beginnings of the Mormon temple. He pictured the gold mines of Sacramento, messy patches of scrabbled earth, and the descent into San Francisco, from where Mr Thomas Cook and his tour group had already departed across the Pacific for Japan. He read that there was a ten-day sleeper train back from San Francisco to New York which, if all went according to plan, would meet the steamer to Liverpool.

On the day the steamer was scheduled to arrive, Mr Fisher went to the docks and bought a garland of white flowers. There was such a press of people that he could hardly breathe. He drew his oilskin coat around him, and clutched a box of dark chocolates which he had bought as a gift for Ursula. The flowers were in his other hand, and he held them out so they would not crumple. He strained his neck to look for Sally, but there was too much of a crush, too much stamping and pushing and waving for him to see anything.

A brass band trumpeted behind him. He remembered standing with George Bridgewater to wave Sally and Ursula off on their excursion. There had been white flowers then too, roses perhaps, and a bright blue sky. He had seen the girl standing on the deck, her hands gripping the railing, but he had not waved, had not tried to catch her attention. She would only have raised her hand and waved, too politely, and he would have felt guilty that he had caused her to be taken so far from home. He would have told himself that he had done it for the best, and really, what more could he have done? But he would have been unable to convince himself, and the guilt would have lingered uneasily in his stomach.

And so, if he did not see Sally Walker descending from the boat, thronging her way through the passengers and toffee-sellers and red-capped porters with Ursula at her side, it was because the earlier image of her was fixed too strongly in his mind, her head bowed and her collar buttoned. Indeed, he did not see her arm flapping for his attention, did not hear her calling to him, did not see how she dropped her case and ran, and it was only when she flung her arms around his waist that he recognised her at all.

*

There was, however, one incident which was not recounted to Mr Fisher.

In a field next to Niagara Falls, Sally Walker touched Toby O'Hara's face with her fingers. She lay on the grass next to him and blew gently on his flickering eyes until he looked up at her. There were scratches on his arms and his neck, a red bump on his head. He smiled drowsily at her as he blinked.

'Wasn't that something?' he whispered. 'I mean, really something.'

She nodded. 'It really was,' she said.

The torn flying machine hung in the trees in front of them, one wing snapped cleanly off. Toby reached for Sally's hand, and grinned at her in the bright sunlight. And then Sally Walker, who had dreamed of falling all her life and so was sometimes slow to distinguish between one sort of falling and another, had leaned forward and pressed her soft, hot lips against Toby O'Hara's bruised mouth.

Because, of course, this is a love story.

Author's Note

Although all other characters are fictional, the character of Thomas Cook in *The Opposite of Falling* is based on the real person, although all direct speech and described actions are imagined. The trips taken by Ursula to Scotland, Switzerland and the Holy Land were based on actual trips organised by Thomas Cook in his early years as a tour guide, and which he personally conducted. In addition, the first Round-the-World Cook's tour set off in 1872 and was led by Thomas Cook, following the route detailed in the novel. Incidentally, Jules Verne's novel *Around the World in Eighty Days* was published the following year, quite possibly inspired by Thomas Cook's letters to *The Times* from various stages of the tour that seemed to catch the contemporary public imagination.

The flying machine built by Edmund O'Hara and later by Toby is based on the designs of Jean Marie Le Bris's Artificial Albatross in 1856 and Clement Ader's Eole and Avion no. 3 in 1890 and 1897 respectively. Mr Rufus Porter's Aerial Locomotive for travel between New York and California was designed and advertised as described in Chapter Five, but was unfortunately never completed. In researching the history of flight, Octave Chanute's *Progress in Flying Machines* (first published in 1894) was particularly illuminating, being written before the Wright Brothers had actually managed to achieve flight, and detailing the many theories and near-misses abounding in the nineteenth century, as well as giving a sense of the ambition for flight among amateur inventors at that time.

Acknowledgements

I'd like to thank everyone at Aitken Alexander Associates and Chatto & Windus for helping in so many ways with *The Opposite of Falling*. In particular, I'd like to thank Clare Alexander for her unfailing support and unsurpassed rallying abilities, Clara Farmer for being such a wonderful editor at every stage of the process (including preventing over-sized cutting at the last minute), Juliet Brooke for her editorial input, patience and willingness to provide cake at crucial moments, and Suzanne Dean for designing such a stunning cover. Paul Smith at the Thomas Cook Archive was also incredibly helpful in locating sources, as were the staff at the Washington Air and Space Museum and the Musée de l'Air et de l'Espace in Paris.

I'd also like to thank the many kind and indulgent readers of the manuscript at its various stages, whose advice and suggestions have been invaluable, specifically my mum (Pluse), who was generous enough to read the manuscript more than once, literary experts Peter, Ann and Tammy Holmes, Kath Haydn, Sarah Beckett, Tubs, Lil D and Jonathan Lee. I'd also like to thank Kit and Da-da for their historical nit-picking, Della for being in her prime yet still scared of apples, and Mark, for lots of things.